# Flatwoods
# and
# Lighterknots

*A Cultural Visit*
*to the*
*Coastal Plains of Georgia*

James F. Elders

PublishAmerica
Baltimore

© 2005 by James F. Elders.
All rights reserved. No part of this book may be reproduced, stored in a retrieval system or transmitted in any form or by any means without the prior written permission of the publishers, except by a reviewer who may quote brief passages in a review to be printed in a newspaper, magazine or journal.

First printing

ISBN: 1-4137-8737-1
PUBLISHED BY PUBLISHAMERICA, LLLP
www.publishamerica.com
Baltimore

Printed in the United States of America

*The words in this book are dedicated the memory of
Captain William D. (Bidd) Sands, Commander,
Company A, 1st Bn., 8th Reg., 4th Infantry Division.
Killed in action, Vietnam, March 23, 1967.*

# A Soldier's Elegy

Tree of liberty soaked in blood
Gift from patriots long in mud
Brave souls their memories reside
In men of courage honor and pride

Such are men who pay the cost
Protectors of freedom never lost
Giving their best for others to see
Not without price comes liberty

Far from home in war torn land
That time did come close at hand
When life departs its fragile hold
And leaves the body ever cold

Reaper comes doth dourly take
A soldier's spirit from man of late
Passing over those who mourn
Grieve him not for he is reborn

Another patriot in glory now rides
With souls of those who early died
Men of courage forever gone
Sleep now brother thy duty done

Canopy of trees now abate my fear
And images of home bring me near
To a brother soldier home at rest
Buried upon a hallowed crest

Should this moment end my time
Deliver my soul to ever shine
In company of those patriots past
Brave men their memories last

Pour my blood upon that tree
Water of life I bequeath to thee
The liberty tree my shade now
My duty done I kept my vow

# Contents

Introduction ........................................................................... 9

Chapter I

The Flatwoods ..................................................................... 13

Chapter II

The Pines .............................................................................. 24

Chapter III

Charlie Horse ...................................................................... 37

Chapter IV

Uncle Jeff and Other Kin .................................................. 45

Chapter V

Election Time ....................................................................... 57

Chapter VI

Cane Grinding Day ............................................................ 66

Chapter VII

Fox Hunting ........................................................................ 76

Chapter VIII

Rattlesnakes and Gophers ................................................ 87

Chapter IX

Tobacco Rogue .................................................................... 96

Chapter X

Turkeys ............................................................................... 107

Chapter XI

Television at the Pines .................................................... 115

Chapter XII

Show and Tell ................................................................... 124

Chapter XIII

As Time Goes By .............................................................. 136

Chapter XIV

The Island Hole ................................................................ 144

Chapter XV

The School Bus .................................................................. 152

Chapter XVI

The Willow Tree ............................................................... 162

Chapter XVII
The Wings of Diana .................................................................170
Chapter XVIII
A Dog Named Patchis ...........................................................178
Chapter XIX
A Place and a Friend .............................................................189
Chapter XX
Pete's Moonshine Still ...........................................................201
Chapter XXI
Wild Thing ..............................................................................210
Chapter XXII
The Bridge ...............................................................................219
Chapter XXIII
Music ........................................................................................227
Chapter XXIV
Christmas .................................................................................235
Chapter XXV
Requiem for a People .............................................................243

# Introduction

*Flatwoods and Lighterknots* is a sensitively humorous, often hilarious, and sometimes penetratingly sad story about a young boy's experiences while growing up in the coastal plains of Georgia during the 1940s and 1950s, an era many people might recall with trepidation or nostalgic reverence; perhaps both. The children who grew up during World War II were born to parents who were still dealing with the social and financial aftermath of a war to end all wars, a great depression, and were again facing the barrels of yet another war. It was a time when many Americans were still alive and who had experienced a war from an earlier century, a war that was continuing to divide a nation and its people. It was also a time when America was still mostly rural and people traveled to town only for those necessities that couldn't be produced on their farms or bartered from their neighbors. Country stores and churches were their social centers while workdays were spent tending to chores on family farms that were slowly fading from existence in a fast changing society. Most families spent their winter evenings huddled around their fireplaces or kitchen stoves listening to the only radio in their house. Summer evenings were spent on their front porches listening to the sounds of the night and telling tales of days long gone.

*Flatwoods and Lighterknots* is a literary pictorial as well as a history of a part of America that captures, for perpetuity, an almost forgotten way of life. It even serves as a guide for the preparation of a few special southern dishes and drinks. A young boy of the times is the reader's tour guide as he makes both comical and poignant observations about a life that was interesting and exciting, yet unpredictable and sometimes even dangerous. Several chapters are introduced by poems written in limerick form that were composed by the young boy as he witnessed the moments.

Cane grindings, fox hunting, and fishing and swimming in waters not yet polluted are described in ways that beckon memories back to more innocent times. Dog lovers, horse lovers, and people who love people will appreciate how the author treats relationships between his characters and various kinds of animals. The characters are actual representatives of their times, people who were attempting to deal with the frustrations of being caught on a time bridge between old ways and new technologies. Electricity, television, paved roads, telephones, and more powerful automobiles were pushing Americans to the brink of an unknown world, a world now taken for granted by the children of this age of instant information and casual pleasures.

Children born to America before the advent of World War II have little to identify themselves as a separate generation. Their contributions have been eclipsed by the antics of their younger brothers and sisters who were conceived during steamy wartime furloughs or passionate reunions after the war. These infants of the post war years would later be known as war babies and baby-boomers. They grew up enjoying national security, economic prosperity, V-8 engines and television, while their parents were fretting over atomic bombs, communism, and tight budgets. They were born too late to remember seeing droves of warplanes flying over their homes, new conscripts going to war to the sound of marching bands, or to smell the bandages on those who came home without a parade. And they were too young to remember seeing men return to broken marriages and women crying over men who would never come home. They were America's first generation to receive the benefits of victory over oppression without having an understanding its price, and they became the flower children of the sixties.

The children who lived the war years, witnessed the happy reunions, and saw the tragedies that war visited upon their lives were blessed with much closer ties to the past. It was a kind of connection to history that gave significance to their lives, a deep respect for the achievements of their forefathers, and a strong sense of responsibility to their nation. Although this book is not about the specific differences between two factions of a generation split by the inconveniences of war, such is the setting from whence the words in this book did spring. Each story portrays an incident that is reflective of a time when life was hard, but good, and challenges were many. People who can remember the war years and are now witnessing the unfolding of a new millennium will be able to identify with the author's characters. Their children and grandchildren might even gain a greater understanding and appreciation for the contributions of those who came before them.

*Flatwoods and Lighterknots* is a cameo peek into the lives of a few people who were attempting to adjust, in their individual, yet sometimes clumsy ways, to sudden changes that were occurring around them in a world that was being overtaken by the courses of events. Each story contains a message that was delivered to a young boy as he experienced the moment, even though the meanings might not come clear to him until much later in his life. The people portrayed in this book are representative of the kinds of souls who keep the home fires burning when there is no one else around to care enough to want to feel the warmth of the American dream.

*Flatwoods and Lighterknots* now invites you to walk down this little path of words and take a glimpse back into a time when watermelons, grapes, and tomatoes were allowed to ripen on their vines, and to a place where people spoke softly of their neighbors and proudly of their forefathers who had given them a kind of life that no human society had ever before experienced, and nevermore.

# Chapter I

## The Flatwoods

Flatwoods full of sights to see
Little critters scurry to flee
Blossoms open to morning sun
Petals close as day is done
Such are things that come and go
Yet pine trees remain to ever glow
Lighterknots on the ground attest
A pine was once their heavenly nest

At the end of the not so civil Civil War, most of the vast fields of cotton that once seemed to stretch to the four horizons of the South lay fallow. During the *Reconstruction Era* (locally referred to as the *Redestruction Era*), the owners of the old southern plantations were unable, and in many cases not allowed, to cultivate their land on as large a scale as in the years preceding the war. The surviving landowners, those who managed to hold on to a few portions of their land that southern scalawags and northern carpetbaggers hadn't confiscated, divided what acreage they still owned into smaller and more manageable tracts. The small southern farm of forty to eighty acres of cultivated land became the norm, and a new class of farmers began tending their fields. They did it with the help of family members who had managed to survive the war, newly freed slaves who had chosen to remain with their previous masters, tenant farmers, sharecroppers, and anyone else who might be willing and able to stand the hard work and blistering heat of those long, hot Georgia summers.

Pine trees, scrub oaks, and wiregrass soon began to reforest the expansive untilled flatlands where cotton once determined the locations of single-track railroad stations and little cotton-gin towns that still dot the countryside today, but with much less human activity than in the days when cotton was king. As southerners began to slowly regain a new foothold on war-scarred lands that their forefathers once tilled, and the black population began to become wage earners instead of wage deliverers, new industries emerged to breathe fresh life into the stagnated southern economy.

Pine trees grow very quickly in the sandy-loamy soil of the coastal plains of Georgia. It wasn't long before the once barren landscape was covered with a carpet of pine needles, palmettos, gall berry bushes, and wiregrass, all shaded by a tall umbrella of shimmering green loblolly, slash, and longleaf pine trees. The translucent resin that oozed from the trunks of the pine trees was soon being shipped around the world for use in an array of products, some useful and some fraudulent. The pungent yet pleasing odor of distilled turpentine could be detected in a variety of liquid agents that were being marketed as miracle spot removers and paint thinners. It was even used as an additive in stock dips for ridding livestock of parasites and skin infestations that were a constant plague upon farm animals.

Distilled turpentine came to be one of the principal ingredients in many patent medicines such as cough syrups, rubbing liniments, and decongestants. Some people might even remember *Energine*, a popular spot remover and clothing cleaner of the 1940s and 1950s. Distilled turpentine even made a fairly effective insect repellent and starter for fires in outdoor cooking grills. Yielding its products of turpentine, lumber, and numerous other by-products, it wasn't long before the pine tree replaced cotton as the new king of a new south.

Jimmy experienced many distasteful moments every time his Aunt Edith thought he might be coming down sick. She would hold his jaws open and force down his throat a couple of tablespoonfuls of a pine-tasting liquid that had been laced with a heavy percentage of codeine. She would pour the evil tasting stuff from a brown medicine bottle that had a handwritten label scrawled on a piece of white surgical tape, designating the bottle's contents as 'TERPIN-HYDRATE.'

Aunt Edith was the head operating room nurse at the Central of Georgia Railroad Hospital in Savannah. Every time a member of the family would come down with some illness, she would ride the Trailways bus back to Claxton and stay with the patient until their health turned for the better. It would be years later and after joining the army before Jimmy would discover that terpin-hydrate was one of the principal ingredients in a famous all-purpose remedy that American soldiers still refer to as *GI Gin*. Aunt Edith's bedroom closet resembled an army aid-station in the way that she always kept it stocked with various medicinal concoctions with scientific sounding names. Her potions seemed to work quite well, provided the patient survived long enough to finish taking her prescribed dosages.

Turpentine strippin', dippin', loadin', and haulin' is sweat popping, back breaking, snakebite-dangerous, downright miserable, and very sticky work. In its heyday, turpentine probably destroyed more denim overalls in the life of just one turpentine worker than modern laundry techniques have since been able to demolish for a whole nation of farmers and mechanics.

The process of collecting the turpentine began at the bases of the more mature pine trees. A rectangular shaped tin cup that could hold about a quart of turpentine was attached to the base of the tree, just above the grass line. A short handled oval-shaped stripping blade was used to cut a few pairs of slashes on the tree, beginning just above the tin cup. The 'V' shaped slashes resembled chevrons of military rank as more slashes were added up the side of the tree. Eventually, the stripping tool had be several feet long in order for the workers to be able to reach up and cut additional slashes on the tree, which often reached up the side of the tree for over twenty feet. The translucent resin would seep from the scarred pine trees and slowly ooze its way down the center of the slashes and into the tin cups.

Armed with wooden paddles and five-gallon buckets, the strippers and dippers would make regular rounds through the flatwoods collecting the resin from the full cups. They used the paddles to scrape the sticky goop from the cups to the buckets and then for shoving it from the buckets and into large wooden barrels that had been previously placed in strategic locations along the tar wagon trails. The largest and strongest turpentine workers always rode on the tailgates of the tar wagons. Their job was to load the heavy barrels on the wagons, drop off empty barrels along the trails, and make sure that the water barrels were kept full of fresh drinking water for the thirsty strippers and dippers. After the barrels were full of turpentine, they would then be hauled to a processing distillery in wagons that each held six barrels and were pulled by a two-mule team. And they sang.

> Loadin' dis wagon anda' haulin' tar.
> Woya mule now yuse gone too far.
> Gees and haws dees mule dun't mind.
> Jest keep on a'haulin' dis turpentine.
> Pay man comes dis Sat'tidy morn.
> Mules gits hay and we gits corn.

Curtis Wright (named after a couple of airplane guys) was the fastest and strongest pine tree stripper and tar barrel loader in South Georgia. He was also known throughout the flatwoods of southern Evans County as the strongest man in Georgia. Every now and then a loaded tar wagon would get stuck in a watery wheel rut, or become lodged on a submerged tree stump or fallen log. The mule team driver would then unhitch one of his mules from the tar wagon and ride off to fetch Curtis. It wouldn't be long before the growing crescendo of the sound of tree branches breaking and water sloshing could be heard as Curtis made his way through the knee-deep water and thick underbrush. A sudden quietness would come over the flatwoods when he stepped in the wagon trail and glared at the disabled wagon. Not a bird chirped, and the other turpentine workers would stare in admiring amazement of Curtis' hugeness. The sun would reflect off Curtis' sweaty bronze shoulders as he reached down with one hand, grabbed the wagon by its frame, and lifted the entire wagon. When the wagon was high enough for the wheels to clear the obstruction, the driver would yell to his mule team, "Yeeup!" Curtis would then disappear back into the thickets, shaking his head in disapproval of the young tar wagon driver's incompetence.

Curtis was also the one who people would call for when they needed to have their house re-leveled. All by himself, he could life the corner of a sagging house off its foundation and hold it up long enough for someone to place a brace under one of the sills of the house. After the required repairs had been completed, he would return and place the structure back on its new foundation.

There once was a famous weight lifter by the name of Paul Anderson who lived somewhere over in the middle part of the state. It was reported that he was the strongest man in the world and that he had even competed in the World Olympic Games. The *Atlanta Journal and Constitution* printed a story about Paul that featured a picture of him lifting the side of a house off its foundation. Curtis carried that newspaper clipping around with him everywhere he went. If anyone ever mentioned anything to him about Paul being the strongest man in the world, Curtis would take that picture out of his pocket and point out the fact that Paul had to use both hands to lift that house.

Curtis often told a story about the day when he finally got a real name. It was back when he was just a baby and his father was standing out in the front yard of their house watching an airplane fly back and forth over a nearby field of tobacco. The plane was diving down and climbing back up as it dusted the tobacco field with a now prohibited insecticide called DDT. It was the first airplane that Curtis' father had ever seen up close. When he asked Uncle Jeff what that thing was, Jeff told him that it was a Curtis Wright airplane.

Curtis always claimed it was on that very day when his father decided to name him Curtis, because he wanted his son to be like that airplane and soar higher than other men. That seemed to be a pretty workable idea since their last name really was Wright. Jimmy often wondered what Curtis would have been named had Uncle Jeff told Curtis's father that the airplane was a 'Jenny.'

Uncle Jeff was a genius. He had to be since he was also the laziest man in the county. No one can recall seeing him walk fast, not even when he was moving to a shadier and cooler spot away from the blistering sultry heat of those Evans County summers. Actually, it wasn't necessary for Jeff to move all that fast. Since he was a genius, he knew exactly where every shady spot in the county would be at any given moment of the day. From shadow to shadow, shade to shade, and with a ghost-like nonchalance, he could navigate through the entire Bay Branch Community without ever having to expose himself to the direct light of the sun. From one tree to another and from one clump of palmettos to the other, he would disappear and then reappear as he made his way out to the flatwoods where the annual road fishing party always took place during the late spring of every year.

Uncle Jeff was a loner who preferred to live in his little shack that he built back near the property line on the north side of the farm. Jeff lived alone in his private little abode except for the company of a pack of Walker foxhounds and his Tennessee walking horse that he named Major. He had been living there ever since Aunt Augusta kicked him out of the big house. In only a few days, and with an unusual streak of energy for a lazy person, he constructed his one-room house of cypress logs and scraps of lumber and then covered it with a roof of orange-colored Ludowici clay tiles. Although it wasn't anything like a modern day architectural dream, it was still a rather cozy looking little cottage. It was shaded by a small grove of oak trees and sat on a hill overlooking a meadow that sloped down to the cool running waters of Cribbs Branch.

Even a young child can tell when there is something strange about an adult, and Jeff was different. He was not strange in an evil way or a bad way, or even a mentally ill way, but there was an aura of sadness about him that suggested a deep loneliness and sorrow about something that seemed to always haunt him from somewhere out of his past. It would be much later in Jimmy's life before he would begin to understand and appreciate Jeff, and to wish that he could have told him so.

All those double-trace mule-powered tar wagons wore deep wheel ruts in the soft flatwoods soil as they hauled the heavy wood-staved fifty-five-gallon-barrels full of tar over the same old trails, week after week and year after year. During the spring rains, the wagon trails would fill with water that rushed in from the creeks and branches that were overflowing their banks and draining the excess water into the flatwoods. As summer approached and the waters began to recede, the wheel ruts that had been created by the tar wagons would be left filled with long strips of water that were anywhere between one to two feet in depth.

Little cypress ponds, not more than thirty feet in diameter and three to four feet deep, dotted the flatwoods like little oases.

And like the wheel ruts along the tar trails, they too would be left filled with water that was stained a reddish-brown color from the tannic acid that leached from cypress trees, pine bark, and dead pine needles. Those little reservoirs of captured floodwaters were the final resting places for thousands of wayward bluegill bream, catfish, red-finned pike (also called pickerel or jack), and the ever present slithering and sly nemesis of the southern wetlands, the cottonmouth moccasin.

Jimmy's father, grandfather, Uncle Wallace, Mr. Thomas, who was one of the last living vestiges of slavery, and Thomas' three boys, Pete, Tommy, and Temp, would show up with garden rakes, field hoes, and several number-three galvanized wash tubs. The grown-ups would push the fish laden water from the wagon tracks with vigorous shoves of their rakes and hoes. The children would run along the sides of the watery trails and collect the fish as they flipped and flopped in the thick wiregrass after being shoved from the wheel ruts. The younger children, those not yet strong enough to carry a full tub of water, were assigned the job of keeping fresh water in the wash tubs so the fish would remain alive long enough for them to be hauled back to the well shelter where the fish scaling and cleaning would be taking place that same evening.

Uncle Jeff, being real smart and all, usually showed up looking like some kind of plantation overseer whose self-assumed job was to inspect other people's work. He would ease along under the shade of the pine trees and point his walking cane at selected wheel ruts and cypress stump holes that he believed would be containing the most fish. Fish were always found in the places he selected and, apparently, another reason was found as to why he really was a genius.

After the fish had been gathered from the road ruts, the cypress ponds were cool and inviting places to take a swim by anyone who might be young and dumb enough to believe that all the snakes had been chased from their hiding spots along the edges of the little ponds of water. The swimmers used their feet to muddy the water until the fish would swim to the surface of the ponds where they would be netted and dumped into the wash tubs. The adults would stand on the banks of the ponds and net the fish by using long poles that had been specially cut from tree branches that had a fork at one end. A burlap bag was attached to the fork of the pole in a way that made the whole apparatus serve as a dip net.

The largest fish that was ever pulled from one of those cypress ponds was a thirty-pound catfish that Temp discovered while he was using his bare feet to muddy the water. It took only one vigorous leap for him to reach the top of the cypress pond and then run across the surface of the water. He looked like one of those fast-retrieving artificial top-water buzz baits that modern fishermen use. He dove onto the bank, hopped in an empty wash tub, and yelled, "I ain't stain' no whar' whar' de fish bees bigger'n me!"

That evening, after the fish had been scaled, cleaned, and the cats and chickens were finished dining on raw fish heads and entrails, the big fish fry and story telling session would commence around an open fire near the well shelter. A large black cast iron wash pot would be filled with hog lard and brought to an aromatic and crackling hot temperature over a fire that had been started with the help of a couple of lighterknots. The fire was kept at an even burning rate by a steady supply of stack-dried split oak logs.

There is nothing in this world that tastes anything like or anything better than a plate full of cornmeal-dipped deep-fat-fried flatwoods fish served up with a generous helping of golden-brown corndodgers and fresh cabbage coleslaw. When a red-fin pike is fully cooked, its entire backbone and rib cage can be pulled from the steaming hot fish, leaving the meat in one piece. When the single rack of bones is detached from the fish, it looks like one of those cartoon skeletal remains of a fish that has just been eaten by a cat. The whole fish can then be eaten like you would eat a roasted wiener. A few corndodgers dipped in cane syrup always rounded off the best meal that Jimmy would ever enjoy, even during all of his future travels around the world. No matter where he would go or in what world-class restaurant he would dine, there would always be the memory of a tale told many times around the dying gray ashes of a pot full of fish-fry grease, a tale about the biggest catfish ever pulled from a flatwoods cypress hole.

Fishing the flatwoods with rakes, hoes, and washtubs will most likely never again be experienced in the lifetime of another human being. The old turpentine trails have disappeared and the cypress ponds are only dusty remnants of another time. But Mother Nature had no hand in that deed. Man's incessant appetite for throw-away paper products and the increasing demands of big industry for more production and greater profits are the guilty parties responsible for destroying one of Mother Nature's most magnificent works of art.

The pulpwood and paper company that owned most of the land around the flatwoods brought in giant earth moving tractors and dug enormous drainage ditches that still stretch for miles through the flatwoods. Years later, while flying over the flatwoods in his airplane, the ditches reminded Jimmy of the long dry canals that appear to cut across the sun-baked surface of the planet Mars. The little streams that once fed the creeks and flooded the flatwoods during the rainy season were severed and drained of every drop of moisture, all for the purpose of harvesting faster growing paper-producing trees that would never be permitted to grow to maturity. The old cypress ponds and stump holes are now just little dry depressions in the ground filled only with wiregrass, broom sage, and memories. That natural environment, which was once so perfect for gallberries, huckleberries, and dewberries to grow in abundance along the damp edges of the cypress ponds, quickly disappeared. And, soon after, so too did the wildlife that fed upon the berries.

The flatwoods are mostly dry now. But, every now and then, and when there is time and an opportunity to visit the old home place, Jimmy takes a long walk through the flatwoods. He sits quietly under the shade of a tall old pine tree that still wears a long chevron-shaped scar down the side of its trunk, and which somehow managed to escape the jagged teeth of a sawmill. He relaxes under its dancing shade, takes a deep breath, and closes his eyes. Soon, he is revisiting old sights, hearing old sounds, and smelling old fragrances as his dreams take him back for another visit with a few old ghosts who still haunt the flatwoods.

# Chapter II

## The Pines

Jimmy has always been able to recall the day when he first became a conscious person. As confused as things can be for an eighteen-month-old child, he nevertheless became suddenly and acutely aware of the fact that he was a separate entity from all the strange things and sights that were occurring around him. The first thoughts that began to take substance in his mind were like a menagerie of all his senses as they simultaneously tested the faculties of his sub-juvenile mentality. It happened at what appeared to him as some kind of special event. New thoughts were feeding his callow brain with lasting mental pictures, which he would later recognize as a collection of reflections having to do with horses, music, and war.

Horses appeared to Jimmy's neophyte consciousness as enormous hairy things that had long legs and emitted a constant stream of wet slobber from somewhere above him. Music was an exciting yet noisy commotion that seemed to be coming from a group of people who were dressed all alike and carrying big brass and silver colored objects. War was some mysterious thing that grown people were talking very excitedly about, but which seemed to be going on in some place where Jimmy was unable to see or imagine. All he understood was that everyone was talking about going to some place called war, and he wanted to go there too. At such a tender age, there is only so much information that a small child's brain can assimilate. That is probably one of the reasons why little children cry so much. It is also a practical reason as to why children should be under constant adult supervision to prevent them from acting on their first impulses.

Those first mental pictures that were captured forever in Jimmy's mind came to him during a time of national uncertainty and preparation for a coming conflict between many nations, a conflict that was to be known as World War II. As an army brat whose first cognitive thoughts were formulated in a military environment in which he was born, Jimmy saw and heard many things that children born to civilian parents will never have and, most likely, will never even have the opportunity to experience. His father was a horse cavalryman and one of the most loyal to have ever served in the horse cavalry, a special breed of men with centuries of history behind them.

Before he was old enough to be responsible for his own carelessness, Jimmy spent the war years and his youth growing up on his family's old homestead that everyone in the family always referred to as the *Pines*. The *Pines* still sits nestled deep in the pine forests and cypress swamp covered coastal plains of Southeast Georgia. And although it is now deserted, as it has been for a long time, it waits for a new era of occupancy and a new coat of paint.

The *Pines* was a place where hard work and reading was mandatory. And it is there where Jimmy's memories often draw him back to the first book that he was able to read from cover to cover without adult assistance. That first solo reading adventure sparked urges in him that, even today, prod him on to discover and do things not yet experienced. As he turned each page of Daniel Defoe's *Robinson Crusoe*, he dreamed of how wonderful it would be if only he could be so lucky as to be stranded on a desert island with someone with a name like Friday. By the time he was twelve years old, he had read most of the works of Dickens, Poe, Stevenson, Huxley, and many of the works of other classical writers of the late nineteenth and early twentieth centuries. During his awkward years of puberty, Jimmy even explored the bizarre literary worlds of Henry Miller and his offbeat literary friends who used to hang out around the hotels and sidewalk cafes in Paris near Cluney Square.

After his evening reading sessions and before falling asleep, Jimmy would write to himself about some of the places that he had been reading about. Many years later, when he was a young soldier stationed in Germany, he managed to finagle a leave of absence and travel to France. He spent most of his time there sitting at a table in front of a Parisian sidewalk café, sipping Pernod, and reading Hemingway's *For Whom the Bell Tolls* and a copy of the first English translation of Remarque's *All Quiet on the Western Front.*

Most of Jimmy's favorite authors wrote about the adventures of fictitious others as seen through the eyes of yet other fictitious others. Envy bears heavy on the soul, and their writings made Jimmy more envious of the authors than did the characters they created with such marvelous strokes of their pens. Although they gave their human representations literary breaths of life that made them all seem real and exciting, Jimmy believed that the lives of their imaginary creations could never match those of their creators. He was sure the ghosts of all the authors that had been sharing his room with him for so many years had once been real living people themselves, people who had untold stories of their own. He even supposed that the authors, themselves, had done many of the things that they had been giving credit to their fictional characters for doing, and that they had sought out difficult circumstances just so they could create and write about special people to serve as their literary stand-ins.

The walls of the living room, den, and hallway of the big house where Jimmy lived from his fifth birthday until graduating from high school were all lined from the floors to ceilings with long shelves that were filled with hundreds of books his family had collected over the years. Not many children get to grow up in their own private library. Even his little bedroom in the rear of the big house was a brothel of virgin literature. And with the desire of a Satyr, he bedded as many as possible. He read much on the subjects of government, religion and philosophy before leaving home at the urgings of a curiosity about a world that had been conceived and born from his nightly liaisons with books of various covers and titles.

As he became more engrossed in reading about places he had never seen and people he had never met, envy faded and admiration grew for his belletristic companions. He could hardly wait until he could leave Claxton High School back in the dustbin of his memories, shed the official bonds of his juvenile existence, and follow in what he was certain were footprints into his future that had been laid down especially for him by his literary friends. Even though he knew he might never be as famous as his old back-room book buddies, he was to experience such a kaleidoscope of life's adventures and pleasures that he would never again feel the need to be envious of another person.

The *Pines* got its name from the tall grove of longleaf pine trees that still stand between the big house and the main road. Those stately trees are a few of the last examples of the great virgin pines that once shaded the southern coastal plains before the days of sawmills and cottonseed. Anyone who might wish to visit the old homestead today must pass through a double wrought-iron gate that opens to a cathedral of glistening and whispering pine trees. Their huge brown trunks give the appearance of Corinthian columns as they rise to support a majestic ceiling of shimmering greenery.

The ground below the giant sun-freckled shadow of the pine grove is covered with layer upon layer of rusty colored pine needles. The constant shedding of the pine needles keeps a fresh and deep carpet of straw around the azaleas, day lilies, spirea, and wisteria that grows in sculptured clumps throughout the grove. It is a place that is perfectly suited for whippoorwills that like to build their nests on the ground amongst the camouflaging straw. This ancient mountain of greenery still stands like a platoon of soldiers guarding a tomb of memories. And although the pine trees now look like a formation of old battle-scarred veterans that are missing a few of their ranks, it continues to serve as a visual navigation aid for pilots flying east and west to and from Savannah.

The old black woman who helped care for Jimmy during the first few years of his life spoke perfect English. She would scold him every time he brought into the house what she referred to as "field-hand talk." Eloise was a stern, yet kind and tender matriarch of the descendants of slaves who once worked the fields that belonged to Jimmy's great grandfather from his paternal grandmother's side of the family. Eloise would read to Jimmy and his brother every Sunday afternoon when the grown-ups were having their weekly adult gathering and the children had already been seen and now were not to be heard. She was wise beyond her education, and she instilled in Jimmy the seeds of respect that would grow into an admiration and appreciation for the earned achievements of the individual human mind.

Jimmy has only a few lingering yet persistent memories of Eloise's mother and father, Josh and Martha Murphy. His most vivid recollection of Josh is of him driving a mule and wagon and speaking in a very deep, but kindly voice. There was usually another white-bearded old man with him who wore the first wooden peg leg that Jimmy had ever seen. When riding in Josh's wagon, the man would sit in an old armchair that had been nailed to the floorboard of the wagon. His peg leg would be propped up on one of the sides of the wagon in a way that made the stubby end of his wooden leg jut over the side of the wagon like a small cannon on a gunboat. His walking cane would always be hanging on the end of his peg leg about where his ankle used to be. The cane would swing back and forth in rhythm with the sauntering gait of Josh's mule. Jimmy's most memorable picture of Martha is of her sitting next to Josh on top of their wagon, using a giant pillow for a seat cushion, wearing a large red brimmed bonnet, and singing gospel hymns in a voice that could drive Mahalia Jackson into vocal retreat.

Every Sunday morning, Josh and Martha would come riding down the white sandy road in front of the big house. The two of them would be perched high on the seat of the wagon while their old mule meandered from one side of the road to the other, tugging them along on the way to listen to Preacher Stewart burn holes through the souls of his little congregation. Jimmy knew it was only the breeze that was blowing through the tall pine trees, but those pine needles sure seemed to dance in resonance with Martha's operatic vibrato. It was a sight and sound to behold, one of those mental paintings from past times and past events that can only be captured and recorded in the memories of those who were lucky enough to have witnessed the presentations of the moment. Such images are destined to be lost forever as they die with the death of the beholder.

Before Jimmy was old enough to have a driver's license, he was driving a ten-wheeler truck and working for his Uncle Wallace (named in honor of a famous Scotsman). They would load the truck with watermelons or cantaloupes and maybe a few dozen three-pound bags of pecans. Jimmy would drive the truck down to the coastal tidelands between Savannah and Kingsland where he would set up his *"Watermelons and Pecans for Sale"* sign on the side of U.S. Highway 17. While relaxing in an old discarded chair under the shade of a sprawling live oak tree, he would open one of the books that he always brought with him and wait for the tourists to pull over and buy his goods.

The tourists would stream down the highway in a convoy of cars that stretched up and down the highway as far as the eye could see, all headed for Florida. The roof of every car would be stacked tall with layers of beach umbrellas, lawn chairs, and at least one ice chest. Jimmy would sell the watermelons for thirty cents apiece or three for a dollar. Maybe the tourists were just being kind to him, but they usually took the three for a dollar deal.

Uncle Wallace would drive his pickup truck along his regular route and sell the watermelons to the people who lived on the banks of the tidal creeks, which were accessible only by narrow one-lane roads of loose white sand overhung by giant live oak tree limbs that were draped in gray Spanish moss. They always saved at least two watermelons to give to Mrs. Johnson who had several children living with her. Mrs. Johnson was a very nice black lady who lived in Pinpoint, a small settlement of mostly clapboard houses on the outskirts of Savannah. Several children were usually playing in her front yard, which she kept brushed clean with a homemade broom made of dead gall berry bushes bound together with bailing wire and tobacco twine. The children were very well mannered, and one of them was named Clarence Thomas.

Uncle Wallace was a tee-totaling, non-smoking, often profane, and very outspoken atheist who did a lot for other people. Jimmy once asked him why it was that he gave away perfectly good watermelons when he could have easily sold every one of them. Uncle Wallace explained that kindness is something everyone needs, but kindness will turn to greed if it is not quickly passed along to someone else. He cautioned, however, that we should be deliberately mindful of our kindness, because misplaced kindness and charity is welfare, which soon breeds contempt for the giver by the receiver and for the receiver by the giver. He said that Mrs. Johnson understood the differences between kindness, charity, and welfare, and her acceptance and appreciation for the few gifts that he was able to give her was an even greater gift to him. For an atheist, Uncle Wallace was a fairly good preacher.

After Uncle Wallace and Jimmy had finished selling all their melons, they would drive over to the fish and shrimp docks near Richmond Hill, a little village south of Savannah that was founded by the automobile magnate, Henry Ford. They would fill up the back of Uncle Wallace's pick-up truck with a mixture of ice and fresh fish, shrimp, oysters, blue crabs, or any other seafood that might be in season. They would haul the dripping load of seafood back inland and sell it to the grocery stores and little seafood markets in Pembroke, Daisy, Claxton, Hagan, and Bellville. Uncle Wallace was a thrifty businessman who didn't like the idea that he might waste fuel by running an empty truck. He was what people used to refer to as a '*cash-and-carry*' man. He even claimed to have never owned a checkbook, never paid a tax, and never charged a tax on anything that he sold.

Henry Ford came to Richmond Hill in the 1920s and bought up most of the land south of the Ogeechee River delta where he soon began conducting his own private experiments in socialism and communal living. His intentions were to turn Richmond Hill into a completely self-sufficient community that would be supported entirely by the industrious and cooperative nature of its citizens. Of course that would all be accomplished under his personal tutelage and benevolent presence. He quickly indentured the local population and furnished them with their own school, their own teachers, their own hospital, their own fields, their own timber forests, their own lumber mills, their own seafood industry, and their own everything that a good communist commune would ever need according to Karl Marx. But he held the liens. They soon began to have their problems too.

It seems that when everything is made equally available to all people they soon become resentful of each other, and, soon after, they become unproductive. When people are left to the mercy of their own devices, personal resentments, jealousies, ambitions, and desires for status, which are natural tendencies existing in the human condition, they begin to breed competition and, therefore, productivity, which is the life-blood of capitalism and insurer of a nation's freedom.

Nevertheless, Mr. Ford was steadfast in his faith in the powers of social welfare. He believed that, regardless of a person's socioeconomic background, anyone can be placed in a significant or responsible position and, simply through such freely given opportunities, they will become enthusiastic and productive members of society. In fact, his belief in the socialist utopian theory was so strong that he decided to take a family of the worst examples of breathing human flesh that were known to reside along the mouth of the Ogeechee River, move them to Detroit, and give them important jobs in his automobile factory. They lasted only a few weeks before the entire family hitchhiked back to the muddy banks of the Ogeechee. Today, the descendants of that experiment still live along the same tidal creeks where they lived before, and still robbing crab traps by day and dragging tidal waters for illegal shrimp by night.

Mr. Ford made a good cheap car, but he was a miserable failure in the social sciences. It is paradoxical how some people are so willing to vehemently condemn the extremes of others while at the same time defending and promoting their own favorite system of feudalism, socialism, or some other example of human slavery and oppression.

It was the end of an era and the beginning of another when Henry Ford finally went back to Detroit to die and Richmond Hill began to live. The old Ford home still stands on the south bank of the Ogeechee River where it remains a constant reminder of how fleeting glory can be when it takes the bride of arrogance. After many years of intermittent vacancies and several changes in ownership, it was an ironic twist of fate when the old place was purchased by an Arabian oil sheik that owed his riches to the world's thirst for petroleum products brought on by Henry Ford's automobiles. After the war in the Persian

Gulf and subsequent diminished effectiveness of the Middle Eastern oil cartel, the old Ford house and its expansive grounds and gardens were again returned to the marketplace of the people.

The old Ford home and its surrounding grounds are now a community of riverside homes that are owned by instantly rich dot-comers, money market speculators, and a few Hollywood movie personalities. These new strangers to the banks of the Ogeechee were so afraid of the local inhabitants that they erected a twenty-foot high earthen wall and fence around their new community in order to keep prying eyes out and protect the new residents in their new but probably temporary xenophobic existence.

Many wonderful Americans, who are finally realizing their dreams, now populate the area around the old Ford plantation, the mouth of the Ogeechee, along the Belfast River, and up and down the banks of other tidal waters of coastal Georgia. They are a people who no longer have to hope for someone else to give them a future; they made their own. God bless America.

Jimmy's grandfather was born a just few weeks after the Confederate forces fired on Fort Sumter, and he was almost four years old when Abraham Lincoln was assassinated. He was born in Bulloch County, but raised by his grandfather who lived in Liberty County on the old family land grant that was named *The Isle of Patmos*. The original land grant of several hundred acres along the banks of the Canoochee River had been deeded to his great grandfather in payment for his services as a Captain of Cavalry in the famous Sparta Regiment. The founder and first commander of that Revolutionary War regiment was Colonel John Thomas, but was later commanded by Colonel Benjamin Roebuck. The regiment is now commonly referred to as Roebuck's Regiment.

An additional tract of land adjoining the original grant was later granted to the Captain's son in payment for his services in the War of 1812. It would be another one hundred and fifty years before the United States Government would take all the land back and build an artillery firing range for a new military camp, which is now called Fort Stewart. Fort Stewart is one of the largest contiguous land mass military installations the United States, and it continues to command the pine forests, swamps, and riverbanks where Jimmy's grandfather spent his youth. The only signs that still remain, and which are indicative of previous human habitation, on the Isle of Patmos is a note on a military map and an old cemetery. The map marks the site of a once active ferry crossing over the Cannochee River that was operated by the Captain during his retirement. The cemetery has only one grave marker, that of the Captain.

It was only recently that the original record of the land survey and transfer of the Liberty County grant was discovered. It revealed that the great-great-great grandfather of Jimmy's wife had conducted the land survey for his great-great-great grandfather. The next time the two family names would appear again on one document would be on their marriage license. It would have been a wonderful thing had Jimmy's grandfather lived long enough to be able to hold both documents in his hands and experience the merging of old memories and the beginning of new ones.

It was in August of 1958, less than a week before Mr. Jim's ninety-eighth birthday and only a few months after he became bedridden. Jimmy was packing a few of his belongings and getting ready to catch a bus to Savannah where he would be inducted into the United States Army. When it was time for him to leave, he went to his grandfather's room to bid him farewell. Jimmy could tell that it bothered Mr. Jim knowing that they would no longer be taking their walks together through the flatwoods and oak ridges. Mr. Jim took Jimmy's hand and, speaking in his old familiar and knowing manner, said, "Jimmy, I know you want to go away and see the world now, but one day you will come back home to stay."

"How do you know that, Grandpa?"

"You have always talked and dreamed about people and places that you were reading about in all those books of yours. Those memories are still fresh in your mind, but the memories of the people and the place you are now leaving were your first memories. Those memories will always be your strongest ones, and they will pull on your soul until your body returns."

That was the last conversation that Jimmy had with his grandfather. In 1959, Jimmy was stationed with the 8th Airborne Infantry Division in Germany and on a trip to Luxembourg to participate in a military ceremony in honor of General George S. Patton. General Patton died in December of 1945 and was buried in an American military cemetery on a hill overlooking Luxembourg City. His grave was placed at the head of a great formation of white crosses; each cross marking the grave of one of the thousands of soldiers who had served in his command and had been killed during World War II. It was when he was standing next to General Patton's grave that Jimmy received the news informing him that his grandfather had died. Mr. Jim was almost a hundred years old. Jimmy sat down by the grave of that great warrior, defender of liberty, and protector of the weak, and wondered where it is that great minds go after their fragile bodies die.

Someone once said that it is impossible to go back home again. But it seems reasonable and proper that it be an unpardonable sin against the memories of those we leave behind to never have a desire to return. The overpowering longing to leave people and places one loves and venture to places visited only in the galleries of an imaginative mind can be a dichotomy of emotions. Such conflict must be resolved by keeping alive the hope of returning, maybe someday when time is more permissive.

Forgetting the past might be possible and even desirable for people who have unpleasant memories of the people they once knew and of the place from where they came. But that would be impossible for people who are fortunate to have fond remembrances. Good memories of past places and past relationships are things that people should pass along to their children so they can cherish them and use them as reference points and foundations for building their own futures and memories.

General Patton chose to rest with the people he loved most, a place where he can serve forever with his troops who had given him the memories that he treasured most during his last days. One day too, Jimmy will return to where his old memories dwell, and he too will rest among the people and the place he knows and loves, a place called the *Pines*.

# Chapter III

## Charlie Horse

The first horse that Jimmy was allowed to call his own, a privilege that came with the responsibility for its care and keep, was named Charlie. Charlie was a horse that Jimmy's father kept on the farm to teach horsemanship skills to members of the family. He even made a little money on the side by teaching a few paying customers that lived in nearby towns. However, when the time came for Jimmy to enter the first grade at Bellville School, Charlie was sold to a man who lived somewhere on the other side of Glenville. It didn't make Jimmy feel any better when his father promised to get him another horse just as soon as he was old enough to properly care for one. It would be four long years and on Jimmy's tenth birthday before Mr. Fet would drive his truck over to Glenville and, after a bit of horse-trading talk, bring Charlie back to the farm where he would spend the rest of his life.

Charlie was not a young horse. In horse years, he was probably several years older than Jimmy's father, who was over fifty at the time. Charlie seemed to be able to sense the difference between his age and Jimmy's age, and he would sometimes appear to assume the duties of a wise old sire when Jimmy's father was not around. A ten-year-old boy has little chance at surviving this world when there are no adults around, of some species, and when his erratic pre-adolescent male human brain kicks into gear. Mr. Fet was probably aware of that when he brought Charlie back home and immediately enrolled the two of them in his cavalryman's school of good horse sense.

Jimmy's father was an expert horseman, and he always stabled at least two or three horses. No one in the Bay Branch Community has ever know of or seen anyone else who could match the equestrian skills of that old horse cavalryman. His horses even seemed to sense his dominance every time he walked through the barnyard. Every horse would turn to face him and then drop their head in acknowledgment of his presence as he walked by each of them on his way to or from the stables and tack room. Actually, horses have no cognitive abilities at all and therefore don't understand anything. Nevertheless, they are amazingly capable of being trained to such a level as to cause them to react to various stimuli and complex circumstances with anticipated accuracy. That one characteristic has made horses very useful to the labors of humanity and one of the most enjoyable companions that humans have ever known to exist among the kingdom of animals.

Charlie was not only Jimmy's first horse, but was also his first really good friend. After school, and depending upon the time of the year, Charlie and Jimmy had several duties that were required of them to be accomplished before nightfall. When the school bus stopped at the head of the lane in front of the big house, Jimmy would run the hundred yards to the back porch of the big house, slip on his riding boots and split-tailed canvas brush coat, grab an apple and his hat, and head for the barn. The entire exercise was an escape and evasion maneuver that Jimmy designed just for the single purpose of getting out of the house before his Aunt Augusta could spot him and give him a list of things to do that might interfere with his own plans for the rest of the day.

After throwing a blanket on Charlie's back, followed by his Sears and Roebuck Ranch Hand Roper saddle, and tightening a couple of half hitches in Charlie's cinch, horse and boy were ready to go. Jimmy's best time from stepping off the school bus to being saddle-ready was just under ten minutes. Even with all the modern conveniences of today, it has become very noticeable that most children are seldom, if ever, required to do after-school chores or work on homework assignments. When they are required to do either of them, both homework and chores are usually insignificant in quantity and quality. They are unfortunate children whose parents will eventually reap the results of their own shortsightedness.

Mending fences and counting the cattle that free-roamed the flatwoods were Jimmy's primary chores. After taking the daily cattle count and checking for newborn calves, he would check a section of fence to make sure that there were no breaks or sags where the cattle might be able to escape into the vast expanses of the great flatwoods.

As the days grew shorter and the evenings cooler, it was time to gather a winter's supply of lighterknots to be used as fire starters in the kitchen stove and the two fireplaces in the big house, one in the living room and another in his grandmother's room. Jimmy would tie two burlap bags together with a piece of rope and sling them over the rear of the saddle, just like they were a pair of pony express saddlebags. After finishing his cattle and fence checking duties, he would ride off into the flatwoods and fill the bags with lighterknots.

Lighterknots are among the abundant gifts that come from Mother Nature. It would be difficult to argue against the idea that such gifts were meant to help humans along in their long struggle to the top of the food chain. Long before the miracle of strike-anywhere matches and charcoal lighter fluid, human beings were looking for something to use to start fires without being embarrassed every time they tried to light a fire with those two stupid pieces of flint and a wad of dry grass. Lighterknots have been lying around on the floors of southern primeval forests for eons, just waiting for some curious homo sapien to come along, pick one up, and discover its magic. It is quite possible that there are more potential BTUs compressed in just one square inch of a lighterknot than there is in the entire tail section of a NASA space shuttle.

Longleaf slash and yellow pines are only two of several species of pine trees that are indigenous to the southern coastal plains, and they are the ones that create lighterknots. The sap that flows through the soft wood of the pine tree becomes highly concentrated at the junctions of the tree's trunk where the bases of the limbs meet the trunk. That is where the tree's annual age rings are tightly constricted, which causes the wood at the junctions to become extremely dense. The annual growing process eventually leads to a heavy knot being formed at that point on the tree. As the tree grows larger and taller and finally succumbs to the natural progressions of age and disease, it is this very hard and heavy lighterknot that is left on the ground as the last remaining evidence of the pine tree's once great majesty.

It was an irresistible temptation for Jimmy to dream up songs and sing them out loudly as he rode Charlie through the flatwoods. Other than an occasional shake of Charlie's head, there was little fear of the intimidating presence of others. One day, perhaps when technology permits, those who were not present for the live concerts might be able to hear the voice of a twelve-year-old boy singing in concert with the whispering pines. It has been said that lighterknots have locked within them the recordings of all the sounds that were ever made in the forest when there was no one around to hear the overtures of the moment.

Charlie and Jimmy had an additional and very noble duty of delivering medicines to some of the older people who lived along the Sara Ace and Cribbs branches. Most of them did not drive, could not drive, or did not even own an automobile. They rarely ventured past the confines of the front porches and back room kitchens of their lapboard houses. One of Jimmy's customers was Sara and her husband Thomas. They lived in a little house that overlooked Cribbs Branch, about four miles by road from the big house but only two miles by cross-country horse.

One sweltering hot August evening, Jimmy and Charlie were returning home after having delivered one of his Aunt Edith's medicinal concoctions to Sara's sister, Bessie, who lived on the other side of Cribbs Branch from Thomas and Sara. Charlie and Jimmy had just forded the waist-deep waters of the branch and were on their way up the hill along a red clay road leading to Thomas and Sara's house when Charlie's feet suddenly slipped. The two of them went down on the hard clay trail that was covered with a loose layer of small volcanic rocks, which are common in that region of the South. As Charlie fell, Jimmy's right leg became tangled in one of the stirrups and his head slammed against the marble-sized rocks on the hard-packed trail.

The sky had already turned dark by the time Jimmy regained consciousness and began to realize that the sensation he had been feeling while unconscious was Charlie's bridle reins being dragged back and forth over his limp body. He managed to climb back on the saddle and ride Charlie to Sara's house where she put him in her bed and sent Cleo for help. During his later career in the military, Jimmy was to have little tolerance for his fellow officers when they failed to perform their duties with at least the kind of dedication and determination as demonstrated by Charlie.

It was a very cold winter evening as Jimmy and Charlie made their way back home after another of their many cross-country journeys. As they crossed the Sara Ace Branch and neared the crest of the hill, Jimmy looked up and out across the fields toward home. A thick black plume of smoke was rising above the tall pine trees that bordered their property to the north along Cribbs Branch. Smoke rising from burning fat tar pine boards has a very characteristic swirl to it as the intense heat of the flames sucks in all the air from around it. Jimmy had spent a lot of time in those woods, and he instantly knew the origin of the smoke. When Charlie and Jimmy reached Sara's house, all that remained was an old brick chimney that was standing among a pile of smoldering ashes and twisted tin roofing.

Sara was one of those people who had nothing, but gave everything, and now she was gone. For the first time in his life Jimmy experienced the surreal shock of being in the presence of violent death. And, after that night, Thomas never was the same again. He never again worked on the farm and never showed up at another cane grinding or flatwoods fishing expedition, and he died less than two years after the fire. Some people said that he died of a heart attack while he was sitting alone on the front porch of his sister's house.

Before Thomas died, Charlie and Jimmy often stopped by Bessie's house where Thomas could usually be found sitting on her front porch and gazing out over Cribbs Branch towards the old place where he and Sara once lived. Jimmy told him how much he used to enjoy stopping by Sara's kitchen window when he and Charlie were out on one of their jaunts. She would give him a large flour biscuit that she had punched a deep hole in with her finger and poured cane syrup in the cavity. Thomas looked up and, in a quiet but matter of fact way, said, "Yep, Sara sure could cook those biscuits real good. And, you know, she's probably cooking some of those biscuits right now. It won't be long before we'll be seeing each other again, and then we'll be able to sit down once again at our old table and share a plate full of her biscuits and syrup."

Thomas' words made Jimmy realize that Thomas was never really alone after Sara died, and he understood just when it was that Thomas' heart attack had actually begun. And ever since that day, Jimmy would often wonder if perhaps Thomas and Sara might have been the last perfect relationship on earth.

Jimmy was barely thirteen years old when Charlie died. Charlie had carried him through many experiences, which in future years would provide him with the kind of stamina, patience, and character that would enable him to overcome the dangerous as well as the ridiculous. But, as all good servants serve their last day, all masters will demand their last favor. Charlie went blind, first in one eye and then the other, and it wasn't long before Mr. Fet had to explain to Jimmy what must be done.

It was on a cool Saturday morning in early spring of 1953 when Jimmy rode Charlie for the last time. His father led the way as he held Charlie's reins in one hand and cradled his rifle in his other arm. Charlie and Jimmy rode together for one last time and for one last mile before reaching the appointed place of life's earthly departure. As Jimmy sat on Charlie's bare back, clutching his mane tightly in his hands, he sensed that it was Charlie's last wish for Jimmy to be the one who must deliver him to graze forever in the vast green pastures that lay, somewhere, beyond the flatwoods.

Before Jimmy left home and began his career in the military, his father often talked with him about horses. Mr. Fet would explain to him about how horses had contributed so much to man's wars, progress, and enjoyment. And Jimmy remembered his father telling him how much he had always wanted to go to the Olympic Games and see the equestrian events.

It was 1972 and nearly twenty years after Charlie's death. Jimmy was now an army officer and assigned to the 8th Airborne Infantry Division in Europe where he had been given command of a tactical airborne company. The World Olympic summer games were being held in Munich that year, and a few tickets for several of the events had been donated to the officers and soldiers of the 8th Division. Jimmy felt as if he had been touched by fate when, of all the tickets that had been donated, he drew the only ticket that was available for the equestrian events. Even a rough and tough commander of airborne troops can shed a few tears as he watches an event that causes him to recall a father's wish and the memory of a horse named Charlie.

# Chapter IV

## Uncle Jeff and Other Kin

Ever wish for days of yore
When men were sure and ladies wore
Frilly things and proudly bore
Virtuous children and patience galore
Upon their souls they carried more
Love and faith till hearts did sore
With home fires burning men could rest
Guarding liberty with a nation's best

There never was any doubt in Jimmy's young mind that his life was about to change the day Aunt Augusta moved his brother and him into the big house to live with their grandparents and her ideas. Soon after the Japanese attack on Pearl Harbor, Jimmy's father received a promotion and was ordered to report for officer's training at a military base somewhere up in the state of Michigan. He was allowed only a few days furlough for moving his wife and two young boys down to the old family home in South Georgia. A war in the

Pacific was a certainty and America's entry in the European War was imminent. Mr. Fet thought it might be a long time before he would be able to come home again, if ever.

During the first two years of the war, Jimmy and his brother lived with their mother in a little house that their father was able to build during the short time in which he was allowed to be at home. He built the house among a grove of oak trees about a hundred yards behind the big house. That made sense, because having two young children and another adult living in the big house would have been an imposition on Aunt Augusta and their bedridden grandmother. It also gave Mr. Fet a little peace of mind knowing that his wife and children would have a safe and private place to live and still be near his family while he was away. The little house was built very well, and it still stands today even though it is now obscured by an overgrowth of scrub oaks, cedar trees, and wild grapevines. It serves now only as a storage place for things forgotten, but not yet discarded.

The few times that Jimmy was allowed to visit the big house were marked by a constant and irritating presence of some adult standing over him and using their knees to guide him in some direction in which did not wish to go. Apparently, they were trying to prevent him from destroying some old bric-a-bracs that had somehow managed to survive the War for Independence, the War of Northern Aggression, World War I, the Great Depression, the 1939 New York World's Fair, and several clumsy childhood's of previous members of the household.

Aunt Augusta's concern for her antiques must have finally been overcome by her even greater concern that her two nephews might have possibly been physically neglected or perhaps even subjected to a depraved social life. That would certainly necessitate her immediate and personal intervention, and it was most likely what prompted her into taking drastic action.

One fateful day, Aunt Augusta stormed into the little house, grabbed Jimmy with one of her hands and his brother with the other, announced to Eloise that she now worked for her, and then marched the three of them up to the big house. From that day on, Jimmy and his brother lived in the big house with their grandmother, grandfather, and Aunt Augusta. And that is when Jimmy first became aware of the fact he had an Uncle Jeff.

While Mr. Fet was in Europe attending to matters of war, it turned out that the mother of his two boys was something less than a perfect kind of little wife who would be willing to patiently and faithfully wait for the war to end and her brave soldier come home to her loving arms. The usual battle over child custody ensued, but that little squabble quickly terminated when the divorce court awarded Mr. Fet full custody of his two sons. That was an occurrence rarely heard of in those days, and it was the event that led to Aunt Augusta being appointed as legal guardian for her two nephews.

Aunt Augusta was married for only a short time to a man from Atlanta, but things didn't work out for them very well either. She was a passionate supporter of her church, the temperance movement, prohibition, and anything else that might present any possibility of preventing men from enjoying a few moments of peace and quiet with a good drink, a fine smoke, and the company of the kind of women who are not prone to complain about and enumerate the many vices of men. It seems that her new husband enjoyed having a couple of drinks every now and then, a fact that he had somehow been able to conceal from her before they were married. But the fault can't be placed entirely at his feet. She had likewise failed to mention anything to him about the fact that she disapproved of such conduct.

It is curious how the visceral urges of men and the social pressures on women to get married will oftentimes cause some people to completely abandon all thoughts of the commitments that are involved in marriage. In addition to her convictions regarding the immorality of imbibing alcohol, Aunt Augusta harbored even more resilient opinions on the subjects of politics and religion. At any rate, she soon dumped her husband and went back home to the *Pines* where she began a long life of caring for others. Other than those few minor dents in her life's armor, she was a perfectly wonderful person who gave everything she had in defense of her family and support of her community. She even came to be the South Georgia resident expert on Renaissance art, hemerocallis lilies, the lost gordonia, blue birds, and the science of hybridizing, grafting, and transplanting gardenias, azaleas, and other flora and fauna common to the South.

Soon after returning to the *Pines* and assuming personal responsibility for the care of her father and mother, Aunt Augusta wasted little time in establishing her rules of order regarding anything that might be remotely connected to the *Pines*. Her brothers and sisters conveniently bowed to her self-assumed authority. Those of them who were able to provide financial support did so in return for her management of the old home place and for caring for other members of the family who were either physical victims of the war or products of broken wartime marriages. Jimmy's grandfather, Mr. Jim, used to say, and no one ever questioned whether or not he was joking, "If you get married, stay married. It is much easier to deal with an angry woman who is living with you rather than having to deal with one who is able to attack you from the cover of another man's house."

Besides his Aunt Augusta, Jimmy had three other aunts. Aunt Eva was married to a *Southern Railway* executive in Atlanta, Aunt Anne was married to a corporate lawyer and lived in New Orleans, and Aunt Edith, the fourth and youngest of the sisters, was the family spinster who never seemed to care much for the company of any man, sober or otherwise. She was devoted to her duties as the head surgical nurse at the *Central of Georgia Railroad Hospital* in Savannah.

Uncle Jeff probably had the highest IQ in the family. He also had the strongest taste for and highest tolerance for any type of liquid that might contain the slightest amounts of alcohol, and he was usually in the process of proving it. He went to college at South Georgia Tech in Cochran where he was the captain of the sorriest basketball team in Georgia. Nevertheless, in one game and from the center of the court, he once personally scored all twenty-six of his team's losing points.

Jeff was one of those naturally talented people who often seem unable to orient their lives or stick with anything of significance for any length of time. He was more involved in transitory endeavors of the types that he could turn on and off at his pleasure, like sports, chasing women, and drinking. He also enjoyed great pleasure in raising Aunt Augusta's ire and then having to dodge her wrath.

Jeff was the youngest of Mr. Jim's seven children, the family antagonist, and professional playboy. Jimmy often wondered if perhaps his Aunt Augusta had decided to adopt his brother and him simply for the reason that she thought it would be much easier taking care of two young waifs rather than having to be saddled every day with the problems of an alcoholic younger brother. Nevertheless, Jeff moved out of the big house soon after the two brothers moved in and, since he was the oldest, Jimmy got Jeff's old room.

Mr. Fet was a professional soldier and the only one of the three brothers to ever hold a steady job for any length of time. He was given the middle name of *Felton* because his father, Mr. Jim, held Rebeca Latimer Felton in very high regard. Mrs. Felton was from up around Augusta and the first woman to ever serve in the United States Senate.

Uncle Wallace was a good-humored atheist who bought and sold produce and seafood when they were in season. His favorite sport, regardless of the season, was debating religion with any local religious leader that might be willing to take his bait.

When they were all home at the same time, Mr. Jim and his seven children would gather on the front porch of the big house and have long and spirited discussions on just about every subject known to mankind. When some point of debate needed to be verified by an outside authority, Mr. Jim would send Jimmy inside to search for and deliver the appropriate book of reference from the living room library. It was through these experiences that Jimmy earned the equivalent of a PhD in politics, history, religion, geography, military science and, even before they came to be recognized as academic disciplines, primary group dynamics and deviant behavior.

Uncle Jeff liked airplanes and began taking flying lessons soon after he came home from serving with the U.S. Army during the 1930s. But, as it happened to so many young men of those times, World War II intervened and he was ordered back to active duty and sent off to the war in Europe. He had a real tough time of it over there. The German Army captured him, but while they were transporting him back to a POW camp, he managed to escape and somehow find his way back to friendly lines. After surviving all that difficulty without suffering so much as a scratch, he suffered the misfortune of having his back injured by one of General George Patton's artillery pieces when it fell on him. His war injury ended his military career as well as his plans to attend the army air corps flight training school.

When Jeff came home before the war ended, everyone talked about how he no longer seemed to care about anything. Worse than that, he was unable to commit himself to anyone or anything, and he would sometimes leave home for weeks and months at a time. No one ever knew where he went during his many absences, but Jimmy imagined that it might be to some place where he could enjoy the company of the kind of people who weren't so prone to condemn him.

Whenever Jeff was home from one of his travels, he would spend most of his time puttering around the well shelter and making things that worked very well, but never lasted very long. He believed that it was against the laws of nature to make anything or do anything that challenged the natural order of things. He often rambled on about things like; "The incompetence of humanity is eventually revealed when they go against the more powerful forces of nature. Now consider what happened to the mule. God, in his infinite wisdom, created the mule so it would have a weak mind and strong back and be capable of working for man all day long. But that wasn't good enough for some people. They invented the tractor, which made God's mule something that people just laugh at. Then, along came all these New Deal programs that give free housing to people who once lived in the country and plowed mules, drove tractors, and planted and gathered crops. Now it's difficult to get crops planted or harvested and no one is breeding mules anymore. The price of tractors has gone sky high, all the farmhands have moved to town to live in subsidized housing where they sit around waiting for free government checks to arrive in the mail, and no one seems to have any further use for God. See what I mean? It's just not natural to make something that will outlast its usefulness or replace something that is still useful. At least the person who designed the whiskey bottle knew what he was doing. Those eighteen jiggers that are in one bottle of Scotch whiskey are perfectly suited for exactly one round of golf."

Jimmy didn't understand everything that Jeff was talking about then, except maybe that part about whiskey bottles. But listening to Jeff was an education to which few people have ever been exposed. That was Jimmy's first experience in dealing with someone who either understood planned obsolescence or who could actually see into the future. All he was sure of was that Jeff was very concerned about how the war had saved the world from the terror of the Nazis, but we were losing another war against something that he called "the tyranny of our own passions."

Some people said that Jeff had just "lost it" when he was over there fighting that war in Europe. But maybe Jeff understood something that most people never think about, and it bothered him that he would never be able to do anything about it. That seems to be a common problem with very smart people. Nevertheless, Jeff's mind was never idle, and he would often create situations that tested Jimmy's problem-solving skills and, what seemed to give him even greater pleasure, tried Aunt Augusta's patience.

Aunt Augusta decided that it would be a good idea to take her two new charges on a trip to the beach. Evidently, she thought that might do their young minds good and they would have a chance to do and see a few things that they had never before done or seen. That was most likely supposed to be some kind of therapy for her two boys for their having missed out on so much culture before coming to live with her.

Jimmy didn't know what a beach was or even where one was. Jeff, being real smart, used his walking cane to draw a huge map on the ground next to the well shelter. He explained all about continents, tides, oceans, and where England was by pointing his walking cane toward some unknown distant place that, to Jimmy's small mind, appeared to be somewhere just beyond the other side of the well shelter. Jeff had just given Jimmy his very first lesson in geography, and with that information well implanted in his head, they packed up Aunt Augusta's 1940 Ford early the next morning and off to the beach they went; Aunt Augusta, Uncle Jeff, and two excited boys.

In 1945, the Atlantic Ocean was about a three-hour drive and at least one flat tire change towards the east on U.S. Highway 280. But a five-year-old boy has no concept of the relationship between time and space, much less of Einstein's theory on relativity. As soon as they were in the car, Jeff began explaining to Jimmy about how far they were going to have to travel and how, if he really kept his eyes peeled, he would be able to see England on the other side of the ocean. With the anticipation of a seasick sailor gazing across the horizon for the first glimpse of land, Jimmy kept his face welded to one of the side windows of the car. When they neared a little town called Pembroke, about fifteen miles east of Claxton, Jeff suddenly exclaimed, "Look Jimmy! There it is! There's the ocean! Look at England on the other side! Can you see the little houses on the other side of the ocean?"

After a short burst of elation, a disappointingly suspicious feeling came over Jimmy as he was quickly consumed by the cold hard facts of reality. That body of water that Jeff was pointing at was not even close to being the size of the little field behind the big house. England was nothing but a grove of slash pine trees, and awww damn; those English houses sure looked a lot like grandpa's beehives.

That so-called ocean was one of those roadside ponds that are created when highway construction crews dig big holes along the sides of roads to provide dirt for building up the roadbeds so they will be high enough to keep the surface of the road from getting flooded during heavy rains. Even Aunt Augusta, the stoic iron mistress of rigidity, gave out a few gleeful cackles at Jeff's humor and the innocent gullibility of a five-year-old.

Mr. Fet was a frequent, yet more formidable target of Jeff's antics. One of the horses that Mr. Fet owned was named Sergeant, in honor of one of his old cavalry buddies who had served with him back in the early 1920s when they were chasing banditos along the border between Texas and Mexico. Sergeant was bred from an old line of cavalry horses, and he was one of the most beautiful animals to have ever grazed the pastures of South Georgia. He was a well-trained, well-groomed, and well-mannered horse that was a perfect reflection of Mr. Fet's combined knowledge of horses, equestrian training skills, and deep respect for practical traditions.

Jeff had a Tennessee Walking horse that he had named Major, in honor of no one that he ever knew. He just thought it would be nice to have a horse that out ranked his brother's horse. Jeff was one of those people who have the unique ability to work with horses while hardly speaking a word that would be loud enough to be detected by the human ear.

Major always seemed to understand what Jeff was thinking, and it wasn't long before Jeff had him trained to do tricks, just like a dog. Sit, roll over, lie down, shake hands, and stay, everything but fetch. Jeff would stand in front of Major and make only slight motions with his hands or body and Major would react to his cues like a concert violinist responding to the silent hints of a conductor's baton. About the only time that Jeff ever gave Major a vocal command was when he wanted him to walk, trot, run, or stop. And those were the exact words that he used to solicit his desired responses. When Jeff wanted to mount or dismount Major he would say, "down." Major would kneel down and allow Jeff to step in or out of the saddle without having to irritate his old war injury. Jeff was always willing to demonstrate that, no matter how perfect anything might be, someone will always come along and corrupt it. Mr. Fet was a purist. Jeff was a realist.

Some people said that Jeff drank because he had problems. Other people said that he had problems because he drank. No one can be absolutely certain about all that, but it was true that Jeff's health had been failing for some time. But that didn't seem to bother him as much as other things bothered him. And although he drank more heavily as the years passed, he was always able to speak intelligently about the relationships between people and their governments. He could accurately quote Rosseau, Hobbes, Locke, Voltaire, Paine, and other great figures of political and historical significance. Jeff just might have been one of those people who are capable of understanding the coming tragedy that is assured when people combine greed, liberty, and power without accepting any degrees of personal responsibility for the results of their unbridled excessiveness. At least those are some of the things that Jimmy remembers Jeff talking about, and maybe that is what influenced Jimmy to take a few things to excess later in his life as well.

Jeff died in December of 1965. It was a time when the war in Vietnam was just beginning and Americans were beginning to pay more attention to the war as the news media escalated it into a national trauma. It was also a time when many Americans were beginning to demonstrate great difficulty in defining simple terms like cowardice, bravery, patriotism, duty, honor, and personal responsibility.

A few months before Jeff died, Jimmy came back home from his army base in Kansas to marry a girl from Reidsville. Her father had recently moved his family to Claxton where he opened a new automobile parts store. Before Jimmy and his new bride said their wedding vows and traveled back to Kansas, he stopped by Jeff's little shack to bid him farewell. The situation in Vietnam was becoming more troublesome each passing day, and Jimmy was sure it wouldn't be long before he would be headed in that direction. Jeff wished Jimmy good luck and told him that he approved of the girl he was going to marry. He said he could recollect being very fond of one of her relatives.

As Jimmy turned to leave, Jeff's voice changed and he seemed almost sober as he looked at Jimmy and said, "You are about to be in a war that is going to create more problems for this country than any war we ever fought."

"What do you mean?"

"There are many people in this country who are beginning to hate their government, and the government is beginning to show contempt for the people. There is a lot of power in the military, and history has shown us that those who control the military have a habit of using it when they are afraid they might be losing control over the people. Regardless of any victories that might be won on the battlefield, when war is waged for the purpose of diverting people's attention from other issues, a different and more important war has already been lost. There will be a lot of dead heroes coming home from that war, but few live heroes will be so honored. A government that is willing to sacrifice the liberties of its own citizens under the pretense of protecting the liberties of the citizens of another nation cannot be trusted. You just be careful over there and try to be one of those to come home alive, no matter what other people might say about you."

As usual, Jeff was drinking that day, but he spoke with great wisdom and prophetic vision. And there is something about whiskey bottles that might lend a bit of validity to Jeff's theory about the natural order of universal chaos. The game of golf was invented in Scotland. The game had little to do with wisdom, but more with practicality. After using their sheepherder's staffs to knock rocks around in their pastures all day long, the Scots decided that the game of golf should end after playing exactly eighteen holes. Their decision made good sense in view of the fact that they knew a fifth of scotch whiskey contains exactly eighteen jiggers. Today, some golfers can be observed having a bit of difficulty finishing all eighteen holes of golf. That just might have something to do with the fact that whiskey bottles no longer come in only pints and fifths, they now come in liters and half-gallons. No doubt about it, Jeff had a mental grasp on a few things that few of us rarely ever contemplate.

# Chapter V

## Election Time

Every summer, just about the time when the grapes were ripe and had turned to a deep purple, all sorts of people would begin showing up at the *Pines*. The women would gather on the large screened-in back porch and the men would join Mr. Jim under the old grapevine arbor that stood, like a fresh-air grotto, between the big house and the well shelter. The old cypress post and split-rail arbor created a huge open-air convention hall that was shaded from the hot summer sun by a canopy of greenery, sixty feet long and forty feet wide. It was an inviting and comfortably cooling place for the men to escape the heat of the day as they strolled around or sat on split-log benches and talked their politics. As the men munched on fresh crackling-cornbread and sucked the juicy pulps from the grapes, they would take intermittent sips of a liquid mixture that Pete would keep bringing to them from his special hiding place that seemed to be somewhere on the other side of the well shelter. The man who drove the ice truck for the Claxton Ice Company seemed to know when the time was just right to come by and leave an ice pick and several blocks of ice piled high in the huge cast iron cane juice boiling vat under the well shelter.

The large group of men would congregate under one of the corners of the grapevine. And after a brief explanation of their purpose, further discussion, and final agreement as to the rules of order, they would separate into several smaller groups. Each little assemblage had a runner that they kept busy delivering messages to and from the other groups. Every now and then, some of the men would get a little disgruntled with their lack of progress and Mr. Jim would have to encourage them on until finally calling them all together for the great compromise.

"Herschel, you know that dog of yours won't hunt. Now you just leave him home and come along with us. You can be sure that things will be taken care of over your way. We need to put that boy with the red suspenders in the state house so he can get on with our list of things that we want him to do for us."

Herschel was Mr. Jim's brother, a lawyer, ex state senator, and county judge from over in Reidsville, the county seat for Tattnall County. Mr. Jim and Uncle Herschel usually pretended to be on opposite sides of major political issues until one of them finally 'caved in' at the last moment. That always seemed to make the compromise appear more convincing to the actual holdouts.

Spiraling wisps of cigar smoke could be seen drifting over the grapevine arbor and there was always a clandestine supply of spirits available. But Mr. Jim never smoked, and drank alcohol only in mild moderation. He believed that the human body was a temple for the soul and often said, "Any man who can't control his liquor will always be a sober man's servant."

Thomas E. Watson, Eugene Talmadge, and Eugene's boy, Herman, may not have been the holy trinity, but anyone who harbored any desires to be elected to public office in the State of Georgia had to pay homage to each of them and then pay his dues to the Treasurer of the local Democrat Party. After dutifully giving his tithes, the political aspirant had to swear that he had the permission of Tom's ghost to run for office. After the local party bigwigs accepted him as a viable candidate, he then had to donate another undisclosed sum of money, in honor of Gene's memory, to the state Democrat Party headquarters in Atlanta. And if that wasn't enough, and it never was, he had to publicly announce his support for Talmadge's road building program or his campaign would be derailed about as fast as a state trooper could pull him over on some trumped-up traffic charge.

Mr. Jim believed that young Herman was a little rough around the edges, but he was still of the opinion that Gene's boy was of good conservative stock and therefore deserving enough to be elected to the office of Governor, even if he did lean a bit towards being one of those New Deal Roosevelt Democrats. Besides, if Herman could get that infernal six miles of dusty road paved, the one that runs in front of the big house from Bay Branch Church to Blocker's Crossing, he was going to get Mr. Jim's vote along with a whole bunch of other Republican votes.

Some of those southern politicians at the national level were getting pretty good at moving money out of the north and spreading it around in the south to finance various social programs, road building projects, government employment schemes, and vote buying conspiracies. That sort of thing hadn't happened since the days before the *War of Northern Aggression,* and it had been sorely neglected during the so-called reconstruction era. Mr. Jim understood the politics of political money; "If you don't get it, someone else will." He blamed President Franklin Roosevelt for bringing us out of the great depression by teaching people who were worth only about one dollar how to mooch off people who were worth two dollars. He called it, "the politics of envy."

Mr. Jim was a progressive Republican in a southern world of dirt-level Democrat politics. And not one of those Roosevelt Democrats was comfortable with the idea that any of their kind might possibly make some deal with any of those Lincoln

Republicans. During the first half of the twentieth century, the Republican Party in Evans and Tattnall counties understood that they would never be able to get one of their candidates elected to any public office. It was often said that, even if Moses himself ran as a Republican against a Democrat in a two-man race, he would still finish in fifth place.

The Democrats would always win every general election, even if the only candidate they had to put up for election was a yellow dog. In the South, the term *yellow dog* refers to mongrels, mixed breed curs, or any other dog or human of ill breeding. They are the miserable creatures that cowardly follow anyone that promises them anything yet will never rate a shady spot on a decent man's front porch. Therefore, the term *Yellow Dog Democrat* applies to all people who blindly follow the ideology of the Democrat Party, whether they understand it or not.

Although the Republican Party was the minority political party in Evans County, they were still able to control the balance of power between the different factions that made up the Democrat Party. That made Mr. Jim the political pivot in the county during the primary elections. In order for any Republican to be able to vote in a Democrat primary, they had to call themselves an Independent or come all the way out of the closet and register as a Democrat. But everyone in the county knew who all the Republicans were anyway, and getting their voting block was essential for any faction of the Democrat Party if they wanted to be the dominant faction and, therefore, in power. The Democrat candidate who could get Mr. Jim's endorsement would win the primary, and whoever won the primary always won the general election. That is why the grapevine arbor at the *Pines* was such a busy place during election time. More deals have been cut under the shade of those scuppernong and muscadine vines than has ever been cut in any Las Vegas casino.

In South Georgia, as in most parts of America's rural south, people used to enjoy the social aspects of political gatherings about as much as they enjoyed community events like county fairs, cane grindings, school projects, and after church meetings. But that was before the days of consolidated schools, mass communications, mass production lines, mass transit, and mass confusion. Television was yet to imprison the simple-minded, welfare was still for only the truly poor, and listening to the radio was an intellectual stimulant that actually required the listener to use a bit of imagination.

Edward R. Murrow, Lowell Thomas, and Gabriel Heater were some of the few links to the outside world. *The Squeaking Door*, *The Great Gildersleeve*, and *The Bell Telephone Hour* were pleasant outlets for mystery, fantasy, and beautiful music. Things were simple, hard, but good, and election time was a periodic diversion that brought people together in a kind of conflicting concert that gave them a sense of local community pride and an even greater national purpose. People knew that professional politicians lied, cheated, and stole as a matter of course. But that was something they understood and even tolerated as long as the politicians never insulted the people's intelligence by being overtly crude or obvious in their shifty dealings. South Georgians are realists who attend to those things that are within their control and leave alone those things they cannot influence.

Bad politics is just bad politics, but bad manners and a bad party are inexcusable. And South Georgia people know how to throw a party. They are not very fond of the kind of parties where people are afraid they might get their expensive tuxedos or evening gowns mussed up, or the ones where everyone keeps looking around like the only reason that they are there is to impress someone. The southern outdoors party is a party where people come to enjoy the uninhibited presence of others without putting on airs or having to tolerate those who do.

After the results of the upcoming election had been properly discussed and agreed upon, the political meeting turned into a party. The men would set up a long table under the grapevine arbor and the women would cover it from end to end with all sorts of good things to eat. Pete would begin to be a bit more discreet in his efforts to make sure that everyone had timely access to sufficient amounts of his more spirited liquid refreshments.

The big grove of pine trees in front of the big house would soon fill with children of all ages, close cousins, distant kin, dog kin, black children, white children, some folks no one knew, and some who would probably never be seen again. The children played the usual hide-and-seek and tag games, but their greatest thrill was taking turns riding bareback around the pine grove on one of Preacher Stewart's or Uncle Wallace's mules. People of both races and economic levels attended the parties, and things like prejudice, segregation, and envy of another person's status were never a part of that life. It would be a few more years before children would learn how to practice such things in the public school system.

Playing little children's games was not for Jimmy. With that many adults distracted, he could do pretty much anything that he wanted to do without having to worry about anyone noticing him. Pete was about twenty years older than Jimmy was, but they had a relationship that was built on mutual trust and an appreciation for the other's tendency to get into things that were better off left unreported.

One of those little girls who came over from Reidsville with Uncle Herschel seemed to have taken a special interest in Jimmy. He was only eight years old but believed he was at least twenty-one and quite confident that he could give Rhett Butler lessons in how to charm women. The two of them charmed each other all the way up to the loft of the well shelter where there was a large pile of fertilizer bags and corn seed sacks stacked up like a giant rag bed. Jimmy was not sure what they were going to be doing up there all by themselves, but the thought of discovering the undiscovered was irresistibly exciting.

As luck would have it, they had not progressed very far before Pete's head popped up from the other side of the pile of burlap and cotton. In an excited whisper, Pete said, "Jimmy, dis here spot be took!" That got the little redheaded girl from Reidsville out of any mood she might have been in that would have been more pleasant for Jimmy. She started crying and acting like it was somehow Jimmy's fault for her being up there in the first place. That was when Jimmy learned a valuable lesson on how the minds of some ladies can work.

Oftentimes, a party would migrate to another house. "Pete, would you please bring me just one more dippah of that marv'lous tea, just so's to last 'till we get ovah' to the Tootle place?" That has to be spoken in a soft low-toned female southern drawl while conjuring up mental images of magnolia blossoms, pink azaleas, and white chiffon gowns flowing gently in a sultry evening breeze. Pete always obliged and helped things along by making sure that everyone was provided with one of his *travelers*. Try one sometime.

*Fill a large glass full of ice and then pour some strong unsweetened Luzianne tea over the ice until it is almost covered. Add a spilling jigger of second-run moonshine (43% alcohol = 86 proof and 50% alcohol =100 proof). If you can't find anyone who can get the real stuff for you, store bought 'corn-licker' such as Georgia Moon or Everclear will suffice. Top it all off with a crushed sprig of freshly picked mint. The ladies usually preferred to sip on their travelers with about two tablespoons of cane syrup stirred in the glass. That makes the drink taste a little sweeter and takes a bit of the edge off the moonshine. For those of you who can't find real cane syrup, you can substitute by using dark brown sugar. Close, but don't count on it tasting exactly like the real thing.*

Eugene Talmadge was elected to the office of Governor of the State of Georgia in November of 1946, but he died the following month, only a few days before he was to be sworn in for his term of office, which was to begin in January of 1947. The state legislature took the unusual action of electing his son, Herman, to serve out his father's full term of office. *Hummon,* as Herman's name was pronounced in Georgia, served as Governor for only a short while before the Georgia State Supreme Court ruled that his election by the state legislature was in violation of the state constitution. A big fight quickly ensued over who was the rightful governor, Gene's son Hummon, the newly elected Lieutenant Governor, Melvin Thompson, or the outgoing governor, Ellis Arnall.

Talmadge, being king of the hill at the moment, had his friend, who was the state Attorney General, arrange for the State Police to change the locks on the state capitol building overnight. Ellis Arnall, finding himself locked out of the state house on the following morning, decided to challenge Hummon by putting a desk at the entrance of the capitol building and then sitting there all day long acting like he was governor. After a few days, Arnall began to realize how stupid he was looking sitting there in his make-believe office that had no walls. He finally decided to give up and went home.

It wasn't long before a few state officials got together and conveniently sided with the State Supreme Court by declaring that Talmadge had not been elected in exactly a legal and proper manner. Hummon saw the handwriting on the wall and graciously gave up the governor's office to Melvin Thompson. However, those crafty good-old-boy politicians were not about to spoil things for Hummon, and they did something about it. They arranged for Melvin and Hummon to go head-to-head in a special election that was to be held in the fall of 1948.

Do not believe that there was not a whole lot of wheeling and dealing going on in every county in the State of Georgia during the summer of 1948 before that special election took place. Herman Talmadge called in every political marker that was still owed to his father, and the political machinery went to work. Mr. Jim's favorite arm bender was, "Now you listen here, this is not about whose daddy was on which side during what war, this is about your farm (your store, your school, your road, your hogs, or your whatever might fit the situation at the moment)."

Herman E. Talmadge, the boy who wore those flashy red suspenders just like his daddy did before him, won the special election. It wasn't long before the road in front of the big house was paved all the way from Bay Branch Church to Blocker's Crossing. And, as promised, Uncle Herschel was satisfied when the Reidsville State Prison was awarded a new construction project that required a lot of electrical work. That was good, because all four of Uncle Herschel's boys were electrical contractors.

Herman Talmadge was elected to a second term as governor and then went on to serve twenty-four years in the United States Senate. Pete went on to become a successful businessman in the clear liquid refreshment marketing business. And how about that little redheaded girl from Reidsville? Well, she finally grew up and used her southern charm to coerce some out-of-state medical doctor into marrying her. They lived unhappily ever after, at least until their divorce. That doctor sure could have used a friend like Pete.

# Chapter VI

## Cane Grinding Day

Grinding sugarcane and making cane syrup was once an annual social event in South Georgia. It was an occurrence that necessitated a substantial amount of commitment from everyone who lived in the Bay Branch Community, which is a farming community that takes up most of the southwest corner of Evans County. The community is bordered to the north by both sides of Bull Creek, to the south by both sides of the old historical Reidsville/Savannah/Sunbury Road, to the west by the Tattnall County line, and to the east by the old Hagan/Glenville Road.

Cane grinding and syrup-making day always occurred in the early winter, soon after the first heavy frost. It was a time when the air around the *Pines* would be filled with the very distinctive sweet bouquet of boiling cane juice swirling up from a large cast iron caldron. The aromatic essence of the cooking cane juice was usually accented with the smoky smell of chickens and sausages cooking over open grills. The air would be so full of flavor that you could taste it, and every dog in the community seemed to be attracted to that smell. There was just no way in the world that one family could manage that many dogs at one time. The only way to solve the problem was to hunt the dogs real hard early in the morning and then give them a good feeding before it was time to begin grinding the cane. That usually calmed the dogs down long enough for them to be willing to spend the rest of the day lounging in hairy heaps of tongue-dripping contentment on the front porch of the big house.

A similar technique seemed to work just as well with the older men, although they never seemed to need much of an excuse for pretending that they were tired. They would sit on the front porch of the big house in a long row of cane-bottomed rocking chairs and talk about old times while taking intermittent sips of fresh cane juice that Pete kept doctoring up with a few splashes of his branch-water special. The old men took turns contributing their favorite tales about a world that existed in earlier times, stories that only they were fortunate enough to have witnessed.

Jimmy and Pete's younger brothers, Tommy and Temp, would hide under the porch and listen to the old men's bawdy tales of yore. However, it was sometimes a bit difficult to discern what the men were saying over the sporadic interruptions that kept coming from a porch full of dogs. The dogs would contribute to the conversation with intimidating growls and compliant yips as they negotiated for the more sunny spots on the porch.

Cane grinding and syrup making day was always preceded by a day that was filled with ritualistic events, which were purposely designed to get people excited enough to show up for just two days of hard work. It was two full days of work and fun that would finally come to closure with the women enjoying a feeling of contribution and the men enjoying a feeling of not feeling anything.

After the cane boiler and juice barrels had been cleaned, the mule fed and stabled, and all the shelves along the walls of the well shelter lined with bottles of fresh cane syrup, the women would gather on the screened-in back porch to discuss the day's work and make plans for future community events. The young men would join the older men and the dogs on the front porch where Pete's evening was about to get very busy.

Not a farm in Southeast Georgia that was worth its allotted populations of fleas, ticks, gnats, and chiggers would ever get caught being guilty of not having a cane patch. The patch didn't have to be a very big one, because just one acre of prime cane can produce many gallons of syrup. Just one gallon of cane juice will yield one gallon of syrup. That was a good thing, because planting and harvesting sugar cane was hard work. It was a lonely backbreaking job that offered few rewards other than a promise that it would all be worthwhile after the effort finally resulted in the first community party following the fall harvest, Thanksgiving weekend, and the Christmas holidays. And there was usually plenty of help available for harvesting the cane stalks, because that was when the kind of fun and socializing began that involved more than just the normal holiday family gatherings. It was a time that signaled the end of summer and fall and the beginning of the coldest part of winter when there would be more time for family leisure and community socializing.

Real soppin' good cane syrup is nothing like that watered down stuff that drips from Yankee trees. Neither is it like that imitation translucent or caramel colored gunk that commercial syrup companies call corn syrup and load down with high levels of refined sugar. Just take a look at the labels on some of that stuff. They use the word artificial more times than a salesman does at a prosthetics convention. That naturally colored and naturally sweet gift from the gods of breakfast is made from nothing but raw cane juice that has been squeezed from common red-stemmed sugar cane stalks and then boiled down to the point that it makes the finished product look a lot like used motor oil.

Most of the containers that were used to store the cane syrup in were old liquor bottles, probably because they were the most natural and abundantly available receptacles, thanks to Jeff's drinking habit. The bottles would be sanitized with boiling water and filled with hot cane syrup before capping each bottle off with a good grade fishing cork. Cane syrup can be a little slow when you try to pour it from a cold bottle, but it can be encouraged to come out a little quicker by placing the bottle next to a hot stove burner or in a warm oven for a while before dribbling it over a plate full of hot buttered pancakes, homemade biscuits, or pan-fried cornbread.

There are several brands of commercially produced table syrup that can be found taking up shelf space in most grocery stores. They can also be spotted sitting on dingy tables in roadside restaurants, usually propping up a greasy plastic coated menu next to one of those spring-loaded napkin holders and little containers of salt, pepper, sugar, catsup, and mustard. Such things are generally thought of as belonging to the condiment family and meant for only occasional use and in very small amounts. Cane syrup, however, is one of those items that people in South Georgia have always considered to be one of the main food groups, and it is used in healthy quantities in preparing and consuming various southern dishes. For example, the pecan pie was invented in South Georgia long before Yankees started making that stale cardboard tasting stuff that they put in those anemic-looking little pecan pie simulations and try sell to unwary motorists at all those tourist traps along Interstate 95. You know, those places that some people actually have the nerve to call 'cultural centers.' Since South Georgia is the best source of supply for American pecans, it would seem sensible for Yankees to do the job the right way and import real cane syrup from Georgia so people up there could learn how to make real pecan pies. The real thing always tastes better and sells best.

Pecan pies are very easy to make. Pour one cup of cane syrup in a bowl, crack three large eggs and, very vigorously, beat them in with the syrup. Make sure that the mixture is a bit frothy and then pour it in a prepared pie shell. Some people have never learned how to make pie shells from flour and hog lard, but they may substitute for their lack of skills by buying one of those dainty pie shells that can be found in the frozen food section of most grocery stores. Sprinkle a cup and a half of pecan halves (don't forget to shell them first) over the top of all that stuff and then stick the pie in the middle rack of an oven that has been preheated to 350 degrees. Do not over cook. When the pecans begin turning a darker shade of brown, and way before they turn black (about 45 minutes), remove the pie from the oven and let it cool naturally at room temperature. That's somewhere between 65 and 80 degrees, depending on whether or not you have air conditioning. Allow the pie to cool until the filling firms up enough so that you can cut it with a dull kitchen knife, a hunting knife, or you can break off a chunk with your bare hands and eat it while you are on your way to the store to get some more of those Georgia pecans. If you just can't live without your jolt of refined sugar, you can dilute the cane syrup with up to a half a cup of that stuff people call corn syrup (white or dark Karo seems to do fine). But keep the flavor of the cane syrup dominant or you will miss the whole point of making pecan pies in the first place.

Some connoisseurs of cane syrup enjoy mixing a little bit of it in with their refried grits at breakfast time. That probably won't work if you didn't eat grits for supper. It certainly won't work if you are one of those unfortunate souls who refuse to eat grits at all. But, if you have and you do, the next time you cook grits, leave some of the leftovers in the pot and store in the refrigerator overnight. The following morning, the grits will be firm enough to cut into bite-sized cubes. Fry the hunks of grits in a skillet with just enough bacon grease (yes, real bacon grease, not vegetable oil) so as to keep the grits from sticking to the bottom of the skillet. When the grits are sizzling real good and turning brown around the edges, dump them in a cereal bowl and pour a little cane syrup over them. That is yummy good.

No matter how you like to eat cane syrup, it is just too thin if it won't break a hot biscuit in half when you drag it through a layer of cane syrup poured in the bottom of a dinner plate. And just a couple more things need to be said about grits. *Grit* is a verb and *grits* is a noun. I *grit* (verb) my teeth every time I go to a restaurant and *grits* (noun) ain't on the menu. Furthermore, if you ever visit a restaurant in the South and someone hears you say, "I'm not very hungry, I think I'll have just one grit," everyone in that place is going to believe you are a Yankee spy. Grits is a singular noun; deal with it.

The main reason that farmers intentionally set fire to their cane patches is to get rid of snakes, spiders, ticks, hairy worms, and many other critters that irritate and bite the people whose job is to go in the patch and harvest the cane. Fire burns very quickly through a patch of dry cane stalk blades, and it doesn't damage the stalks. Also, the thinning of the patch makes it much easier for the workers to cut and gather the cane stalks.

Another reason for burning a cane patch, and the one that is most enjoyable, is to have one heckuva good rabbit, coon, and snake shoot. The smartest and most responsible participant in the event should always be the one to assume the tasks of making sure which way the wind is blowing, placing the hunters around the field with their backs to the cane patch, stationing the fastest runners at the downwind side of the field, and making sure that everyone understands and observes a few ground rules. Never shoot into the cane patch; never shoot down the line of other hunters; and all hunters must wait for anything that comes running out of the patch to get by them before taking a shot at it.

After everyone is in place and properly briefed, a fire is set on the upwind side of the cane field. Then the fun begins. When it gets too smoky and hot for the shooters that are stationed at the downwind side of the patch, they are supposed to stack their shotguns, arm themselves with fire swatters made from green pine saplings, run to the crosswind side of the field, and make sure the fire doesn't spread to the flatwoods. That wouldn't be good.

It all happens very quickly, and a good shooting eye is essential for a cane patch hunter to be able to distinguish the subtle differences between running dogs, foxes, raccoons, or cousin Judy's tabby cat that had been getting fat while dining on field mice that had been getting fat dining on sugarcane roots. As luck would have it, Judy's cat survived at least four cane patch hunts before finally succumbing to the effects of the left rear tire of Uncle Wallace's pickup truck after her cat tried to escape the fire by crossing the dirt road between the burning cane patch and the safety of the barn. At least the hunters didn't shoot the cat, which made it much easier on them since Uncle Wallace was Judy's father and was the one who had to break the bad news to her.

Sometimes, strange things come high-tailing it out of a blazing hot cane patch. That usually necessitated a few slight, although immediate, alterations in the local rules of engagement. There was one particular cane patch hunt when everyone was at their assigned stations, the fire had been set, all shotguns were at the shoulder, but no one was thinking about the fact that Junior and Thomas's granddaughter, Cleo, had not been seen since early that morning. Once that fire gets going real good, all minds are focused on the cane patch, and nothing can be heard above the crackling and popping of burning cane stalk blades, shotgun blasts, and hunters yelling; "Thar one goes; git em!"

Such was the situation just as Junior and Cleo came crashing out of the cane patch, following the same general direction and estimated speed as Judy's cat. The only thing that Junior was wearing was his Evans County High School '*Longhorns*' football jersey that he had cut off about mid-waist. Cleo was wearing nothing but her birthday suit and a pair of brown unlaced ankle-high brogans. Uncle Thomas, as everyone called him, grabbed Cleo just as she went flying past him in an attempt to jump the ditch between the road and the cane patch. He caught her in mid-air, threw her in the ditch, yanked off his overalls, and tossed them on top of her. It was then that Cleo's brother, Tommy, yelled, "Grandpa! You ain't got no draws on!"

Uncle Thomas was a very religious man who had his hands full trying to raise three rowdy but hardworking boys and one wild girl. He calmly reached down, picked up his tattered old straw hat, and made a reasonable and respectable effort at covering his most exposed elements. With full resignation and dutiful acceptance of his situation, he looked up to the heavens and cried out, "Lawd, I ain't ner' axed yo' fo' much, but rat now, I sho' cood use jes' one mo' par' o' pants!" Junior was not heard of nor seen again for the rest of the day.

After the stalks of cane had been cut and gathered, they would be stacked in a huge pile near the cane mill. The mill consisted of two heavy iron cogwheels that turned together and squeezed the juice from the cane stalks while someone, appropriately referred to as 'the feeder', fed the stalks of cane into the mill. The cane juice would trickle down a trough that was made from a section of old tin roof capping and then spilled in a large wooden staved barrel that was covered with a strainer made from an old burlap bag. If a family didn't have a cane mill of their own, they would show up with their family truck or mule and wagon loaded down with cane stalks from their patches, along with generous contributions of cakes, pies, jars of pickles and other great things to eat. Everyone contributed and everyone benefited.

A mule provided the power for the cane mill by pulling a mill sweep in a big circle around the mill. The sweep was made from a cypress or bay tree log that had been specially selected by the way it was naturally bent in a manner that allowed it to be bolted to the top of the mill at the log's balance point. The large end of the log served as a counterweight and the small end extended down and outward to the mules' harness and traces. The mule would pull the small end of the log around the mill in a never-ending circle, stopping only for an occasional drink of water or for someone to empty the full barrel of juice into the boiler.

A gallon jug was always kept full of raw cane juice and kept cool for drinking by storing it in the bottom of the horse trough. Before drinking the fresh juice, it would be strained a second time through double sheets of cheesecloth. It surely must have been the drinking cool fresh cane juice that was responsible for the longevity of South Georgia dirt farmers. When the juice was mixed with a little of Pete's midnight special, it produced a lucid green concoction that surely must have given Al Capp his inspiration for a drink that he called 'Kikapoo Joy Juice' and made famous by his comic strip about people who lived in a place called 'Dogpatch.'

Things are not the same anymore. There is only one person in the county who is still known to be making cane syrup. He is a cantankerous old curmudgeon who stubbornly clings to the ways of the past and allows only a few select people to purchase a bottle or two of his small stock of cane syrup, which he keeps like vintage wine, stored in neat rows along the walls of his well shelter. And the old farm, where Jimmy began his journey into conscious life and where he spent his youth preparing for the day when he would begin another journey into a different life, has been leased out in an effort to satisfy the insatiable demands for pork from people in far off places, people who have never tasted cane syrup, pecan pies, or re-fried grits. And none of them has ever heard of Uncle Thomas or Pete, whose souls have since departed this earth and their bodies left buried in a little cemetery near the cool trickling waters of Bull Creek and Cribbs Branch. It is a place where, in spring and summer, the air is filled with the sweet fragrances of Cherokee Roses and honeysuckle blossoms.

Today, only soybeans, corn, millet, and other crops that are more suited for feeding hogs are grown in the old fields that were once dotted with the brilliant colors of cantaloupes, tomatoes, and watermelons, fields that were once alive with the laughter and shouts of black people and white people working and enjoying life together in a bygone world that time seems to have forgotten. They were a kind of people who shared each other's personal joys, successes, trials, and sorrows in untarnished ignorance of the prejudices and hatreds that, once again, were soon to invade the South.

# Chapter VII

## Fox Hunting

A few weeks after World War II ended, Mr. Fet retired from the army, came back home, and moved in his little house among the oak trees behind the big house. The house had been vacant ever since his two sons moved to the big house and their mother went back home to North Georgia. Mr. Fet spent many lonely nights in that house studying agricultural extension courses that had been made available to military veterans through the GI Bill program. It wasn't long before the old barn was full of various kinds of farm animals, the fields were being cultivated, and the old familiar sounds of people and machinery working on a farm could be heard once again. New wire fences were strung around the flatwoods where only a few half-wild cattle had grazed during the war years. There was even a new tractor for plowing the fields that had been leased out during the war to provide fresh produce for thousands of soldiers stationed at nearby Camp Stewart.

Although many items that are usually necessary for operating a farm were not rationed during the war, it was still difficult for small farmers to compete with the larger and more politically connected landowners that were able to manipulate the sources of farm supplies and influence the availability of credit. A few families who owned their farms free of mortgage were able to survive the war years by leasing their fields out to large corporations that imported low-wage migrant workers. The descendants of white and black sharecroppers, who had lived on and worked the land since the Colonial days, were faced with being forced to move to town or hire themselves out as cheap field labor. Many of them chose to move to town and live on public assistance, a practice that was becoming more and more popular.

The economy began to strengthen during the months following the war, and jobs were becoming more available for anyone with an education or who possessed special skills. Many farm laborers, encouraged by dreams of getting one of those big city jobs, migrated to urban areas only to find themselves qualified to do nothing more than the similar kinds of labor that they had been doing on the farms, loading someone else's truck or cooking for another man's family. The increasing availability of new social welfare programs was encouraging many such people to stay in the cities where they became the inner-city poor of the 1950s and 1960s. But Mr. Fet somehow managed to convince one black family to stay on the farm and work it with him. He believed that, because of the increasing migration to urban areas, there would be a corresponding increase in the demand for fresh produce, pork, and beef. He was right, and that was why he began taking those agriculture and farm management courses just as soon as he came home from the war.

At the end of the harvest season of the first year following the war, Mr. Fet had a thousand dollars left over after paying expenses, supporting the family, and purchasing a few luxuries. He was even able to purchase another automobile. In the 1940s, anyone who was ahead by a thousand dollars going into the

Christmas holidays was what people around those parts of the country referred to as "doin' real fine."

After the family finished eating their evening Christmas dinner at the big house, Mr. Fet invited his brothers and sisters to join him in the living room. He placed his thousand dollars on top of the fireplace mantel and informed Aunt Augusta that the money was hers for taking care of his two boys while he was away during the war. He explained how there could be even more money the following year, but since the land was divided among all seven brothers and sisters, he would need their consent to mortgage some of the land so he could purchase more equipment, supplies, and livestock. To show his good faith, he offered his entire share of the estate as collateral. There was a moment of dead silence before everyone in the room seemed to go nuts.

Aunt August was first to break the silence. "What? Our family managed to get through the Civil War, World War I, and the Depression without a mortgage on this land and I am not about to permit it to happen now!"

Mr. Fet's older sister offered to buy his portion of the land just to keep him from running the risk of losing it to those devil Republican bankers. His youngest sister started complaining to no one about how no one in the family ever consulted her about anything.

Uncle Wallace kept pacing around the floor and repeating, "Fet, now do you see what I mean? I told you it would just get things stirred up again! Dammit, I told you! Didn't I tell you?"

Jeff walked out of the living room and into the great hallway where many old paintings were hanging on the walls. He took a big gulp from a bottle that he always kept hidden in the bottom of the old wind-up RCA Victrola.

Mr. Fet looked squarely in the eyes of each of his sisters and retorted, "Well, you can keep the damned money and farm the place yourselves, or you can put the land in the soil bank like so many other quitters in this country have done." He then stormed out of the room and went back to his little house back in the oak grove. A few weeks later, a house-moving rig came and hauled the little house as far back towards the north property line as possible without putting it square in the middle of Cribbs Branch.

It was not that Jimmy's father and his siblings didn't love each other; it was just that, together, his four sisters owned four-sevenths of the entire estate. Most of them believed that anyone who would ever admit to so much as touching even one drop of alcohol was an irresponsible drunk and would eventually piss away everything that he owned.

Jimmy's father, his grandfather, and all his aunts and uncles even had different opinions regarding subjects of a political nature, and they took their views very personal like. Jeff called himself a constitutional libertarian and didn't care what anyone else did as long as they didn't do it to him. Uncle Wallace was an atheist who claimed that he would never belong to any political party since all politicians were nothing but liars, pimps, and thieves, and not one of them could ever be trusted any more than you could trust a traveling preacher with your daughter.

Mr. Fet was one of the last true conservative Democrats in the country. He was convinced that the Democrat Party was leaning toward socialism and would eventually bring on the collapse of the party. Mr. Jim was always trying to convince him that, since he was so sure of the imminent demise of the Democrat Party, why didn't he just go ahead and become a conservative Republican like him?

Aunt Eva, the one who lived in Atlanta and whose husband worked for the railroad, was one of those New Deal, Eleanor Roosevelt, give it all away, socialist democrats. She believed that it was the duty of every American citizen to give money to the needy, but not before it had been funneled through some government agency that would guarantee equality of distribution and provide some bureaucrat with another government job. She was the first person that Jimmy ever knew of who argued that the purpose of government was to provide financial security for everyone.

Aunt Ann, the one who lived in New Orleans and married to a lawyer, was a true independent. She claimed that she would vote for anyone who could protect the nation, preserve our individual liberties, and promote domestic tranquility without taxing everyone to death.

Jimmy's spinster aunt, the one who was the family nurse, had no political leanings at all. She claimed that she had enough problems just trying to keep the family healthy without having to worry about all their personal and political idiosyncrasies.

Aunt Augusta was a dictatorial right wing Republican and religious absolutist long before there ever was such a thing as the Christian Coalition. Any person or any living creature whose politics were even mildly to the left or right of hers, no matter if they were democrat, republican, or whatever, was in danger of getting run over by her right-wing extremist views.

Jimmy and his brother continued living in the big house after their father came home from the war, but they were occasionally permitted to take turns spending the night with their father back in his little house. Aunt Augusta disliked that practice, but had to tolerate it in order to maintain a little peace and quiet around the big house. She was in constant fear that her two adopted boys might discover the primary purpose of empty beer cans, wine bottles, and numerous other objects of her derision. And there was always plenty of beer, wine, and other more potent refreshments in ample supply during the great foxhunts and annual cookouts that took place every autumn back in the oak grove near Mr. Fet's little house.

Before Jimmy was successful in wearing Aunt Augusta down to the point that she finally gave up trying to keep him from hanging out with the grown men, he would slip out the window of his bedroom and spend the evening carousing with the men and enjoying the musky aroma of horses and dogs. For two weeks in every October, the oak grove would be filled with all sorts of vehicles, everything from old pick-up trucks to new Cadillacs. It seemed as if very man in the county would come driving in sometime during that two-week event. They would stay a while, eat a little bog, have a drink or two, and then drive out just as another vehicle was driving in to take its place.

Pete and Uncle Jeff were always in charge of making arrangements for the food and liquid refreshments, although there was never much effort needed to get things together and keep the festivities going. A large cast iron kettle was placed on a stack of firebricks and a couple of lighterknots got the fire started. When the water came to a boil, the goodies would be added to the pot, all in proper order. Pork, beef, and a few de-boned chickens were used to get the bog started. After the meat was almost done, rice, cornmeal, and grits were tossed in to give the bog a little body. Corn, lima beans, tomatoes, okra, onions and pretty much any other kind of vegetable that was available during that time of the year would be added to the pot. A few peppers, a good helping of Louisiana hot sauce, and a few special and secret spices gave the bog the right kick.

The bog was ready to eat when it reached a consistency that allowed it to be dipped on a slice of cornbread or hamburger bun without getting the bread so soggy that it couldn't be held in one hand without slipping through your fingers. The texture, thickness, and general viscosity of a bog are important and indicative of how a perfectly prepared bog got its name. A good bog clings to the face of a Claussen's hamburger bun sort of like swamp mud clings to your boots, but the bog tastes a heck of a lot better. For the duration of the two-week event, the bog would be kept in proper working order by adding various donations from Mother Nature's pantry. Squirrel meat, raccoon, rabbit, quail, dove; it really didn't really matter as long as an acceptable proportion of meat, rice, cornmeal, grits, vegetables, and spices were maintained.

No one ever concerned themselves about the source of the liquid refreshments that Pete always made sure was readily available and in adequate supply. Everyone knew that it was there and everything would be just fine as long as no one did anything stupid. Of course that was back when most county sheriffs actually knew the difference between real criminals and people who were just having a good time on their own property.

After failing to become a gentleman southern planter, Mr. Fet took up breeding fox hounds, bull dogs, horses, game chickens, transplanting wild fox, and doing those things that most men work their entire lives to be able to do after they retire. When he was in England preparing for the D-Day invasion, he spent much of his free time riding to the hounds, British style. He enjoyed the kind of fox hunting that they did in England even though it was a bit different from the way it was done back in South Georgia.

When the American soldiers arrived in England, the only people in Great Britain who had enough money to own horses for pleasure or even the spare time or inclination to chase a fox just for the sport of it were members of the aristocracy. The native red fox of England had become almost extinct after years of being killed off by English farmers who regarded them only as threats to their domesticated geese, ducks, pigeons, and chickens.

The British aristocracy had to keep a few wild fox in captivity in order to be able to maintain some semblance of their traditional manner of riding to the hounds. But every time one of those over-fed and over-weight caged up critters was turned loose for the great chase, it turned out to be a poor runner. The kind of fox hunting that allowed the hounds to catch the fox before the hunters could catch up with the hounds was beginning to reduce the fox population in England about as fast as the farmers had been depleting their numbers. If the British were going to maintain their old tradition of having a foxhunt that lasted more than a few minutes, they were going to have to come up with a better plan.

Some lowly English stable keeper, while in the process of cleaning fox cages and turning up his nose at the pungent odor, realized that just one soiled fox cage smells stronger than a whole forest full of free-roaming fox. The hunters soon had their stable hands collecting fox feces and urine-soaked straw from underneath the cages and stuffing the smelly stuff in potato sacks. The hunters would tie a rope to the sack and lay down an aromatic fox trail through the forest and countryside by dragging it behind a galloping horse. With a fox trail scented like that, they could keep the hounds running all day. And that, so it has been told, is how and where the term *'potato sack race'* originated and which, with a little modification as to the contents of the sack and manner and purpose of the race, became a favorite church social and school playground game.

In America, the English style of hunting a fox was mostly centered in the State of Virginia and a few other places up north where people still observed some of the old English horse riding methods. Riding to the hounds was also practiced by American military officers who had been exposed to the sport while serving in the cavalry. In the traditional English manner of fox hunting, the *red* fox is chased while the riders are in sight of the hounds during the entire chase. However, fox hunting in South Georgia is a completely different sport that is characterized by a more casual manner of hunting a species of fox that is indigenous to the southern United States, the *gray* fox.

Hunting the southern gray fox evolved from the sport of coon hunting rather than from the English fashion of red-coated hunters riding on horses behind a pack of hounds in hot pursuit of a fast running red fox. The gray fox is mostly a nocturnal animal that doesn't usually run cross-country like his English cousins. When a gray fox becomes aware that hounds are on his trail, he dodges, turns, doubles back, and generally trots an escape and evasion course that is designed to keep him just outside the reach of the kind of hounds that are trained to trail rather than chase. Oftentimes, while being trailed by hounds, a gray fox will double back, cut across his own path, double back again, and then climb up to an elevated perch where he will sit and watch the hounds as they continue in a giant circle of canine confusion around his observation point. The hunters would usually stay in one place and listen to their dogs while trying to identify the individual sounds of each of their dogs. They would talk a little politics and maybe even have a few social drinks.

Fox hunting in South Georgia was a sport that involved the expenditure of a lot of leisure time. It never was meant to involve hard work. Although rare, the hounds would sometimes pressure a gray fox into taking refuge, usually in a hollow log or up a hollow tree trunk. That always required a couple of hunters to go to the place where the fox had been cornered, dig him out, and then turn him loose in some area that wasn't being hunted that day. The purpose of the southern foxhunt is not to catch the fox or demonstrate the hunter's horsemanship or, for that matter, demonstrate any skill. Any southern foxhunter will get down right verbally abrasive whenever someone even suggests that fox hunting might be for any reason other than for socializing and listening to the sounds of the hounds.

The southern foxhunt is a long drawn out affair that is best begun early in the morning just before the dawn of light, preferably after a late evening rain shower and fox have put down fresh tracks. That is a time when the moisture in the air is close to the ground and the scent of a fox is strongest. The first hound that picks up a hot fox trail sounds out with a "Yaup, Yaup, Yaup, Har-Oooooo!" The other hounds soon chime in, each voicing their individual and distinct manner of vocally reporting the fact that it is in agreement that the hunt has begun in earnest. Experienced foxhunters can recognize the individual sounds emanating from the mouths of every dog he owns, and many hunters can distinguish the sounds of the dogs belonging to their usual hunting buddies.

Mr. Fet was determined to mix the English style of hunting the red fox with the heavily wooded and swampy terrain style of hunting the gray fox in the coastal plains of Georgia. He imported several pairs of red fox and placed them in hand-dug dens all over the sand hills of Evans, Tattnall, Bryan, and Liberty Counties. He even imported a few special breeds of foxhounds that are called Julys and Trigs. These are a kind of hound that have been bred to run fox rather than slowly trailing them like Walker hounds, which are the most common breed of hounds in the South. His intention was to capitalize on the red foxes' habit of going to high ground and running. He figured that, by taking shortcuts around the swamp thickets and creek bottoms, he could ride his horse and still manage to keep up with the hounds while they were chasing the fox.

Too much hope and not quite enough forethought guided Mr. Fet's plan. Like those smart scientists that import plants and insects into the country in hopes that they might control some undesirable species, he failed to anticipate the sexual prowess of the American southern gray fox. It wasn't very long before the flatwoods, oak ridges, and swamps of South Georgia were full of a kind of fox that didn't look or act like either the indigenous gray fox or the imported red fox. Although their colors may vary, they usually have a salty-colored brown body with black ears and a reddish tail that is capped off with a tuff of black hair. Every time the hounds would jump one of those little genetic cocktails of fox blood, it would either take off and head in a straight line toward the next county or just run around in a big circle in the middle of a swamp without ever taking a break. The trailing Walker hounds were subject to being led out of the county, never to be seen again. The Julys, Trigs, and other running hounds would get their faces and ears cut to pieces trying to keep up with the smaller and sleeker hybrid fox as it led them through blackberry briars, ty-tys, clinging wild grapevines, and those infernal nettle weeds that grow almost everywhere in the coastal plains, especially around those darned swamps and along every creek bank.

Fox hunting is fast becoming a rare sport in South Georgia. Modern fish and game management techniques were successful in bringing the whitetail deer herd back to numbers that even surpasses their pre-colonial populations. Most of the sons of the old foxhunters have now changed their quarry without having to alter their hunting style. It is now a common sight to see deer hunters lined up along one side of a road, wearing bright orange colored vests, leaning against the fenders of their trucks or sitting next to a beer cooler, and waiting for a pack of dogs to chase a deer past them. Their fathers would turn over in their graves if they knew that their sons had allowed all those high-priced Walkers, Trigs, and July hounds to cross breed and the resulting mongrels used to chase deer. But, one must remember that hunting anything in the South was never meant to take a lot of energy. Maybe hunting deer from the back of a pick-up truck while sitting in the comfort of an old over-stuffed chair next to a beer cooler might not be such a bad idea after all.

# Chapter VIII

## Rattlesnakes and Gophers

Here be words fer all to know
Why it tis dat snakes slither so
No legs him had since days o' yore
Nary any wings wid which to soar
Ever to crawl on him belly he must
Fo' givin' dat woman de sin o' lust
Whilst scornin' him like de devil foe
Still we runs fo' fear o' losin' de toe

There is much snake lore in South Georgia. It is a kind of local wisdom that has managed to survive through several generations with very few modifications except as occasionally deemed absolutely necessary by the narrator of the moment. South Georgia is a wonderful place to live, but if anyone believes they might have a little difficulty coexisting with all four species of poisonous snakes that are indigenous to North America, not to mention their many slithery, but harmless cousins, perhaps they should consider living in some other part of the world. It has been reported that there are no snakes in Hawaii or Ireland.

Coral snakes are the most rare of the four poisonous snakes native to North America. It is a beautifully colored reptile that seldom grows to a length of more than eighteen to twenty-four inches. Its head is rounded like that of the head of a worm and its body is decorated from head to tail with alternating bands of black and red, the red bands being about twice as wide as the black bands. Much narrower bands of yellow separate the black and red bands. There are non-poisonous snakes that have the same colors as the coral, which makes the differences in color combinations difficult to remember. Just remember the old saying, *"Black on yeller kill a feller."* Humans are rarely presented with an opportunity to see a coral snake. But, when they do encounter one and disturb its dark refuge, which is commonly under a log or thick pile of brush, the intruder is usually bitten on whichever extremity is used to invade the coral snake's private space.

The venom of the coral snake is much like that of the cobra snake. Both are very poisonous and attack the nervous system of their victim. However, few humans have ever been known to die from the bite of a coral snake because the coral's venom-injecting fangs are not like those of the more common pit vipers. The coral has multiple rows of small teeth that inject venom in amounts that are not usually fatal to humans or other large animals. Nevertheless, it has been reported that some victims of the coral snake have actually committed suicide rather than experience the ordeal of trying to bear the lengthy and excruciating pain that soon follows a bite from that colorful little demon.

The copperhead is probably the least poisonous of the four venomous snakes that inhabit the United States. But caution is warranted, because that fact does not mean that medical attention should be delayed after receiving a bite from a copperhead. It only means that the victim will probably survive an extended state of pain and misery.

Copperheads get their name from their dull copper-colored skin, which is accentuated by their much brighter copper-colored head. While most harmless snakes have thin tails that taper down to a fine point, copperheads, corals, cottonmouths and rattlesnakes all have rounded stubby tails. Copperheads are usually found in one of two places in South Georgia. They seem to have an affinity for living in cane patches and hiding under piles of building materials that have been left in one place for more than a few days. A pile of old boards, bricks, or stacks of cinder blocks are magnets for these silent creatures of stealth that never give prior warning of their presence, not even when they decide to strike.

Speaking of stealth, the cottonmouth moccasin is a snake of a different story. These troublesome critters are champions of stealth and cunning, and they rarely give ground to intruders of any size.

While on one of his many ventures in the flatwoods, Jimmy witnessed the actions of a cottonmouth just before the critter was aware of his presence and then how the snake maneuvered after being detected. As Jimmy approached the dark mass of waiting danger, the snake seemed to not notice his presence as it slowly and slyly moved to a more advantageous location along Jimmy's direction of travel. The cottonmouth coiled his body and pointed his head in a direction that was best suited for launching an effective ambush. It actually appeared as if the snake was pretending to be asleep as Jimmy tied his bandanna to the end of his snake stick, held it out in front of him, and then slowly moved along the trail towards the snake. SMACK! The explosive strike of the cottonmouth almost knocked Jimmy's snake stick from his hand.

Anyone who might be thinking about venturing into the woods of the southeastern United States should heed this warning. Never, never, and I do mean NEVER, go for a walk in the woodlands of South Georgia without being armed with a snake stick that is at least as long as you are tall. Everything humanly possible should be done to reduce the chances of stepping into the kill zone of the master of the ambush. A good sturdy snake stick is useful not only as a weapon but is also an ideal tool for testing the path in front of you. It even provides a means for maintaining your balance when trying to navigate unsteady ground or when crossing a stream of water.

The cottonmouth moccasin may be the big boss around the creeks, swamps, and wetlands of South Georgia, but the eastern diamondback rattlesnake is king of the scrub-oak hills and pine forests. The largest rattlesnake that Jimmy ever encountered was just over seven feet long and eighteen inches around its girth. The snake's two fangs, which enabled him to deliver a stream of venom with hypodermic accuracy, were over two inches long. The end of the rattlesnake's tail was adorned with twelve pairs of rattles.

The rattlesnakes that live among the flatwoods and sandy oak hills of Georgia have developed a strange, but symbiotic relationship with another creature that is common to the coastal plains of the South. The *Gopher Tortoise* is a hard-shelled animal that many people often mistake for a large turtle or terrapin. Most people in South Georgia simply call them gophers, but that term is scientifically incorrect. But, what the heck, it is much easier to say, 'I screwed up and busted my leg in a danged ol' gopher hole' rather than attempting to stumble through a verbal contortion like, 'I inadvertently stepped in the entrance of a gopher tortoise den and fractured my fibula.'

The gopher tortoise digs a den in the ground that slants downward and laterally for about twenty to thirty feet until reaching a depth of about three to six feet. It then tunnels back up for another twenty or thirty feet and exits a few yards from the first entrance. The tortoise builds himself a perfect southern home, a front door, rear door, and a long breezeway between the two entrances.

Some people claim that tortoises and rattlesnakes never share the same den. But that contention is not based upon sufficient observation. Rattlesnakes choose whichever tortoise hole suits them, whether it is occupied or not, and the tortoise doesn't seem to be bothered by the presence of the snake. All that these two animals desire out of life is food, a little water, and a cool place to sleep without being disturbed. Actually, such joint occupancy seems to be a very practical arrangement of reptilian cohabitation. The snake keeps other undesirable critters out of the den and the in and out movement of the tortoise keeps the walls of the den from falling in and trash from clogging the entrances.

Jimmy and his grandfather, Mr. Jim, often took long walks together, sometimes in the flatwoods that lie to the south of the *Pines* and other times through the scrub oak hills to the north. Jimmy was only seven years old when his grandfather was eighty-six, but Mr. Jim could still out-walk, out-talk, and out-think anyone in the county. The two of them would take occasional restful breaks under the shades of scrub oaks and persimmon trees and eat whatever wild fruits and berries were in season. Their snacks would sometimes consist of ripe persimmons, wild fox grapes, blackberries, or dewberries. When they were lucky, they sometimes found fresh chinquapin nuts that grow along the edges of the sandy trails.

While sitting among the wiregrass and enjoying things that few people ever see or could even imagine, Mr. Jim contributed to Jimmy's education in ways that no public school system could ever hope to achieve. When he was a young man, Mr. Jim held some of the most prestigious positions that a person could hold in South Georgia. He was a school headmaster, postmaster, founder of the Evans County Republican Party, and a delegate to the 1908 Republican Party convention in Chicago. Mr. Jim never spoke in great detail to children about his political views, but later in life, Jimmy was to realize that the things his grandfather had been teaching him were the building blocks of sound values, political or otherwise.

Brenda was Mr. Jim's half-English bulldog and half-Staffordshire terrier that usually accompanied them on their journeys into nature. Brenda hated snakes and served as a more effective snake detector than did their ever-present snake sticks. Her favorite trick was to grab a snake with her teeth around the middle of its body and ferociously shake the life out of the snake without ever allowing the snake an opportunity to bite her.

Jimmy was sucking on a sweet ripe persimmon when Mr. Jim said, "I think Brenda is after one of those gophers." He had been watching Brenda digging in a tortoise hole with the kind of ferocity that she always demonstrated when she was confident that she had something cornered. Mr. Jim and Jimmy sat on the ground next to the entrance to the den and began helping Brenda by pushing dirt away from the hole. Jimmy looked up at his grandpa and saw in his eyes that his old computer-like brain was whirring away. He had one of those expressions on his face that made Jimmy suspect that his grandpa had just made a big mistake. Mr. Jim suddenly began spouting out everything that he was thinking at the moment. "Snakes live in gopher holes, it's mid-morning, snakes like to sun themselves on cool clear days, and Brenda acts this way only when there is a snake somewhere near." Just as he finished speaking, something very huge and heavy flopped over Jimmy's shoulder, knocked him backward, landed on top of Brenda, and then disappeared down in the tortoise hole just as suddenly as it had appeared.

Grandpa yelled, "By jing! What a big snake! Jimmy, did he bite you?"

"No, grandpa! Did it bite Brenda?"

"No, but she'll never be able to get her mouth around that big boy's body!"

Mr. Jim quickly located the other end of the tortoise den and plugged it with dirt and an old rotten log. "Jimmy, go back to the barn and get a pitchfork and shovel and drain a bit of gasoline from the gas tank in the tractor." Anxiously, Jimmy ran all the way back to the tool shed, collected the items, and dashed back to the tortoise den as fast as he could run. He knew that he and his Grandpa were going to have a snake diggin'.

The tool house and tractor shed was nearly a mile away. When Jimmy returned, almost out of breath, but with the prescribed tools and one of Uncle Jeff's half pint liquor bottles full of gasoline, Mr. Jim had already figured out which way the draft was blowing through the tortoise den. He told Jimmy to hold Brenda while he went to the back door of the tortoise den, pulled the log from the hole, poured some gasoline in the shovel, and then shoved the blade of the shovel down in the hole as far it would go. He then walked over to the other end of the tortoise den and waited with his pitchfork at the ready, poised like Captain Ahab taking aim at the great *Moby Dick*. A few seconds later, the rattlesnake came charging out of the hole and Grandpa came down hard with the pitchfork, pinning the snake's head to the ground with the tines of the pitchfork.

They began their walk back home. Jimmy was dragging the shovel behind him and Mr. Jim was carrying the pitchfork with the handle slung over his shoulder. The snake was dangling from the tines of the pitchfork and its tail was dragging along the ground behind Mr. Jim, carving out one last slithery trail in the sandy white path.

Mr. Jim was much quieter than usual as they walked along the path between the big field and the little branch that fed the waters of Cribbs Branch. Jimmy was wondering if maybe his grandpa might be thinking about something that he wanted to say to him. When they came to the little spring that supplied water to the branch, they stopped for a drink of water. Grandpa kneeled down, captured some of the cool water in his cupped hands, took a long sip, cleared his throat, and then began to speak with a soulful firmness in his voice. "Jimmy, you should know that people should never kill anything unless it is for some just purpose, not even a snake. However, this snake is going to make a fine matching hat and belt that will be donated to the church charity sale, and he is going to have his picture in the *Claxton Enterprise* for being the biggest rattlesnake that has ever been found in Evans County. This snake is going to serve the Lord and entertain more people in a way that no preacher in this county has ever done on any Sunday morning." Grandpa had a way of making things turn out all right.

It was a pleasantly cool evening in late summer, and dinner was being served on the large table on the screened-in dining porch. As usual, Brenda pushed the screen door open with her nose and came in. She scooted under the table, sat down beside Jimmy, and placed her head in his lap. This time she had come home a little later than usual and didn't seem to be her usual spry self. Jimmy slipped a biscuit to her as she leaned against his chair, but she refused to eat it. It was then that Jimmy felt a warm wetness soaking through his blue jeans. Grandpa and Jimmy both knew what had happened to Brenda after they saw the two telltale side-by-side punctures in her throat. Brenda lasted most of that evening. The following morning, Mr. Jim and Jimmy buried her in the back yard next to the big sycamore tree where she often brought home her trophies and displayed them after a good day of snake hunting.

## True and False Quiz about Snakes

1. Rattlesnakes can strike a distance equal to their length.     T or F
2. A rattlesnake's age is determined by counting the
   number of rattles on its tail, one pair for each year of age.  T or F
3. A hoop snake is a snake that can put its tail in its mouth
   and roll downhill.                                            T or F
4. Some snakes bear their young by spitting them out of
   their mouths.                                                 T or F
5. Snakes can run faster than humans.                            T or F
6. Snakes are unable to bite while under water.                  T or F

## Answers to Snake Quiz

1. False. Rattlesnakes can strike only about a third of their length but
   when one does decide to strike, that is usually far enough.
2. False. Rattlesnakes, like most other snakes, shed their skin more
   than once a year and they reveal a new pair of rattles with each
   shedding.
3. False. Southern people tell that story to tourists when they want to
   test their IQ.
4. False. Snakes are strange critters that bear young only in two ways.
   Some lay soft leathery eggs that hatch like bird eggs, turtle eggs,
   and alligator eggs. Other snakes give live birth the old-fashioned
   way, like mammals. It appears that Mother Nature has never been
   quite able make up her mind if she wants snakes to be birds,
   amphibians, or mammals.
5. False. Snakes can't run because they don't have legs. But some
   snakes can crawl much faster than humans can run. The good
   news is that the fast ones are usually not poisonous. The bad news
   is that running where snakes might be present is a very
   dumb thing to do. Remember, walk softly and carry a big stick.
6. False. Southern folks like to irritate tourists by telling that just
   before suggesting a nice place for them to go for a cool swim.

# Chapter IX

## Tobacco Rogue

Most people understand what is meant when they hear someone describe another person as being *'salt of the earth.'* Jimmy's family was fortunate to have actually known such people, and to even have them as neighbors. The old Daniel's farm is located on Bay Branch Church Road between the *Pines* and where Bay Branch crosses the road. Herbert Daniel became the principal owner and manager of the Daniel's farm after his father died and his two brothers left home to pursue other careers in different parts of the world. He soon married Cecile Darsey and they built their new home near the *Pines*, just west of the big field.

When Jimmy wasn't tending cattle, mowing the grass, or doing one of the many other routine chores around the farm, he spent his summers working on the Daniel's farm suckering, topping, picking, hauling, grading, and bundling tobacco. He began working for Herbert soon after he was introduced to the astonishing fact that girls and cars are much more expensive to keep up than are horses and their associated riding gear. Such leisure related activities required a level of financial support that was greater than his adult kin was willing to pay him for doing chores around the farm. Jimmy's father explained to him that *work* provides what people *need* in life but *hard* work is what provides the things that people *want* in life. The more comfort one desires, the more work must be performed. That was Jimmy's first lesson in the economic principal having to do with the fair exchange of goods and labor.

Picking tobacco is a job that is about as dirty as dipping turpentine. The task begins at daybreak while greeting the rising sun and walking between narrow rows of tobacco stalks. Your back is bent over and your face is just above the ground, about snakebite high. The job entails plucking the sap-laden green tobacco leaves from their stalks with one hand while holding the collected leaves under the other arm until you have an armload full. You then walk over to a mule-drawn sled and dump the dew-heavy leaves in the sled. You keep going back and forth picking armloads of tobacco leaves until all of the tobacco is picked, hauled to the tobacco barn, strung on four feet long sticks, and stacked next to the tobacco-curing barn. A full morning of that kind of drudgery was followed by an afternoon of hanging the heavy sticks of tobacco leaves in a sweltering hot thirty-foot tall wood-fired curing barn. At least one person had to stay up all night for the next few weeks keeping constant watch over the barn to make sure that the tobacco was curing at the proper temperature and the barn didn't catch fire and burn down, along with the line of credit at *The Claxton Bank* or *Tippins Banking Company*.

When the tobacco leaves were fully cured to a golden brown, they were graded, wrapped in large burlap sheets, and hauled over to the Farmers' Tobacco Auction Warehouse in Claxton where it would be sold to the highest bidding tobacco company. Tobacco buyers from the big tobacco companies would arrive in town a few days before the auction and check in at the Claxton Hotel or one of the few one-room motels along highway 301. Most of the buyers spent their evenings being entertained at a not so secret place just north of town near the Cannochee River. On auction days, the buyers would stroll through the warehouse examining the tobacco as the farmers laid it out for display in long rows on the warehouse floor. The buyers inspected the tobacco, verified the grades of each pile, made notes to themselves, and wrote down the prices that they would be bidding for each pile of the golden-brown leaves.

After his sisters voted Mr. Fet out of the farming business, much of the farmland was leased to other farmers who, in his four sister's collective agricultural wisdom, were more established in the farming profession than their retired career soldier brother. It seemed that there was a different sharecropper farming the fields every year. And since Aunt Augusta was the only one of the four sisters who actually lived on the farm, she became the resident manager while her sisters assumed positions as silent partners. Mr. Fet's two brothers, realizing that their sisters had them out numbered, eventually decided to sell their shares of the farm to their more financially endowed, yet absentee, sisters. However, the sisters reluctantly allowed Uncle Wallace to farm the fields for a couple of years during the time when their mother was in need of constant care.

Aunt Augusta's home nursing duties didn't leave much time for supervising sharecroppers, all of whom she suspected could never meet her requirements of not being an alcoholic, an atheist, or other form of scoundrel, and certainly not a living male member of her family. Although Uncle Wallace never touched alcohol, the other three major strikes against him would prevent him from ever gaining permanent control of the family farm. Nevertheless, the three years in which he farmed the place and the year that Mr. Fet farmed it were the only years after World War II that the farm ever turned a profit while under management of a member of the family.

The fields around the Pines were very fertile except for the little field behind the big house that seemed to produce only abundant crops of sand spurs and broom sage, at least until

Uncle Wallace discovered that it was a perfect place for growing watermelons. Even during times of severe drought, the corn in the other fields would stand tall and green while cornfields in other parts of the county wilted and dried in the sun. The land around the *Pines* was situated in an area where the water table was near the surface yet there was enough drainage to keep the soil from getting boggy during the rainy season. Even during the driest spells, there was always adequate moisture wicking up from somewhere below the surface to feed the roots of the crops. That is what made the fields at the *Pines* such an excellent place to grow tobacco.

One of Aunt Augusta's attempts at leasing out the farm resulted in the fields being farmed by a man who owned a large farm on the road between Bellville and Mendes. She decided to allow him to rent the fields because he claimed that he needed more farming acreage in order to justify his tobacco allotment, which the government assigned to farmers based upon a formula having to do with how much land a farm had under cultivation. Aunt Augusta knew that he grew tobacco on his own farm, but overlooked that one indiscretion because she respected the fact that he was a hard-working man who always took good care of his family and seemed to meet her other prerequisites. Besides, good Southerners understand that what people do on their own land is their own business, and no one should criticize them for good intentions. Without much thought of it, the man planted a tobacco patch in the middle of the big field that he had planted mostly in corn. That farmer didn't know about Aunt Augusta's passion regarding tobacco, and it is fairy certain that he didn't plant that patch of tobacco in the middle of the big field knowing that tobacco grows slower than corn and would soon be hidden by the tall stalks of green corn. He was probably just a good farmer who knew that the big field was a fine place to grow tobacco.

It was early in the summer when Aunt Augusta was serving one of her scrumptious Sunday evening dinners at the table on the screened-in dining porch. As usual, Mr. Jim was talking about things that he had seen while he was out on one of his walks through the flatwoods, oak ridges, and around the fields. He nonchalantly looked over at Aunt Augusta and commented, "You know, that new plowboy that your sharecropper hired really knows how to hold a straight furrow. You can look down those rows of corn and tobacco and, except for the fact that everything is green instead of white, you would almost believe that you were in one of those national cemeteries."

"Papa, you didn't walk all the way through the flatwoods and over to that man's tobacco field and then back here did you?"

"Oh no, I just walked across the road to the edge of the flatwoods, around by Wallace's place, crossed the big corn field, went down along the branch, walked up by the little field, and then back here."

"Well, just where do you think you saw tobacco growing?"

"Right there," he said, pointing through the screen and out towards the western sunset. "Right there where that fellow planted it, right in the middle of the big cornfield."

Aunt Augusta stared out over the grapevine arbor, past the well shelter, through the tool shed, and right through the tall rows of corn that was growing between the tobacco patch and her penetrating eyes. Jimmy was positive that she could actually see the tobacco growing in the middle of the cornfield. He had been reading *Superman* comic books and knew that such things were possible. Aunt Augusta dropped a pan of hot biscuits on the table, threw a pair of quilted potholders on top of the biscuits, stomped through the kitchen, slammed the back door, and headed for the garage. She cranked up her new 1951 Chevrolet Deluxe, the one she had bought with some of the money that she got from leasing the farm, drove through the pine grove, and headed west down Bay Branch Road towards the Bellville/Mendes road and to that farmer's house.

Grandpa rarely drank alcohol, never smoked, only occasionally used mild profanity, and he never used the name of the Lord in vain. He looked around the table, asked for a couple of those biscuits to butter before they got cold, and shaking his head from side to side, said, "You boys don't know it, and that farmer down the road doesn't know it quite yet, but the good Lord and your aunt knows that there is about to be a big change in that tobacco farmer's life."

No one ever knew exactly what transpired during that discussion between Aunt Augusta and the tobacco farmer, but one can be sure that it involved one of her 'one-way' conversations. Nevertheless, the situation was quickly managed when she broke the lease on religious grounds. Herbert Daniel became the new renter of the farm and there never has been another stalk of tobacco grown in any of the fields at the *Pines*.

Aunt Augusta seemed fairly satisfied with her arrangement with Herbert. He was a good friend, active member of the Bay Branch Primitive Baptist Church, didn't drink alcohol, and, to her knowledge, met all of her other requirements. Besides, she stood to gain a little more money from her new deal. And it sure was fortunate for Herbert that he was successful in keeping her from discovering that, on occasion, he enjoyed rolling his own cigarettes from a can of fine cut Prince Albert. Anyway, Herbert still leases the farm today just as he has been doing since 1952. He quit smoking too.

Unlike Herbert, Jimmy wasn't quite as successful at keeping his conduct concealed from Aunt Augusta, and that caused him to suffer the effects of her radical beliefs regarding alcohol and tobacco. Although it would be years before the consequences of alcohol and tobacco abuse would prove her academically correct, but not necessarily morally right, at the time, Jimmy had to deal with the present. Still, after years of observing both overindulgent and temperate use of alcohol and tobacco, it seems that many of the activities that people call vices, when indulged in with intelligent moderation, can actually be small blessings. It is the inability, perhaps refusal, of man to control his temptations for exceeding his capacities that is the real vice. Good liquor, good tobacco, good conversation, good sex, and good prayer, all when indulged in with the thoughtful temperance of a mature mind, can be very wonderful and beneficial experiences. When taken to excesses, they are apt to be a curse upon the body, mind, spirit, and soul. As Mr. Jim used to say, "Be ye temperate in all things."

The intemperance of Jimmy's youth once prompted him to ask his grandfather; "Does being temperate in all things include being temperate in our moderation as well?" Jimmy's mouth often caused great troubles to come his way.

It was a Friday evening in late October and Aunt Augusta was driving Jimmy and his brother over to the fall festival at Bellville School. The annual autumn school event was always a pretty big affair. Almost everyone who had ever attended Bellville School would come to enjoy the festivities and catch up on all the local gossip. There was a Halloween horror house, all sorts of home-made foods, crafts, rows of booths with all kinds of games, a local talent show, cake walks, and real country singing stars that came to the school in a big colorful bus, all the way from a place called *The Grand Ole Opry*.

The three of them drove through the pine grove and headed west. The big field stretched out toward the horizon, and Jimmy was looking out across the big field through a side window of the car. The corn had already been harvested and dead stalks lay broken on the ground waiting for the tractor and harrow to chop them into the soil in preparation for planting a winter graze for the cattle. That was when Jimmy saw it. It was standing in the middle of the field, and he knew it was something that few people in South Georgia had seen in many years. It was a deer that had a tall rack of antlers on its head. Jimmy yelled, "Look! In the big field, it's a deer!" But Aunt Augusta kept her eyes glued to the middle of the road in front of the car. "Look! See it?

It's a deer, a big deer right there in the field!" Still, there was no response. She kept her chin tucked back in her throat with her eyes glaring over her bifocals and looking straight down the hood of the car.

Jimmy decided that he had better let things go for a while. Maybe Aunt Augusta had something on her mind that outweighed the importance of witnessing the greatest historical event to happen at the *Pines* since Uncle Jeff and one of his old army buddies landed an airplane in the soft soil of the big field and couldn't get it to fly out again. Lucky for Jeff that it was a small airplane and he was able to get several people help lift the tail section and balance the plane on top of Uncle Wallace's wagon. Preacher Stewart's mule pulled the wagon and airplane out of the field and down to a straight stretch of Bay Branch Road where the errant aviators were able get up enough speed to make a successful take off. That was when Jimmy received his first lesson in aerodynamics. It is much easier to get an overloaded airplane down from the sky and safely on the ground than it is to coach an overloaded airplane into making a successful take off.

When it appeared that his Aunt Augusta might be a bit more receptive, Jimmy asked her why she had not looked at the deer when he told her that it was standing in the middle of the field. Coldly, she responded, "I knew it was a deer, and I knew where it was. I was not going to look at it because of where it was standing."

"Huh?"

"It was standing right there! That deer was standing right in the middle of the big field where they planted that filthy tobacco patch! It was there that we allowed God's land to be fouled!"

Jimmy was young enough and dumb enough to respond with, "I bet that deer just came all the way over here from Pete's place where he got drunk as a coot on some of Pete's corn squeezings. That deer was probably just out looking for a young doe and a good smoke." Although Aunt Augusta preferred to deliver corrective action in a more formal fashion, she never had any qualms about dishing out instant retribution, usually in the form of a quick, hard, and twisting pinch to the upper arm of a smart-mouthed kid.

Aunt Augusta had two basic forms of corporal punishment, which she administered according to the severity of the offense. Both methods were applied after a great deal of ritualistic preparation, much like what happens at one of those special church services where the preacher mumbles a few indistinguishable words and then does a lot of arm waving before making you gag on a piece of stale bread just before giving you a thimble-sized shot of grape juice to wash it down your throat.

If the guilty party's offense was one of physical defiance or one that Aunt Augusta considered a crime against her rigid code of conduct, the offender had to go to the hedge behind the house and cut a switch that was not less than three feet long, trim off the leaves, and bring it to her. She would be standing on the back steps of the big house, arms folded, and mumbling something indistinguishable, sort of like that preacher. The convicted felon had to lean over, grab the dinner bell post, take his medicine, and then report to the living room for a reading of some special bible verse that she considered appropriate for the crime. If the offense was one of vocal desecration of her religious domain or some audible utterance of a word that she considered to be a violation of her code of oral syntax, the punishment was a soapy rag in the mouth followed by another dose of biblical verse.

The morning after the big autumn festival at Bellville School, Jimmy was in the kitchen with his head poked inside the refrigerator. He was doing what most boys do when they are near a refrigerator, staring in the open door with his head bobbing up and down like one of those novelty shop carved wooden birds that sit on the rim of a water glass. That was Jimmy's unwieldy position just as Aunt Augusta came storming in the kitchen. Her left arm was stretched out and the palm of her hand was cupped upward like she was carrying something that she rather not touch. Her right finger was pointing, more like pecking, at the object in her hand. "Jimmy! What on earth are you doing with this thing?"

Jimmy jumped back, smacked his head real hard against the bottom of the freezer door, spun around, and took one glance at the object in her hand. That was when he said it. Jimmy said the really big one. Without thinking, out came the big 'F' word. "F—"

Jimmy didn't know when or where it was that he first heard that word. Heck, at eleven years old he was not absolutely certain what it even meant. He just knew that it was one of the most powerful words that a kid could have stashed away in his verbal arsenal. Nevertheless, he suddenly became acutely aware that the word had a great deal to do with what Aunt Augusta was holding in her hand. The only reason that he had the danged thing in the first place was that every kid at school had one squirreled away somewhere, just in case it might be needed for something or other, later on, whenever, or for whatever.

After that one fateful exclamation, a deathly silence came over the kitchen, broken only by a barrage of screaming yet silent thoughts that were shooting through Jimmy's head, like a volley of bullets spraying from a machine gun. 'Damn! She found that rubber thing I left in my pants pocket last night. I forgot to put it in my special hiding place when we got home from the festival. I need some kind of an excuse. I need to think, fast! Oh, what the heck, there's no use. It's all over and I'm up for the big one. I'm going to get a whipping, my mouth washed out, and then I am going to have to memorize every word in that Bible of hers. Worse than that, she might just go ahead and kill me right here and bury me back in the oak grove with all of her dead cats. No way! I'm getting out of here.' Jimmy ran through the back door and made it all the way to the big sycamore tree out by the smoke house gate before her screeching voice caught up with him, penetrating his ears like the stings of a thousand wasps. Images of a wicked witch in hot pursuit of a little girl from Kansas twirled through his mind like a tornado.

"Jimmy! You stop right there or I'll…"

"I'm dead. It's over. When she says, 'or I'll,' that's the ultimate threat. I'm just going to have to surrender and walk the plank like a brave pirate."

Jimmy stood by the sycamore tree and waited for the end. After what seemed like ten years on death row, Aunt Augusta came out of the house holding a steaming hot wet washrag full of powdered *Tide* detergent soap. She pulled Jimmy's mouth open like she was going to give her dog a worm pill and then began scrubbing every crevice in his mouth. When she was satisfied that his mouth was clean enough to suit her, she looked down over her bifocals at him and said, "Jimmy, that thing you had, well…boys will be boys. But, in the future, you better watch your mouth or I'll wash it out again. And I do mean but good! Now get in the house and bring my Bible to the living room."

Jimmy made a quick security check of his room while on his way to fetch Aunt Augusta's Bible from where she always kept it on top of the piano in the dining room. He wanted to make sure he had covered himself regarding a few additional pieces of evidence of his crime spree from the night before. Mumbling too himself, he said, *Good, the photograph that little dark haired girl from Bellville gave me is still here. The box of .22 caliber bullets that I traded my homemade slingshot for is still here too. And, yep, at least that other thing is still in my special hiding place. Aunt Augusta would have really killed me and buried me back there with all those dead cats had she found my pack of Camel cigarettes.*

# Chapter X

## Turkeys

Wild turkeys are probably the most cautious birds on earth, except during the early spring of each year when the male turkeys begin to act real stupid, like college kids on spring break. Depending upon the local weather conditions and natural seasonal changes in daylight hours, turkeys usually begin to mate around the last week of March and continue their ritual until about the end of May. Like most males of other species, when that certain thing gets on a wild turkey's mind, they throw all caution to the wind and begin thinking with a different region of their bodies than with the little pecan sized gray piece of matter that occupies the tiny cavity between their ears.

During most of the year, the hens and young jakes (one-year-old males) are the ones that can be heard doing most of the clucking and yelping. The older males (toms or gobblers) remain to themselves and keep their mouths shut. By the time the young toms are about three years old, they have developed a more refined understanding of the art of survival among the sexes, an ability that adult male humans seem yet to develop.

However, during the spring mating season, male turkeys begin to exhibit reckless aberrations in their behavior that is much removed from their usual display of cautious logic. They become careless in concealing their locations, a mistake that oftentimes proves fatal. The older gobblers distance themselves from the hens and young jakes and begin hanging out at their old favorite watering holes of ill repute and arguing with every other male turkey that they encounter. They spend their days gobbling at each other, answering the calls of every hawk, crow, owl, blue jay, and mocking bird, and trying to seduce every little brown-skirted turkey hen they can find. After about six or seven weeks of dawn to dusk carousing, partying, and gobbling about their latest conquests, they return to their males-only club somewhere deep in the thickest parts of the flatwoods. They remain there and are rarely heard or seen again until the following spring when the dogwoods and azaleas begin to bloom again.

Mr. Jim kept a flock of about fifty domesticated turkeys that he enjoyed walking amidst and feeding them cracked corn during the early morning. His personal attention and daily handouts usually kept his flock from straying too far from the barn, tool shed, well shelter, or the wooded edges of the fields near the big house. At least his turkeys started out being domesticated birds.

One spring evening, while eating supper on the large screened-in dining porch, which was the usual place for the family to eat their meals during the more comfortable months of the year, Mr. Jim was wearing a studied and concerned look on his face. He put down his usual after-dinner glass of water, which he always sweetened with two tablespoons of cane syrup, glared out the window toward the barn and pecan trees, and declared; "You know, someone or some thing around here is stealing my turkey hens and, by jing, I'm going to go find out what's afoot here!"

Mr. Jim's turkeys roosted high up in one of several giant pecan trees that shaded the barn. He always counted them every evening when they would fly up to their favorite limb and begin the process of jostling each other over the best roosting spots. For the next several days, he never missed an evening counting his turkeys. He even got up early in the morning and counted his turkeys again when they flew down from their roosts.

Satisfied that nothing or no one was stealing his turkeys while they were roosting, his next plan of action was to follow the turkeys to the edge of the east field where they would go every morning to scratch for nut grass roots and dust themselves under an old cedar tree. That was when grandpa heard it. "Thump, Thump, Thump, Skirrrrrrrrr", followed by a short pause and then, "Jaba-Jaba-Jaba-Jaba!" It was the unmistakable sound of a wild turkey gobbler in full strut, drumming, strutting, and gobbling his seductive message to the receptive ears of one of grandpa's cute little turkey hens that the wild tom turkey had decided to court that day.

"Jimmy! Go get my Purdy piece from my room and bring it to me!" The wild turkey gobbler was in the oak grove behind the house and grandpa was not about to let one more of his hens go eloping off to the flatwoods with that scoundrel. Jimmy ran through the dining porch, scrambled to Mr. Jim's room, grabbed two shotgun shells and grandpa's Purdy piece (Mr. Jim's name for his side-by-side double-barreled shotgun), and passed it to his grandpa as he was sneaking around the side of the house to take up a firing position by the smokehouse. Grandpa poked his shotgun over the wooden gate by the back corner of the smokehouse, braced himself against the side of the smokehouse, and BLAM!

As his family was sitting around the table on the screened-in dining porch and enjoying their Easter dinner of home made cranberry sauce, dressing, and baked wild turkey, Mr. Jim commented, "You know; I feel a bit sorry for having to shoot that wild turkey. He was doing a much better job of taking care of my turkey hens than that sorry tame gobbler I bought from that sorry turkey breeder over in Reidsville. Nevertheless, that scoundrel had to go. My hens haven't laid one egg around the barn since that wild turkey became a problem. Because of him, several of my hens are still out there somewhere in the flatwoods sitting on their nests and hatching more little wild turkeys."

Grandpa's pen-raised tom turkey had done everything he could to keep his harem of hens under control, but all those wild turkeys that the Wildlife Department turned loose in the flatwoods had him outnumbered. Old Tame Tom's dominance was being seriously jeopardized as Grandpa's hens eloped, one by one, to experience the sweet adventure of prohibited love.

Out of pure frustration and a determination to salvage what little pride he had left, Tame Tom turned his jealousy and rage upon Jimmy and his brother. Jimmy was sure that Tame Tom was holding him personally responsible for his downfall ever since Jimmy began spending so much of his time in the flatwoods, out there in enemy territory. Tame Tom's favorite tactic was to stand guard under the grapevine and every time Jimmy or his brother tried to come out of the house the turkey would chase them back inside. The two boys spent the entire summer negotiating yard space with that obsessively compulsive, sexually frustrated, and paranoid old tom turkey. It was downright aggravating having to worry about the possibility that they might grow up to be afraid of birds!

That following November, Mr. Jim and Jimmy were out by the well shelter cutting little round holes in dried gourds and hanging them on tall posts so that martin birds would have a place to make their nests. Martins are very useful birds and great fun to watch as they swoop through the air and dive down to feed upon the many kinds of flying insects that come out during the early evenings. The martins were always followed by thousands of bats that came out in the afterglow of the evening to feed upon mosquitoes. Nowadays, people use insecticides and electric bug zappers to deal with pesky insects. The martin birds and bats have all but disappeared while the mosquitoes remain a problem. Should we wonder why?

Jimmy looked up just in time to see Crazy Tom (Tame Tom's name had been appropriately changed) running straight at him. Crazy Tom had his head down and his eyes seemed to be zeroed in on Jimmy's center mass. Jimmy nervously looked up at his grandpa who, with an air of condescending authority, said, "Jimmy, that turkey will stop bothering you if you would just hit him with something." Bravely but nervously, Jimmy reached for the nearest object that he could find to use as a weapon, a wooden shingle from a pile of cedar roofing. Holding the shingle high over his head with one end of the shingle clutched tightly in both hands, and with an excellent estimate of timing and perfect range acquisition, he closed his eyes and brought the shingle crashing down on Crazy Tom's head. Jimmy never saw a thing, but the crisis was over very quickly.

The momentum of Crazy Tom's kamikaze attack knocked Jimmy backward and in the horse-watering trough that had been carved out of an old cypress tree log. When Jimmy opened his eyes, he found himself flopping around in one end of the trough and Crazy Tom floating in the other end, his wings flapping their last earthly flaps. Grandpa walked over to the horse trough, looked down at Jimmy, and in his matter-of-fact manner said, "Jimmy, I said hit him, not kill him and give him a bath!"

Crazy Tom joined the family on the screened-in porch as guest of honor for Thanksgiving dinner. Nevertheless, by then, most of grandpa's turkeys were roosting somewhere in the flatwoods. But Crazy Tom got in the last lick. In South Georgia, when a half-eaten turkey is left on top of a warm stove with nothing but good intentions and a promise that someone will put it in the refrigerator, food poisoning will often reward the negligent and forgetful.

The books that Jimmy read as a child, the ones that ever mentioned anything about cooking a Christmas dinner, referred mostly to cooking and eating a Christmas goose. Very few people in South Georgia owned geese or even thought much about eating one. There was only one man in that part of Georgia that anyone ever heard of who knew anything about geese, much less owned any. He lived somewhere near Glennville and called his geese 'alarm clocks' because they woke him up at the same time every morning with their honking. They would sound the alarm every time anything or anyone came near his house. One morning, the geese failed to wake him up at the usual time. When he went out to check on his geese, he discovered that his dog had silenced every one of his alarm clocks. Dogs may be man's best friends, but they are jealous friends.

Down south, Christmas dinner has always been about baked turkey served up with all the customary trimmings that go with it. It also meant that people could have several fun days of going to turkey shoots during the Thanksgiving and Christmas holidays. The turkey shoots that were held in Evans County were not like a bunch of rednecks blasting away at paper targets that are tacked to a fence post where people try to hit the target with enough bird shot to win a store bought hunk of frozen turkey, those genetically engineered mutations that, when alive, couldn't walk, fly, or gobble. When those commercial alternations of nature are cooked, they taste a lot like the cellophane paper they are wrapped in, not to mention the fact that they deposit a deadly layer of cholesterol on the walls of human arteries. The turkey shoots at Nathaniel Fennel's place were real 'live' turkey shoots.

Nathaniel Fennel married into preacher Stewart's family and opened a little store down the road from the big house, about half a mile towards the Sara Ace branch and close to where the old Level Road dead-ends at Bay Branch Road. Nathaniel stocked his store with just about everything that Mr. Sapp sold from his rolling store except maybe Watkins liniment, blocks of ice, men's sock garters, hog feed, and forty-pound sacks of *Clabber Girl* flour. But Nathaniel was always home and would open up his store anytime anyone would come by and beat on the metal barrel hoop that was hanging from a piece of rusty bailing wire on the side of his store.

Although Mr. Sapp stopped by Nathaniel's store in his rolling store at least twice every month, there never was any competition between the two businessmen. That was because Mr. Sapp was the one who stocked Nathaniel's store. And it didn't take much to keep Nathaniel's store fully stocked. His store was only about 12 feet long and 10 feet wide and had just enough space in it for a nickel drink cooler, a few shelves, one stool that was always occupied by his cat, and a burlap floor mat that was embedded with enough dog hair to fill an entire kennel of dogs.

The turkey shoots always took place behind Nathaniel's store. Ten shooting posts were cut from young pine tree saplings, placed in a row, and numbered one through ten. A wire pen that could hold several turkeys was improvised from a roll of the kind of wire that chicken coops are made of and held up by tobacco curing sticks that were sharpened at one end and hammered in the ground. The makeshift pen was located down a freshly cut lane that was prepared for the event by mowing a firing lane from the posts to the pen through an old field, which was usually grown over with a bitter weed called *dog fennel* (no kin to Nathaniel). The front of the pen was built up with pine logs and dirt piled high enough so that only the heads of the turkeys and about four inches of their necks would be visible to the shooters when they were standing at their assigned posts. A turkey's brain is wired in a very nervous manner, and that makes it impossible for them to hold their heads still for more than a few seconds. And at twenty-five cents a shot, anyone who wasn't a crack shot with a .22 caliber rifle could run up quite a turkey-shooting bill.

Jimmy ran a scam with some folks who always came to the turkey shoots. He knew that most of them were not financially well off and would really appreciate having a cheap turkey for their Thanksgiving or Christmas dinner. They would give Jimmy a dollar and he would miss the first shot or two with his single shot model 63 Winchester rifle. He would then take careful aim and take out one of the turkeys with a clean shot to the head. His customers would buy the turkey from him for another twenty-five cents. Everyone won and no one's pride ever got hurt. By the time he was twelve years old, people were saying that Jimmy was probably the best rifle shot in the county. Besides, it seemed to Jimmy that missing a few shots at a turkey could never damage his reputation, especially since it was for such a worthy cause.

Liquid refreshments of the adult kind would be available for purchase from the back door of Nathaniel's house, but only after the turkey shoot was over. No doubt about it, Pete had every commercial opportunity covered. Everyone would be served soft drink chasers, smoked turkey, and barbeque from a temporary table that was made of split-pine slabs and set up along one side of Nathaniel's store.

Today, every now and then, when Jimmy has an opportunity to drive by the spot where Nathaniel's little store once stood, he sees the mobile homes that now offend those old hallowed grounds of memories. He wonders which direction it is that people now call progress. And are the wild turkeys still out there in the flatwoods? Well, all those efforts by the Fish and Game Department to reintroduce wild turkeys to South Georgia were successful beyond anyone's imagination. And although many years have passed, its a good feeling to still be able to go back to the old place and spend a few early spring mornings listening to the 'Jaba-Jaba-Jaba-Jaba' and imagine that those wild turkey gobblers just might be descendants of a couple of old tom turkeys that Jimmy once knew.

# Chapter XI

## Television at the Pines

Yo ho, Yo ho,
What's the weather going to be?
Here's the man who knows.
Let's take a look and see.

Here is Captain Sandy
with the weather he has found,
For Savannah and for Chatham,
and the counties all around.

*Weather jingle, WSAV-TV*
*Savannah, GA circa 1950*

That little weather jingle was the first human sound that Jimmy heard when it accompanied the first distinguishable picture that emanated from the first television set to work very well when it was plugged in and turned on at the *Pines*. That pioneering peek into the electronic wasteland of the future was the result of one of Aunt Eva's many trips to the *Pines*. One of the many responsibilities her husband had as an executive with the *Southern Railroad Company* in Atlanta was to oversee the disposition of iost and damaged goods that ended up in the freight room of the main train terminal. That new television set was just the latest in a series of household appliances, furniture, and other useful items that Unkie had rescued from the damaged freight room and found a home for in the homes of various members of Mr. Jim's extended family.

The first television set was a Zenith black and white table model. It had a round viewing screen that was about the size of a salad plate, and the thing took eons to warm up before anything could be recognized on the screen that remotely resembled anything familiar to the human brain. The sound seemed to work just fine, but the shadowy images of the people behind the snow-white flickering screen kept on talking as if they were unaware that no one could see them.

The second television set that came to the *Pines* lasted only about a week or so before it began to smell, smoke, sizzle, and finally spew out one last *Pfffsssst* just before falling into the eternal darkness of some electronic afterlife. However, the third television set was a new one and had arrived in its original packing box. It even came with a little book that described in simplistic cartoon detail how to turn it on, turn it off, change the volume, change the channels, and even how to fix the wavy lines on the picture screen.

In the early 1950s, the only television stations that were anywhere near the coastal plains of Georgia, and which could be depended upon to produce any discernible signs of reception in the Evans County viewing area, were WTOC-TV and WSAV-TV. Both stations were in Savannah, and that was over fifty air miles towards the east. The 'TV' was put on the end of the radio station's call signs so people wouldn't confuse the station's television call signs with the call signs that were supposed to identify the radio station. Mr. Jim didn't think that made much sense. He said it was easy for him to know when he was listening to a radio or looking at a television set. "Any fool can plainly see that a radio doesn't have one of those little viewing screens attached to the front of it." Mr. Jim never let much slip by him.

There was another television station somewhere over in Macon that could sometimes be tuned in. The only way to get it to come in clear enough to be able see anything worth watching was to rotate the big antenna that ran up the side of the big house so as to make it face to the northwest. Every now and then, when the weather was just right and there were no disruptive astrophysical events going on, the antenna could be pointed to the south so the television would receive some station in Jacksonville, Florida. It was one of those stations that transmitted a lot of religious and educational programs. Those were always special occasions when Aunt Augusta considered it permissible for Jimmy and his brother to sit on the floor in front of the television and eat their dinner, a practice that was soon to be popular with millions of future TV addicts all over America.

The peculiar thing about television is that the video (the part you see) is a result of a method of transmission that electronics folks refer to as *amplitude modulation* (AM). The audio (what you hear) is transmitted by *frequency modulation* (FM). Because of its line-of-sight characteristic and inability to penetrate natural and manmade barriers, FM is relatively free of electromagnetic interference (static) but is limited in range. However, AM can span thousands of miles, although it can be, and often is, inhibited by all sorts of static that collects on its carrier wave. That distorts the signal as it makes its way at the speed of light to radio receivers and television sets. That is the reason why the audio that comes from a television set might sometimes sound very clear while the picture will appear distorted and covered with a blanket of visible static that has the appearance of falling snow. That probably sounds a little technical to some people, but back in those days, had Jimmy understood such basics in communications and electronic theory, he might have been able to rescue his family from the throes of what very nearly came to be a major domestic revolution. But, his knowledge of communications and electronics was not to improve for years to come.

Mr. Jim understood absolutely nothing about the mechanics of things that had to be plugged in a wall before they did what they were reported to be capable of doing. However, he did appreciate the electronic revolution of the twentieth century and often mentioned that he would like to live long enough to see how people would deal with all the new changes that were coming. One of the greatest marvels to him was the radio, of which he remarked, "...represents the beginning of man's dominance over either his vices or his virtues, but it will be man's character that will dictate which will prevail. A simple fool with too much information becomes a dangerous fool." That was about as far as Jimmy's grandfather ever ventured into the world of electronic communications, but it was one of the most profound observations that he would ever recall his grandfather making. Mr. Jim decided he was not quite ready for television, or maybe television was not quite ready for him. The unreliable picture took too much effort for him to keep looking at. Besides, when he closed his eyes, it was just like listening to the radio anyway. No one ever witnessed Mr. Jim watch another minute of television for the rest of his life.

During its early years, television was like politics, local. Every little baton twirler, talking dog, ventriloquist, giant watermelon, boxing match, local ball game, and grammar school May Day pageant was given airtime that any modern-day politician would kill for. Uncle Wallace took one look at that television set and said he would get one of those things just as soon as he gets a telephone, and that would be sometime after his funeral.

Aunt Edith came home for a weekend visit from her nursing job in Savannah. After a futile attempt to watch some opera show on the television, she started telling everybody how the television set in the nurse's lounge at the hospital was a much better television than the one at the *Pines*. "The television in our nurse's lounge doesn't have all that white flaky stuff on the viewing screen." Uncle Jeff, being real smart and all, tried to explain to her that the reason her television had a better picture was because the hospital was sitting right under the TV station in Savannah while the television set at the *Pines* was over fifty miles from the nearest station. She said that was a silly notion because the window fan in her room at the hospital didn't blow air any better than the one in grandpa's room, and her power company was just down the street from the hospital while the power company for the *Pines* was all the way over in Reidsville. Jeff had no way of responding to that kind of logic. He went to the big hallway and pretended to be looking for a phonograph record in the bottom of the wind-up RCA Victrola where he always kept one of his bottles of stress relief. It didn't matter to Aunt Augusta what anyone else wanted to watch when one of the television stations was showing Norman Vincent Peale, Bishop Fulton J. Sheen, or some new preacher by the name of Billy Graham. When one of those preachers was on television, everyone had to watch what she was watching and be quiet about it or they would just have to leave the room.

Trying to watch television at the *Pines* was getting out of hand by the time the winter of 1950-51 arrived. That was one of the coldest winters in South Georgia ever since the government began keeping accurate records, and there were only three rooms in the big house that could be kept warm. There was a fireplace in the front bedroom where the television was, another one in the living room, and a big stove back in the kitchen that could burn either wood or coal. Except when it was absolutely necessary, no one went outside during the worst days of that winter. With everyone staying in the house most of the time, there was usually much hubbub, quarreling, and mental consternation going on as to which television program the family was going to watch.

Winter days and evenings were much more tranquil before television came to the *Pines*. Everyone in the family would gather near the fireplace in the huge living room where all the walls were lined with shelves filled with hundreds of books. It was a warm and cozy feeling sitting near an open fire and falling asleep while listening to Mr. Jim read some passage from the works of one of his favorite old literary masters.

Before Jimmy's grandmother died in December of 1948, the family would migrate back and forth between the living room and her bedroom where she had been bedridden for many years. A fire would be lit in the living room every other morning and all social activities of the day would be carried out there. The ashes in the fireplace in Grandmother's room would be emptied and that fireplace prepared for lighting the following morning. Her fireplace would be kept burning throughout the next day and the family social activities would take place in her room. The fireplace in the living room would be prepared with fresh kindling and oak logs so it would be ready for lighting the next day, and so on. When Jimmy was old enough to be able to carry firewood, it became his job to set the fireplaces each evening and light them the following morning.

Before Grandmother died, the evening gatherings in her room always began with her reading a verse from her Bible. Each member of the family was required to explain to the other members what the verse meant to them. Sometimes, Jimmy's efforts at comedy met with mild disapproval. After the Bible reading session, they would all sit near the fireplace, eat sweet potatoes that had been baked in the hot fireplace ashes, and listen to the radio, or grandpa and grandmother tell stories about old times and relatives who had long since passed away. After grandmother died and television came to the *Pines*, the family began to spend every evening in her old bedroom where the television was placed. Most likely, it was put in her room in an attempt to replace some of the emptiness that everyone was feeling after her death. Nevertheless, it wasn't long before the television set began to disturb the peace and tranquility of a lifestyle that had once dominated the *Pines*.

Uncle Jeff was the youngest of his six brothers and sisters and Jimmy's brother was the youngest son of Mr. Fets's two boys. According to Aunt Augusta's twisted logic, that made Jeff and Jimmy the most physically able males at the *Pines*, which undoubtedly had something to do with the fact that every time she wanted something done around the house it was either Jeff or Jimmy, or both, who were selected to do it. Every time Aunt Augusta decided to watch a program that was coming from some station that was located in a direction other than the one in which the antenna was pointing, someone had to go outside and rotate that dumb television antenna. Those were the days before there were conveniences like electric antenna rotators, automatic channel changers, or cable TV. Channel surfing at the *Pines* meant that Uncle Jeff or Jimmy had to go outside in the blistering cold, climb a ladder, and twist the ice-cold antenna mast until Aunt Augusta yelled out the window to inform them that the picture was clear enough to suit her.

It was a good thing for Jimmy that Jeff was both lazy and smart. Jimmy was walking back to the house from the barn where he had just tossed a bucket of shelled corn to the chickens when he saw Jeff standing next to the big house and staring up at the top of the television antenna. Jeff looked over at Jimmy and said; "Jimmy, go back to the well shelter and get that lasso I gave you for Christmas. It's time we fixed things so we won't freeze to death every time we have to turn this danged thing."

Jimmy retrieved his new sisal lariat from the well shelter, handed it to Jeff, and up the ladder Jeff went. He bolted the middle of the rope to the antenna, wrapped both ends of the rope around the mast a couple of turns, and then dropped the loose ends of the rope to the ground. With the help of a pair of posthole diggers, he planted a large post in the ground and mounted a double pulley on top of the post. He ran the two ends of the rope through the pulley and placed them on a hook next to the window where Aunt Augusta always issued her instructions regarding channel clarity. Damn! Jeff really was smart. He had just invented the first automatic antenna rotor. From that day on, the orientation of the antenna could be changed without anyone having to leave the warmth of the house.

The news that there was something at the Pines called a television set soon spread throughout the Bay Branch community, even to the other side of the Sara Ace Branch. Jeff, being the real smart person that he was, as well as somewhat of a troublemaker, had been tactically dropping word around the community about the magic of television that could be seen at the big house at the *Pines*. He even mentioned that the snow scenes on the television were especially beautiful. He was laying the foundation for an event that was similar to the one that unfolded when Dr. Albert Schweitzer arrived in Africa with a cigarette lighter. Albert could have chosen to be a god, an educator, or an imp. Albert chose to be an educator. Jeff decided to be an imp.

It wasn't long before curiosity managed to get the best of Bob Smalls and his son, Junior. One cold day in late February, about sunset, they both arrived at the big house riding on Bob's mule-drawn wagon. Bob hitched the mule to one of the two magnolia trees that guarded both sides of the gate in front of the house and then rang the rusty cowbell that was hanging on one of the magnolia trees and which served as a means for visitors to announce their presence. Whenever the bell rang, Grandpa always went out and stood at the top of the steps of the front porch to meet any visitors. He would invite them to get down, hitch their rig, come on in, and visit for a spell. Bob thanked Grandpa for the invitation and said, "Wees jes' wanna sees dat radio thing what got dem real livin' pitchers on it, and maybe sum o' dat snow what's supposin' to be fallin' in it. Junior ain't neva' befo' seen no real snow."

Since Grandpa was someone who rarely let anything slip by him, he immediately suspected that something strange was going on, and he wanted no part of it. When Jeff stepped through the front door, Grandpa wisely and diplomatically turned the hospitality duties over to him. Jeff invited Bob and Junior to come in the house and then escorted the two visitors to the room where the television was. Like a classical imitation of a mad scientist in one of those science fiction movies, Jeff methodically referenced the television instruction book and, with scientific-like procedure, slowly turned one of the two big knobs on the front of the television set. Following Jeff's previous instructions, and in his best imitation of a mad scientist's assistant, Jimmy went to the window and pulled on the two ends of the rope. The antenna began to rotate until the television screen displayed its best electronic imitation of a Nordic snowstorm.

Bob leaned over, placed both hands on his knees, stared directly into the television screen, and with utter amazement exclaimed, "Looka dat, Junior! Dat bees real snow! An' hit bees a comin' frum way up dar in de Noth!"

# Chapter XII

## Show and Tell

Uncle Wallace was a self-professed atheist who lived in a Christian dominated community with his two daughters from his second marriage. Jean, his oldest daughter from an earlier marriage, had already graduated from high school and was attending nursing school in Atlanta. Both of his marriages had ended up in divorce and somehow resulted in the male member of the broken unions gaining custody of the three daughters. Apparently, the family court judge that presided over the two divorces must have been privy to a few extenuating and mitigating facts and circumstances that were better off not being revealed to children.

When Uncle Wallace wasn't traveling around selling his fresh produce, he drove a school bus for the Evans County Department of Education. But that was before a majority of so-called experts in the public school system decided that they would consolidate all the public schools in the county. Evidently, there were not enough members on the school board that were favorable to the idea that people who lived in the rural areas of the county might prefer their children be educated near their homes. It makes one contemplate how it was ever possible for so many great minds to have been produced by a nation whose children used to have to walk to school and were educated in one-room country schoolhouses.

After the county officials managed to herd every elementary and high school student in one big school complex in Claxton, they went about rearranging the county school bus routes. It sure was strange when some of the new bus routes began and ended where many of the relatives of the school board lived and all of a sudden several of those relatives had jobs as school bus drivers. The only thing that all those changes meant to the children who lived in rural areas was that they would now be spending an additional thirty minutes riding the school bus each way between their homes and the new school.

Jimmy asked his Uncle Wallace why it was that he even bothered to drive a school bus in the first place. His uncle explained that, since he had to go to town almost every day anyway, he might as well do it on the county's dollars. That man never quibbled with logic. He even kept an old truck parked in the lane in front of his house and another older and even more beat-up truck parked at the school bus maintenance yard. He always had transportation wherever and whenever he needed it for making his produce deliveries.

The *Pines* was one of the few farms in the Bay Branch community that had electricity and inside plumbing during the 1940s. It was also one of the first in the county to get a telephone right after the telephone company finished stringing telephone lines along Bay Branch Road. The telephone number at the *Pines* was 276J1, which signified that it was the 276th telephone connected to the regional telephone exchange system. The suffix J1 (jingle one) meant that the telephone ring was one long jingle on a party line system, a system that allowed everyone on the line to hear everyone's jingles and everyone could listen in on every conversation. The Daniel's telephone number was 276J2, indicating their ring was two short jingles. The next family had three short jingles, the next two long jingles, and so on until things got much more confusing than was surely intended by the *Southern Bell Telephone Company* or the guy who started the whole mess in the first place, Mr. Alexander Graham Bell.

Everything worked just fine as long as there were no more than four or five families connected to the party line. But, the system grew. Eventually, it got to the point there were so many people on one party line that it became difficult for anyone to figure out which jingle belonged to which house. Some folks on the party line simply didn't care how many jingles the phone made. All they wanted to do was to find out what other people were talking about.

The party line system seemed to bring out the best and worst in people. The worst were those who used the telephone as a way to stick their noses in other people's business. Every time the phones would start ringing, you could be assured that one of those characters would be listening in on the conversation. It finally got to the point that the phone would get in only a fraction of a jingle before some nutcase on the party line or their rude child would lift the receiver. That made all the phones on the line stop ringing and no one would be able know for whom a call was intended.

The situation was finally managed in a very uncharacteristically inefficient manner compared to the ingenuity that was usually demonstrated by country people of those times. Everyone would answer the phone as soon as it began ringing. Some responsible person would then have to take control of the situation and keep the line open until the right person picked up the receiver. It was either that or someone would have to take a message from the caller and then go knocking on the intended receiver's door. No mechanical invention or social system in the history of the world has ever survived very long without being modified by human necessity, convenience, or stupidity.

It is quite likely that the people who lived in the rural areas or this country during the 1940s were responsible for the future gasoline shortage of the 1970s. Someone was always cranking up their pickup truck or tractor and driving over to another family's farm to tell them that they had a telephone call from so-and-so from over at wherever. It didn't matter for whom a telephone call was intended; all work ceased when that stupid telephone started ringing and nothing happened in the community until the darned telephone situation was resolved. It might even be probable that it was about that time when the telephone began doing to society what we later permitted television to do to modern day society.

"Jimmy, go tell your Uncle Wallace that he has a telephone call."

"But he is in the new-ground field all way on the other side of the big field planting tomatoes so he can sell them to all those poor people in China."

"You go tell him right now! It's a *'telephone'* call!"

The first long distance telephone call that anyone can remember being connected to the Bay Branch party line came to the *Pines*, but only after several conversations with a series of manual switchboard operators, all of whom seemed to have been selected for their jobs because of their unique ability to talk through their nose. It was an event that ushered out all remaining doubt that the age of communications had finally arrived in the Bay Branch Community. Everyone on the party line tied up the telephone system for weeks talking about the time when someone called Mr. Fet to inform him that he had to give up his Christmas leave and get back to his military base because America was at war with Japan and Germany. "Someone called Mr. Fet, and they were talking on one of those *'long distance telephones'* that they have all the way up there in Washington!"

After the introduction of the long distance telephone call, local telephone conversations came to be routine, even mundane, and interest waned in such things as what kind of vegetables people were going to be planting in their garden or whose daughter was trying to get a date with which boy that had access to a car. People began thirsting for more interesting, unusual, bizarre, and even shocking news. Some folks would even call all over the country trying to unearth some obscure tidbit of news from some far off place. All they wanted to do was to call *The Claxton Enterprise* so they could get their names in the paper for knowing something about something that no one else in the county knew anything about.

Mr. Jim proposed his theory that the telephone might very well be an instrument that was invented by the Devil as a devious way to turn us all into a nation of voyeurs and busybodies. Judging by the way newspaper reporters in those days could be seen clamoring for the only telephone within several city blocks; it is quite possible that the invention of the telephone is also what gave birth to the modern-day phenomenon that we know of as 'Pavaratzi' mania. And, has anyone noticed that, with the increasing popularity of telephones and technological advancements in wireless communications, like cellular phones, there seems to be a corresponding decrease in the ability of people to effectively express their thoughts in writing. Does anyone remember that form of communication? *Writing*; a lost form of human communication that facilitates the thoughts of one person to be transmitted to another in such fashion as to permit the receiving person to savor the words and contemplate their meaning without electronic instant replays or having to ask the sender to repeat themselves.

The years during World War II and the years immediately after the war was a time when many people had to make major adjustments in their lives and ways of thinking. A telephone salesman from the *Southern Bell Telephone Company* stopped by Uncle Wallace's house one day and tried to get him to sign up as one of their new telephone customers. The man from the phone company told Uncle Wallace that he would be charged an installation fee and an additional fee every time he used the very gadget that he would already be paying a monthly rental fee just for the pleasure of having the thing in his house in the first place. He informed the telephone man that if they put that confounded hindrance to peace and tranquility in his house he would cut down every telephone pole that was standing between his house and to wherever that place is where someone keeps ringing that infernal bell.

A couple of years after the war ended, the *Rural Electric Administration* (REA) came through Bay Branch Community and began running new electric power lines along the main road in front of the big house. That was a time when a lot of federal money was being spent on rural development. The new power lines were supposed to be capable of handling more voltage and current than the old lines. Uncle Wallace decided that electricity might not be such a bad idea after all and told the man from the REA to go ahead and hook some of that electricity up to his house. They ran a line from the main road to a big pole right next to his house and then asked Uncle Wallace where he wanted them to install the main switch box. Since he did a lot of reading and thought electricity might be one of the better things to have come along, he showed the electricians exactly where he wanted them to put the switch box. From that day on, Uncle Wallace had a big nickel-colored 50-ampere main electric breaker switch and a four-line fuse box mounted on the wall of his bedroom, right next to his bed. "How in seven hundred hot hells was I supposed to know? I never had any of that electricity stuff before. Well, at least I'm the only person in the county who can turn on and off my radio, my new electric fan, and every damned light in the house without having to get out of bed." No one was aware of the significance of what Uncle Wallace had accidentally stumbled upon, but in years to come, it would be recognized as the first working model of a contraption that was to eventually prove to be a curse upon all humanity, the remote control.

A few days after the REA completed installation of the new power lines along the road in front of the big house, they came back to hook up the individual houses to the main lines. Uncle Jeff was watching one of the REA men strapping on his climbing gear before climbing up the pole to string the new lines to the house. Jeff walked up to the lineman, poked his walking cane out at him, tapped him on his pole-climbing gaffs, and in his best back country redneck drawl asked, "Whacha' doin' der, feller?"

"We're stringing new electric lines to your house."

"Whacha' doin' dat fer?"

"Because the old lines don't carry enough electricity."

"Uh hu. So hows much mor'uh dat 'lectricity weuns gonna' be a gittin'?"

"Oh, you won't be getting any more electricity than you got before."

"So how come dat be?"

"That transformer on that pole over there will keep you from getting more electricity than you need."

"So how's much weuns be a needin'?"

"Well, that depends upon how much you use."

"I sees. So iffen weuns be a needin' more o' dat 'lectricity, dayl' be some more of it in dat der black barrel up der on dat pole o'er der. Dat rat?"

"No, sir. That's a transformer. It just keeps you from getting an overload."

"Uh huh, I sees. So youse'ar a puttin' in dem new lines what be holdin' mor' 'lectricity, but dat won't be a comin' over'n dose new lines cause'n o' dat black barrel o'er der dat nozes how much 'lectricity weuns beez a needin', but hit won't be a givin' hit to us no way 'cause dat'ud be too much'ava load down. Dat rat?"

"Uh, well, uh."

"So hows much mors'hit gonna be a costin' usn's fo' a havin the priv'lige o' gettin' more o' dat 'lectricity dat weuns ain't a gonna be a gettin' no way?"

Jeff had a way of turning simple matters into complex issues, usually at the expense of other people.

Modern advances in technology often clash with the natural order of things. For years, probably eons, wild birds of various species have been flying along the edges of forests that provide cover and concealment from birds of prey that fly in circles over the open spaces in search of victims to sate their hunger. The pine grove in front of the big house provided excellent cover for woodcocks, snipe, ducks, and other species of birds that would fly along the edge of the big field on their way to and from their morning feeding and evening roosting places. The multiple power and telephone lines that were strung along the road dissected the flight paths of the birds and created a waiting disaster for unsuspecting low-flying birds. The telltale noise of a bird meeting its sudden demise could be heard all the way to the front porch of the big house every time one of the birds 'thongggged' into one of those tight wires. Wood ducks, snipes, and other delicious fast flying delicacies were gathered up just as soon as one of those wires sang out its song of death.

Judy was Jimmy's cousin and the youngest of Uncle Wallace's daughters. They lived in a little two-story clapboard house that was nestled among a stand of pine trees across the road from the big house, about a ten-minute walk up the road towards the Daniel's place.

One Saturday evening, just about sunset, Jimmy was sitting on the front porch of the big house. He was watching Judy and one of her friends, who lived somewhere over near U.S. Highway 301, playing in the white sand along the dirt road in front the pine grove. Thonggggg! Something slammed into one of the power lines. Judy and her playmate ran over to examine the results of the collision. Judy picked up the lifeless carcass, carried it to the front porch, and asked Jimmy what kind of bird it was that had just met its sudden aerial demise. That was when the plot began to hatch in Jimmy's mischievously fertile mind.

"It's a black mallard that was headed down to Florida for the winter, just like those Yankees do every year when they drive down U.S. 301." Judy's little friend looked at Jimmy like he suspected something might not be all that accurate, but didn't say anything that might spoil Jimmy's gag. He even agreed with Jimmy's suggestion as to what Judy should do with the bird. "Let's take it to school." That sounded like a great idea to Judy since she was in the second grade and very concerned about not having anything to take to Bellville School for 'Show and Tell' day.

Jimmy began building upon his plot by telling Judy that the bird was a very rare kind of duck. He told her it was a member of a special species that always sent a lone scout duck down south to check on the weather before the rest of the ducks flew down for the winter. Since this was obviously a scout duck, the word would not get back to all the ducks that were still up north, and they would probably freeze to death during the coming winter. Jimmy thickened the plot a little by telling Judy that, since her father didn't have a telephone and the one at the *Pines* wasn't strong enough to reach all the way to Florida, it would be an act of kindness for her to take that *black mallard scout duck* to school for show and tell. The other children in her class would learn about ducks and the teacher would know what to do about all those ducks that were stranded up north. The teacher would probably call down to Florida, check on the weather, and then call back up north so someone up there could tell the other ducks that it was okay for them to fly south. Jimmy warned her, "Don't tell your daddy, he'll just cook the duck and eat it like we usually do with the other birds that hit those wires."

That '*duck*' was actually a common loon, a kind of water bird that local folks call a '*diadaper*.' It was just one of the many different kinds of birds that had met their doom after getting whacked by one of those power lines. Judy wrapped the loon in some old newspapers, stuffed it in a shoebox, and then hid it under one of the seats in the school bus where her father wouldn't see it when he began his bus route the following Monday morning. The next day, Judy spent the entire Sunday practicing her show and tell speech and checking with Jimmy for verification on some of the 'facts' of which she was still a bit unclear regarding that very rare black mallard scout duck.

It took a few years, but Judy managed to make sure Jimmy paid dearly for his little ruse with the loon. A new family had recently moved in the house next to the Sara Ace Branch, about a mile from the *Pines*. One of the children was a little blonde girl who was about Jimmy's age. Never before in his life had Jimmy seen anything like that little girl. Not even one of those girls that model underwear in the *Sears and Roebuck* Spring and Summer catalog could ever come close to matching her beauty. Since they both rode the same school bus to and from school every day, Jimmy knew he had a distinct advantage over the other boys at school. Riding on the bus with her gave him a solid strategic advantage, excellent tactical positioning, and perfect opportunity. All he needed was a little inspiration; something to say to her that would help him break the ice. Just the right words and she would surely tell him how much she had longed for the day when someone like him would come along and take her to wherever it is that those actors in the movies go when the movie is over. Of course the movie would be one of those where the hero has his arm around the girl, the music is fading away, and everyone is smiling as THE END signals another happy ending. A fourteen-year-old boy with strange new hormones vibrating through his body and bouncing against his brain probably should not be let out of the house until things get a bit more stabilized.

It was on a Saturday and about the fourth anniversary of that duck trick that Jimmy pulled on Judy. She was now about the same age as he was at the time of his practical joke. The *Pines* had a new telephone number and the party line system had finally been relegated to history. When the telephone rang, it was Judy calling from Claxton. She and her father and everyone from the *Pines* had gone to town to shop, see a movie, and visit some people that Jimmy didn't know and didn't really care anything about seeing. He had decided to stay home, saddle up his new horse, Diana, and take a ride over to Jerry Salter's house. Jerry was a new friend who had recently moved in a house that was across the flatwoods from the *Pines* and next to thousands of acres of land that was owned by a big paper company in Savannah.

Judy told Jimmy that they had stopped by the girl's house and the girl's mother and father had gone to town with them. She informed Jimmy that the girl told her how much she wanted to see him and would like for him come to her house while everyone else was in town. Judy instructed Jimmy to not go to the front door, but go around to the big window in back of the house and call for her. That way, if someone drove by the little girl's house, they wouldn't be able to see anything that might seem out of the ordinary. Judy failed to tell Jimmy that the girl and her mother were the only ones who had actually gone to town and the only person who was at the girl's house was her father.

The really embarrassing part of the whole charade was that Jimmy's father, Uncle Jeff, Uncle Wallace, and the girl's father had all been in on the deal. They even helped Judy arrange the big trap, and the little blond girl never knew anything about the great plot. But that made everything turn out pretty good for Jimmy. Judy's little trick had given him the icebreaker he needed.

Thanks to that little episode, Jimmy was able to arrange a few after school hours of curious and youthful pleasure with his very first real live girlfriend. No more mooning over scantily clad images in the Sears and Roebuck catalog, he had now seen the real McCoy. But, as events occur and luck will sometimes dictate, the little girl's family moved away after having lived there for only a little over a year. Jimmy often thought about her and wondered where she might be living. It finally came to him that she was one of those special people that most of us keep hidden in one of those secret places in our memories, the same place where all those people on the movie screen go when the show is over.

# Chapter XIII

## As Time Goes By

Time is often wasted on speed about as much as it is lost on idleness. The kind of people who lived in rural South Georgia before the advent of such conveniences as paved roads, television, cellular phones, fax machines, air-conditioned cars, and climate controlled houses never concerned themselves very much with the passage of time. But neither were they idle. As they watched the seasons slowly change, time always announced its presence with gentle nudges in the air to remind them of the time for planting and the time for harvesting. When they were able to spare a few moments of time, rather than submitting to the seductive conveniences of the instruments of modern-day time keeping, communications and travel, country people usually involved themselves in such pastimes as reading, family discussions, writing letters, and reading aloud letters that they received from far off friends and family members. After the rural postman delivered the mail, Mr. Jim's family would gather on the front porch of the big house and listen to the reading of letters from distant loved ones. As the written words were spoken, they would imagine the writer's faces, wonder what they are doing, and wish that they could see them again, sometime soon.

After the evening dinner, families would gather around the only radio in the house and listen to *One Man's Family, The Great Gildersleeve*, or *Fibber McGee and Molly*. The familiar and authoritative voices of Morgan Beatty, Gabriel Heater, or Lowell Thomas always introduced the evening's entertainment with their delivery of news from the outside world. The Saturday drive to the nearest town was an occasional event that, while always an enjoyable diversion, was necessary only when there was a need to replenish essential items that couldn't be produced from their labors on the farm. Time goes by in South Georgia just as it goes by everywhere else. But there, it passes in dutiful service to the people who are closest to the land.

Country people in South Georgia have always guided their lives more by daily attendance to things that are necessary for sustaining life rather than things that are not within their ability to control. This innate and intimate knowledge of man's capabilities and understanding of his limitations produced a strong attachment to the earth and to those things that it is capable of producing. It was only natural for such people to become one of this nation's strongest vestiges of mans' spiritual connection to a higher being. Those things that can be witnessed by man, but cannot be duplicated by him must be within the realm of a higher domain. This is the manner in which humanity has always explained things and events that they perceived to be beyond the control of mortal man. Even today, with our ability to irrigate large tracts of land, we plant our fields and then begin a prayerful vigilance for the blessing of rain to come from the heavens.

The people of rural South Georgia have always demonstrated a special connection to the kinds of values that are represented by a love of family, respect for the sovereignty of others, commitment to death and duty before dishonor, loyalty to one's country, and a unified feeling of the presence of a higher being. Growing up in that kind of culture can cause people to develop a deep sense of responsibility to the earth, those things born from it, and to those who protect it. It's no wonder that the cemeteries of South Georgia are marked with graves of thousands of men who forfeited their lives and futures so that others might benefit from their personal sacrifices. But, as time goes by for the living, time for the noble dead continue only as captured moments in the minds of the living who are willing take a few moments of their time to remember those who have gone, who they were, and to contemplate why it was that they had to leave us.

As time went by for Jimmy, he came to understand that time is well used when spent in thoughtful respect and remembrance of those, past and present, who gave and still give of their time in contribution to the enrichment of others. That may explain why he has always felt a close connection to his indigenous native ancestors who permitted only their elders to make important decisions that would affect the entire tribe. Much can be said for a society that was responsible enough to ensure that the gravest judgments were placed in the hands of the wisest and most experienced of their representatives. One advantage of the human condition is the ability to redirect the impertinence of youth. But when that duty is neglected, humanity is condemned to repeat the bad times of its history.

When Jimmy's father was leaving Troop F of the 6th Cavalry Regiment to join the war effort in Europe, the men of his troop gave him a watch as a going-away present. It was one of those types of watches that can often be seen on the wrists of military officers in old movies about World War II. Mr. Fet was proud of that watch and, as time went by, he began to wear it only on special occasions. He always kept it in a special place on his bedroom dresser, as if it were a small monument to all his old friends who once served with him during his days in the horse cavalry.

Mr. Thomas and two of his boys, Tommy and Temp, were sitting on the front steps of Mr. Fet's house listening to him tell tales about the days when he was in the horse cavalry and how he used to patrol the border between Mexico and Texas during the 1920s. They loved to hear him tell about his adventures and narrow escapes, and they would egg him on as long as possible. He showed his watch to them again and told another story about how the watch stopped running and caused him to be late getting back to his airbase when he was in England during the war. When he finally made it back to his base, he came upon the remains of a German rocket that had destroyed the building where he lived. He said that had it not been for that watch stopping he would have died that day. Thomas mused, "Yep, we is all gonna die one day 'lessen we can stop ol' time frum a'tickin' on."

Corn, tomatoes, melons, and other cash crops provided an income for the *Pines,* but it was the garden that provided an assortment of special vegetables and trimmings for the dining table. The annual ritual of preparing the garden for planting would begin every year about the time when the morning frost began to turn to morning dew. It was on such a crisp Saturday morning in early March when Thomas drove his mule and wagon up to the gate in front of the big house. Tommy and Temp were sitting on the tailgate, dangling their feet behind the wagon, and sharing a *Royal Crown Cola* that they had just bought at Nathaniel Fennel's little roadside store, which was about a half-mile down the road from the big house.

Thomas instructed Tommy to go to Mr. Fet's place and tell him that everyone would be waiting for him at the garden and getting it ready for planting. Tommy headed down the lane towards Mr. Fet's house and Thomas headed for the garden. Thomas unhitched the mule from the wagon, pulled a two-handled single-blade side-busting plow off the back of the wagon and hitched it to the mule's harnesses and singletree. When Tommy returned, everyone was in the garden and had already begun mending the wire fence, straightening bent over fence posts, busting the first furrows with the plow, and throwing cow manure over the newly turned soil. Newly turned South Georgia soil has a special aroma to it that refreshes old memories and beckons the soul like a magnet.

Mr. Thomas asked Tommy if he had told Mr. Fet that everyone was ready to begin planting the garden. Tommy replied, "I told'ed him and he say he be here d'rectly." No one was aware of it at the time, but Mr. Fet had gone to town earlier that morning to buy seed and bundles of young vegetables for planting in the garden. It was nearly mid-morning when Mr. Fet drove his truck up to the garden, backed it through the gate, and parked it close to the freshly plowed rows where it would be easier to unload. He told Mr. Thomas that he was going to walk back to his house and would be back just as soon as he had time to change into his work clothes.

Not a person in the garden said a thing, but it was clear to everyone that Tommy had not seen nor talked to Mr. Fet that morning. The coolness in the morning air seemed to be accentuated by the manner in which Thomas finally spoke to Tommy. Thomas was not a man to call anyone down in front of other people, but it was evident that Tommy was going to be having a discussion with Thomas sometime later when they would have an opportunity for a little more privacy, and Mr. Thomas was going to be the one who would be doing the talking.

When Mr. Fet returned to the garden, he was walking very quickly and went straight to his truck where he began ransacking the inside of the truck like he was looking for something specific. He stepped out of the truck, walked around in a little circle, looked down under the truck, and then scraped around in the grass next to the truck. He mumbled, "I don't think I took it to town with me. Where the heck could it be?"

Mr. Thomas reached for a dipper of water from a bucket that was hanging on the corner of the garden fence, took a big gulp, and asked, "Mr. Fet, where is what?"

"My watch, it should have been on my dresser at the house, but it wasn't there when I got back. I'm pretty sure I wasn't wearing it when I went to town."

The cool crispness of the morning air turned to solid ice as Thomas placed the water dipper back on the fence next to the water bucket, gave Tommy a freezing stare, and then ordered, "Tommy, come over here." Cautiously but obligingly, Tommy slowly walked the few steps over to where Thomas was sitting on the running board of Mr. Fet's truck. "Come here closer, boy!" Hesitantly, Tommy nudged closer as Thomas turned his head sideways and pressed one of his ears to each of the pockets on Tommy's overalls. "Boy! Do you have that watch what be belongin' to Mr. Fet?"

"Nawsir! I noses I ain't got no watch and I noses I ain't stole no watch needer!"

Mr. Thomas reached in one of the breast pockets on Tommy's dungarees and retrieved Mr. Fet's gold 'Gruen Precision' wristwatch. He stared deep into Tommy's soul and said, "Boy, yuse knows only two things in dis world. One o' dem is dat yuse be in trubble and de other is dat yuse be in trubble wid me! Rat now, yuse gonna be a tellin' me why it tiz dat yuse be a havin' dat watch o' Mr. Fet's in yo' dungaree pocket. And no foolin' now!"

Tears cut little muddy channels through the soft dirt on Tommy's cheeks as he sobbed, "Yuse dun' bin tolded us dat yuse a gonna' be dyin' iffen' time dun't git stopped! I wuz jist a gonna see iffin' I could stop time frum a goin' on like Mr. Fet dun back when he wuz in dat big wah and kepped dat big ol' bumb frum a killin' him."

For a few moments, time stood still in the garden as silence prevailed. Then, one by one, everyone began to realize that Tommy had just unknowingly, yet very neatly extricated himself from the jaws of certain doom. It was about that time when Jimmy first began to think more seriously about time and its relationship with the inevitable and impending finality of death.

We would all be well advised to apportion our time wisely, for our mortality is fixed in what little time that has been allocated to each of us. It must be a terrible thing when, upon their deathbeds, some people finally realize that their life is over and they have permitted time to pass without having given themselves an opportunity to take with them pleasant memories of places cherished and people loved. When people fail to master the time that has been allotted to their lives, they will become only forgotten servants of time. At any rate, time marches on, trampling the lazy, taking revenge of the hasty, and rewarding those who patiently and generously give of themselves. The rewards of fond remembrances are the greatest rewards of all.

Jimmy's grandmother died a few days before Christmas of that year. He had never really seen much of her except when it was his turn to tend the fireplace in her room or when it was time for his reading lessons. She had been bedridden long before he knew her and no one ever told him exactly what ailed her. He just knew that she had to stay in bed most of the day, and it was she and Eloise who had taught him how to read.

Eloise read to Jimmy in a way that made him appreciate great literature. But it was his grandmother who forced him to read for the purpose of gaining useful information. It was through their joint efforts that he was able to read long before he entered public school. His grandmother required him to spend at least an hour each day sitting on a stool by her bed while she made him sound the phonetic elements of language, recite the alphabet, and understand the purposes of vowels and consonants. Although he thought his time was being wasted during those lessons, as time went by, he came to realize it was those times that are some of his most cherished times of all.

The old watch that once belonged to his father now rests on Jimmy's dresser where he often gazes upon it and remembers the good times and the good people who no longer live in Bay Branch Community, except in spirit. Although Jimmy never chased Mexican bandidos or fought in that great European war like his father did, each time he looks upon the watch he senses the presence of all the memories that once were his father's. And he remembers those times as his father remembered them, and how he told of the times when he rode a horse named Trixie through dusty Mexican border towns and the times he watched B-17 bombers, P-47 Thunderbolts, and P-51 Mustangs limp back home over the cliffs of Dover. Those are times when time stands still, as time goes by.

# Chapter XIV

## The Island Hole

Oh deep dark watery hole
What might your bottom hold
Did evil men do their best
To hide there a treasure chest
Or are you just a fisher's dream
Yielding up only big fat bream

Bull Creek emerges from the watersheds of Tattnall County and flows along an easterly course before entering Evans County near the old Tattnall Campground where many church congregations still come together for their annual religious retreats and revivals. The waters from small streams like Bay Branch, Cribbs Branch, and the Sara Ace Branch gradually push Bull Creek along its banks, making it wider and deeper as it slowly slices its way through the southern half of Evans County.

Guarded on both sides of its banks by thick scrub brush and waste high briar bushes, Bull Creek finally succumbs to a watery marriage with the Cannochee River at the Bryan County line near the old historic Sunbury Road. But it doesn't meet its demise until after cutting a heavenly chain of fishing holes for people who have a passionate taste for the fattest fresh water red-breasted bream in the world, and for those who have sufficient fortitude for dealing with cottonmouth moccasins and squadrons of biting yellow flies.

Many large bream, which would easily out-strip the official world record but never reported, have most likely been gutted, scaled, fried, and eaten soon after being hooked and pulled to the banks of those waters. The favorite rig for catching those pan-fried delicacies was usually a bamboo pole, a few feet of Dacron line weighted down with a split-shot lead sinker, and a red-wiggler worm or cricket attached to a number six hook. An old bottle cork is still the best thing to use as a float for keeping the bait suspended in the water at a very top-secret depth.

It's a good thing that most country boys are blessed with an abundance of time and energy. It takes plenty of both to find a good fishing hole that is full of bream, and even more to cut a path through the thick vegetation that usually surrounds every water hole in South Georgia. There is probably some scientific name for those pesky bushes, but most people who live in that part of Georgia just refer to them as '*ty-tys.*'

Perhaps the most famous of these fishing holes is the one that is near the junction of Bay Branch and Bull Creek, the one that people call the *Island Hole*. Only a few people know the precise location of the Island Hole, and no one knows for sure just exactly how deep it really is. It is said by those who claim to know that it is still a watery grave for an unknown number of adventurous, but unfortunate souls who managed to stumble upon it and then foolishly tried to determine its depth. One thing, of which is very certain, it was much deeper than the length of any of the many spools of fishing line that Jimmy bought from Bowen Rogers's hardware store in Claxton.

After his Saturday morning haircut at James Smith's barbershop, and with his leftover change from his haircut burning a hole in his pocket, Jimmy always stopped by Bowen Rogers's hardware store. He never knew when he might find something that he needed, like more fishing or hunting stuff, and he always needed more fishing and hunting stuff. The manager of the store, Mr. Cribbs, never seemed to be nervous about children browsing around in his store like so many other storekeepers in town. As Jimmy wandered through the rows of bins, shelves, and glass display cases, Mr. Cribbs understood that he was only looking for that very special, but never actually found, unknown thing that every twelve-year-boy spends his entire adolescent life in search of. He probably remembered the days when he was a young boy because he seemed to have a sense for what young boys were thinking. And he always threw in an extra fishhook or just one more 20-gauge shotgun shell.

Although Jimmy had a fresh supply of fishing line, lead sinkers, hooks, and an itch to get home, his younger brother and he would spend a couple of hours watching a movie at Mr. Tos's movie theater. They would watch the first run of the Saturday afternoon matinee, which was always preceded by a weekly serial episode of *Buck Rogers, Sky King,* or *Buster Crabbe,* and then a whole string of cartoons.

When a movie that starred Roy Rogers came to town, the marquee above the entrance to the theater always billed Roy as the *King of the Cowboys.* Jimmy's brother cited that as proof that Roy was the best cowboy in the world. But Jimmy liked Gene Autry for more practical reasons. Gene carried only one six-shooter in his one-holster belt, while Roy wore two six-shooters that were tucked down in a pair of fancy basket-weave holsters, which seemed to Jimmy as being more suited for wearing to a Saturday night dance than for diving off cliffs and nabbing fleeing bandits.

Jimmy's brother had a box full of Roy Rogers' comic books, pictures of Roy, Trigger, Dale, Buttermilk, Bullet, Pat Butram, and Pat's Jeep, Nellybelle. The walls of Jimmy's room were decorated with pictures of Gene, his horse Champion, and one of Gene's funny talking sidekicks. It was Jimmy's valued judgment that any cowboy who was not able to handle a gang of black-hatted desperados with only one gun and six rounds of ammunition would never rate his admiration. That was often a real sore spot between the two brothers.

During the cartoon break between the main feature and the next round of short features, Mr. Fet would always be standing in the theater behind the back row of seats waiting to drive his boys home. When the double feature started over again, he would walk down the dark isle calling out their names. Jimmy thought, *Oh yeah, like he never believes we know how to get out of the theater without his help.* In a futile attempt to keep from being recognized and publicly humiliated in front of his friends, Jimmy would sneak out the theater through one of the side exits that led to the back alley. It was a nonchalant effort at keeping other kids in the theater from getting the idea that he was the one that his father was calling for. Adolescents do not like to be embarrassed by their parents, especially in front of their peers.

During the drive home, and when the weather permitted, they would sometimes stop at the old bridge over Bull Creek and go for a swim. But not this time, Jimmy wanted to get home as quickly as possible. He had a pocket full of new fishing gear and another body of water on his mind.

Meanwhile, back at the ranch (I always wanted to write that), old Charlie was waiting for Jimmy. As soon as his father's Pontiac rolled to a stop in front of the big house, it took Jimmy only a few minutes to throw his saddle on Charlie's back and gallop three miles of anticipation before throwing his baited hook in the Island Hole. The best place to drop the bait was as close as possible to a big cypress tree that stood in the middle of the Island Hole. The old cypress had a collection of grass, weeds, and bushes growing around the base of its trunk in a way that made the whole arrangement look as if the tree was growing on a little island in the middle of the water. And that is how the *Island Hole* got its name.

While he was sitting on the bank by the fishing hole and enjoying the cool shade of towering cypress, poplar, and water-oak trees, an idea breached the defenses of Jimmy's brain, an idea that soon developed into what seemed to be a practical thing to do. While waiting for the inevitable tug on his fishing pole, Jimmy was reliving the experiences of the hero in the movie that he had just finished watching not more than an hour before. It seems that Lash Larue had managed to find himself in another tight fix after being captured by a gang of bad guys. They threw him in the bottom of a deep pit that was full of snakes, and there seemed to be no apparent way of escaping the imminent torture of all that hissing doom. Undaunted, Lash whistled for his horse. With his trusty bullwhip, which always seemed to be long enough to reach anything within the width of the movie screen, he expertly snagged the saddle horn, easily pulled himself to safety, and then rode off in a renewed chase after the bad guys.

*That would be it,* Jimmy thought to himself. *The Island Hole can't be any deeper than that snake pit Lash Larue just got himself out of. Besides, the lariat hanging on my saddle is much longer than Lash's bullwhip. All I have to do is tie one end of the rope around my waist and the other end to the saddle horn on Charlie's back. I can then find out how far I can go down in that hole.* Jimmy even figured out how he would overcome his body's tendency to float back up while trying to sink deeper with his lungs full of air.

Although Jimmy wasn't yet familiar with the laws of physics as they apply to such things as the dynamics of fluid displacement and buoyancy, he still knew that all he needed was an effective counter-weight. So, he put a big rock in a burlap bag that he brought with him to use as a fish tote and then tied the sack to one of his legs with a quick-release slipknot. No sense in not being able to dump that rock if he got in any kind of trouble. He even had the foresight to arrange the rope in a neat coil on the bank of the creek so he could determine how deep he had gone down in the Island Hole by measuring how much rope was wet after climbing out.

Yeah, I know. He could have just tied the rock to one end of the rope and tossed the rock in the hole. But he had his mind set on finding another one of those things that twelve-year-old boys dream about, gold! Hey, come on, it could happen. Some dastardly fellow probably stashed his ill-gotten treasure in that old water hole and then ventured on to some place where he met his well-deserved, but untimely demise. All that gold was probably still down there, just waiting for the right person to come along and find it. Besides, it wasn't as if Jimmy didn't have permission. One of his aunt's favorite Bible verses was, "Seek and ye shall find."

With everything figured out, his plan properly rehearsed in his mind, and all riggings and knots secure, he waded into the cool waters of the Island Hole. As the water began encircling his neck, he took a few last deep breaths of fresh air and then plunged into the deep and dark watery nothingness. Everything seemed to be going as planned until he felt a sudden and strong tug on the rope, sorta' like Lash Larue lassoing a train.

*Darn! I forgot! Old Charlie never liked being left alone, and every time he is, he always heads for home!* As long as Jimmy was within sight or sound, Charlie would always stay in one spot provided that his bridle reins were draped over a bush, fence, log, or anything that might appear to a horse as being immovable. But, if Charlie couldn't see or hear Jimmy, and the loose ends of his reins weren't connected to something tangible and not just wrapped around the saddle horn, Charlie always figured that it was time to head back home. Before that day, Jimmy never really had much of an urgent reason for breaking Charlie of that one bad habit.

When Jimmy's head popped through the surface of the water, the first thing he caught sight of was Charlie moving away in a slow sideways trot, his body straining against the rope that was connecting the saddle on his back to the dead weight of Jimmy's body and that dumb rock-in-a-sack idea. Jimmy bounced off the bank of the creek with such force that it caused the cinch on Charlie's saddle to break. The saddle ricocheted off an oak tree and Charlie's trot straightened out as he accelerated to a full gallop. He gave one glance back, apparently to verify Jimmy's safety, before heading home to the peace and quiet of his stable.

Jimmy limped back home with little more than a sprained shoulder, skinned knees, and an education. Some people say horses can't really think. But it is a good bet that Charlie was just too embarrassed to be seen with Jimmy that day, and he had made a conscious decision to teach a lesson to Jimmy, one that he would not soon forget.

Years later, as a responsible and dignified officer in the United States Army, Jimmy participated in many after-action briefings on combat training exercises. The briefings were supposed to be a critique designed to identify what the army high brass evasively referred to as "lessons learned." The army used the lessons learned technique to teach military commanders that the mistakes they make in training should not be repeated in actual combat situations.

Jimmy learned two valuable lessons that day at the Island Hole. First, if you don't want field mice and other critters to eat your saddle or anything else that is made of leather, never leave it in the woods overnight. A picture of a twelve-year-old kid dragging a rodent-eaten saddle through the woods on a Sunday morning is a pitiful sight. Second, having relatively high intelligence does not necessarily guarantee personal success unless the mind in which that intelligence resides has been disciplined with regular and adequate doses of education and practical training.

Over the years, dozens of big fish have been caught from the banks of that old fishing hole. During his future travels around the world, Jimmy would catch many more fish from many other holes. But no fish he would catch would ever be as large as the one old Charlie pulled from the Island Hole on that Saturday afternoon in the summer of 1952.

# Chapter XV

## The School Bus

America's addiction to the conveniences of modern day transportation methods is most likely the reason why we allowed our public school system to deteriorate to such a detriment to the intellectual pursuit of educational excellence. Jimmy's grandfather used to tell stories about the days back when he was a young boy and had to walk to and from school. He said that the walk was over three miles but, on occasion, he was allowed to ride the family horse to his little one-room school. His teacher would use the wide cracks between the floorboards of the schoolhouse to explain such geometric principles as straight lines and parallels. Numeration was demonstrated by making the students count the dogs that could be seen sleeping on the cool ground beneath the floor. The school had only five books, and only the most responsible students were allowed to take one home with them to study.

Rainy winters can be penetratingly cold in Liberty County, Georgia. Getting an education in those days must have been very important to children who had to get to school by walking muddy trails, wading swamps, or rowing a boat up the

Cannochee River. Their parents obviously devoted much time to family survival just as much as they did to their children's education. It would be much later in life when Jimmy would come to realize that many children of today don't appreciate how lucky they are to be living in a time when opportunities for learning are so easily available. Nevertheless, their resistance should not be used as an excuse to allow them to wither on the human vine of progress. Education is something that must be forced upon young people. Their appreciation, although delayed, will be their parent's most cherished reward. And the gift of perseverance that children receive from their parents could become one of their most valuable assets. But it doesn't seem to be.

Achievement milestones such as the two-car family, automatic dishwashers, and microwave ovens have enhanced the conveniences that have been made possible by good schooling. Such things have provided welcome relief to parents of today whose parents had to get up early in the morning in order to have enough time for preparing their children for daily trips to school. It is now common for families to have at least two means of transportation, one for work and one for ancillary activities and pleasure. It didn't take long before parental interest in what their children were learning at school would wane and their involvement in recreational activities and supplemental employment would increase. In their pursuit of fun, convenience, and more disposable income to purchase more fun and more conveniences, many people are now making excuses for what has become nothing more than child neglect and abandonment.

There once was a sphere of influence around children that was controlled almost exclusively by two parents and close kin. It was a kind of influence that was supported by schools that were administered by responsible people who lived in the local community. That kind of close parental control and monitored community influence provided a solid base from which children could develop into responsible adults. They were provided at least some knowledge of proper social skills and a chance to grow into adults that might understand the benefits of being people of good character. This daily influence over children is now dominated by television, other children with no parents, adults who have no children, and distant schools that are administered by strangers with untested skills and undetermined character. Perhaps Uncle Jeff was right. We are indeed becoming victims of the tyranny of our own passions.

Jimmy's first day at school started out with busy preparation and much anticipation, but it ended in great disappointment. He had been reading a book about the days when Will Rogers was a young boy and the things he used to do while riding his horse to school. Remembering the stories that his grandfather told him about his school days, Jimmy decided to saddle up old Charlie and ride him to school.

Bellville School was only eight miles from the Pines when driving on the road that runs by the big house. But several more miles were added to the trip when the school bus had to weave its way through dusty side roads picking up children. Jimmy knew he could beat the bus to school if he rode Charlie cross-country. Furthermore, since he was the son of an old cavalryman, he had even figured out where Charlie could spend the day at school. He would string one of those horse cavalry picket lines between two trees down by the little stream behind the schoolhouse where Charlie would have easy access to fresh water. Jimmy even put a quart of oats and a couple of apples in a feedbag the night before so Charlie would have something to eat during the day. The only thing that he had failed to make plans for was his Aunt Augusta. She had her own idea about how he was going to be transported to school that day.

Jimmy's tactics were simple enough. He was going to pretend to be anxious to ride the school bus, but delay long enough for the bus to leave him after failing to meet it at its 6:15 a.m. arrival time in front of the pine grove. He was going to pretend that one of his shoes had come off and then fake efforts to put it back on long enough for the bus to leave without him. His plan was working fine until he began employing his final delaying action. As he sat on a pile of brown pine straw in the middle of the pine grove, fumbling with his shoelaces, taking his time about it, and obviously overacting his part, Aunt Augusta approached his little stage. She stood over him with the backs of her wrists resting against her hips and the palms of her hands facing outward. Looking down at Jimmy over her half-frame reading glasses, she said; "Jimmy, go back to the house. Your father will be driving you to school today. I think he wants to talk to you about something." Ever since his father moved in the little house in the oak grove behind the big house it was not often that he had a reason to come up to the big house. Whatever it was that he wanted to tell Jimmy, it must have been important.

Although Jimmy thought he had kept his plan fairly confidential, it suddenly became obvious to him that everyone in the family had known what he was planning to do. Even worse, he never suspected that his father had already made plans for Charlie that day. While they were driving to school, Jimmy's father told him that he was going to sell Charlie to someone who would be in a better position to take proper care of him. Jimmy's father offered him a small concession by telling him that he could ride his horse, Sergeant, anytime he wanted. Jimmy didn't appreciate it at the time, but his father and his Aunt Augusta understood his passion for riding horses and, because of his tender age, they had taken steps to ensure his safety and place more emphasis on his education. They knew that a young boy with a horse would spend more time with his horse than with his school studies. Like it or not, the school bus was going to be Jimmy's riding partner for the next few years. And that was the way it was until Charlie came back to the *Pines* on Jimmy's tenth birthday.

Riding a school bus for an hour and a half twice a day for 180 days a year for twelve years provides 6,480 hours or 810 eight-hour days that are full of opportunities for school age boys to get into a lot of trouble. And Jimmy applied his talents liberally during those twelve years he was forced to ride the bus to and from elementary and high school. He did so, not as a passive participant, but as an instigator and co-conspirator.

The school bus was always an uncomfortable place for Jimmy. It was even more so after he witnessed several convicts from the state prison in Reidsville being carted around the county in an old school bus. He had to force himself to get on that bus every day. Every time he stepped through its doors he had a feeling that some unknown force from somewhere beyond the reality of the farm and the flatwoods, with which he was most familiar, was in control of him. And every time he stepped off the bus when it stopped in front of the pine grove, a sense of freedom would come over him, probably much like the feeling that the victorious patriots must have felt at the end of the American Revolution. Nevertheless, like those convicts from the state prison, he had been sentenced to twelve years with the Evans County Department of Education, and he knew he might as well make the best of it. It has been said that it is helpful in rehabilitating prisoners and makes their time pass more quickly when they are required to exercise their bodies and use their imaginations in creative endeavors. Jimmy decided to be a model prisoner through juvenile creativity.

Jimmy first met Jerry Salter soon after he got on the school bus the first morning of the first day of the ninth grade. When he stepped through the door of the bus, begrudgingly as usual, he discovered that the first stop for the school bus route was no longer at the *Pines*. The school system had recently consolidated all the schools in the county and the bus routes were rearranged to fit a new Gerrymandered educational demographic of the county.

Jerry and his older sister were sitting together on the front seat just behind the bus driver. Like Jimmy, Jerry appeared to be having a problem adjusting to the fact that he was being held hostage by the county school system. It even appeared that his sister was aiding and abetting the efforts of the school officials. Jimmy figured that Jerry might be someone with whom he could relate. It wasn't long before the two boys became the founders and first charter members of the *Evans County School Bus Route Number One Boys Club*. Their first and only rule was to take all possible measures to keep from going nuts while being cooped up for three hours a day in a yellow sweat box that had windows all around it, windows that the bus driver would never allow a single one of them to be opened.

Uncle Wallace quit driving the school bus the year before the school system was fully consolidated. He said he quit before the end of the school year because it was interfering with his wholesale and retail fresh produce business. The county therefore had to quickly hire a substitute until they were able to find a new permanent driver. There was, understandably, very little supervision on the bus during the interim. Jerry Salter, Martin Glisson, and Jimmy used their golden opportunity to surreptitiously and very successfully assume command and control of the school bus. But that lasted only until Babe Todd was hired as the new bus driver.

Babe's life would never be the same again. He spent the next several years before the three boys graduated trying to re-establish Evans County sovereignty over school bus route number one. Babe was a faithful, honorable, and loyal field commander in the service of the Department of Education, but he never fully succeeded in regaining complete control over his little command. However, he did earn his combat stripes by maintaining a valiant perseverance and keeping those three rowdy boys fully engaged. His bravery in action probably prevented them from expanding their kingdom to include the entire Evans County Department of Education.

During the 1950s, more and more young people were beginning to drive cars to and from school, or were driven to and from school by their parents. The school buses were mostly ridden by children whose parents were smart enough not to let them drive automobiles, children whose parents didn't have time to drive them to school, and children whose parents couldn't afford to furnish them a car of their own. This change in school transportation habits caused the school bus to become a negative status symbol in the minds of high-school-age children. The significance of that was; if you rode the school bus, you must be a member of the lesser privileged and therefore a member of some lower class of humanity. Children can often be very mean, and that is why they should be punished when they do mean things. Mostly, they just do very stupid things, and that is why they require constant and adequate adult supervision until they demonstrate that their conduct can be reasonably predicted to meet acceptable standards.

A large family moved in an old house that was about a half mile off the normal school bus route. The house was located at the end of a narrow dusty side road that the school bus had to travel on in order to pick up the children who lived there. The bus driver had to make several tight turns in front of the house in an effort to get the bus pointed back towards the main road. Every time the children got on the school bus, everyone in that sweatbox would begin to cough, gag, wheeze, and beg Babe Todd to allow the windows to be opened. Living on a farm had provided Jimmy a tolerance for strange odors from such things as soft cow patties, dead animals, and other producers of stifling fragrances. But the odor that was coming from those children was one that could peel the vinyl right off the seats of the school bus.

The problem was persistent, and it became obvious to everyone on the bus that it was not going to be solved by school officials employing the transactional analysis method of adult-to-adult dialogue. It certainly wasn't going to be solved by the County School Superintendent writing letters to parents who probably couldn't read anyway. The three Rebels of the Dusty

Trail would just have to take things in their own hands. So, with very little planning, but with amazingly precise execution, that is exactly what they did.

They scheduled their attack to commence on a Friday. That way, if anyone became overly angry with them for their little stunt, they would have the weekend for things to cool down a bit. When Jimmy stepped through the doors of the bus that Friday morning, he walked to the last row of seats in the back of the bus, sat down next to Jerry, and asked him if he had his equipment with him. Jerry had a cake of lye soap and a stiff brush. Jimmy had a cake of lilac scented soap and a bottle of cologne that he had swiped from his aunt's bathroom. When the bus arrived at Martin's house, he got on the bus carrying a bag full of wash rags wrapped in an excellently written note that described the benefits of personal sanitation and what the rest of the people in the world means when they refer to people as 'close' friends. Jerry and Jimmy knew there was no way on this green earth that Martin had written that note.

Martin had a really cute sister and, by the way she was smiling at Jimmy when she got on the bus, he knew that she was the one who had actually written the note. Her smile struck him in a way that made him realize that he was not about to let another week of his life go by without asking her for a date. But that little moment of teenage ecstasy had to be a fleeting one. It was time to get back to the business at hand. The next stop that the bus was going to make would be at ground zero, and they had to be ready to deliver their barrage.

As soon as the bus rolled to a stop in front of the smelly kids' house, the three boys jumped out through the rear emergency door and fired their ammo in the direction of the front porch. They quickly ran around the bus and jumped back in through the front door, just as Babe was opening the door to let the smelly kids in. Their timing and accuracy had been perfect. The barrage of sanitation supplies landed squarely in the threshold of the front door of the house just as the smelly kids were coming out to meet the bus. But everything started going downhill from there.

A brigade of teachers' aides was waiting in the school parking when the bus pulled in. When the door of the bus opened, one overly excited aide stuck her head in the door and shouted, "Mr. Todd, the principal wants to see you, and he means right now!" When the school bell sounded the signal for the beginning of the first class period, Jerry, Martin, and Jimmy were already standing at attention in the principal's office and being blasted with a vocal dissertation on the differences between gentlemen of honor and common roustabouts. The session ended with a severe paddling for each of the dynamic trio and strict orders for them to apologize to the entire offended family, and they would do it that very afternoon when the bus would be returning to their house.

As they rode the bus back to the scene of the crime, Jerry was looking at Babe in an accusing manner and said, "You finked us out!"

Calmly but with authority, Babe said, "No, you boys finked on yourselves. All those times that you were being so aggravating, I kept things to myself. The things you boys were doing up until now were the kinds of things that mattered only to us, and they could stay between us. You boys went too far this time. You publicly humiliated some people you had no business bothering. They did the right thing by calling the school principal instead of taking things in their own hands the way you boys did. The principal asked me to tell him what happened and I had to tell the truth. Now you boys know the rest of the story."

After each offender finished delivering his very humiliating and public apology, the smelly kid's parents gracefully accepted their expressions of regret. They even said that they understood how some children oftentimes fail to live up to their parent's expectations. Wow! That stung! Nevertheless, when those smelly children got on the school bus the following Monday morning, something else happened that had not been expected. There was a very noticeable and especially pleasing fragrance permeating the humid morning air, somewhat suggestive of lilac blossoms and Hoyte's cologne.

Babe opened the windows.

# Chapter XVI

## The Willow Tree

Emerald leaves on evening sky
Boughs swaying reaching to fly
Such a sight never seen by thee
My willow dances only for me

A willow tree is a very restful thing to behold, even when the beholder is engaged in the immediate necessities of survival during the deadly conflagrations of war. Many years had passed since Jimmy was a young boy growing up at the *Pines*. But this was another place and another time, and his body was pressed tightly to a jungle floor. Dark images of human danger skulked through the dense forest only a few feet from where he lay. They moved closer and closer to Jimmy's hiding place, cautiously examining every suspicious clump of vegetation. In spite of his fears of impending capture, perhaps even death, there still seemed to be an air of restfulness and comfort that was surrounding the spot were he lay in hopeful concealment.

Peeking through overhanging limbs at a star-studded moonless night, Jimmy realized that his umbrella-like shelter was a willow tree. His nerve-racked body then settled into a state of relaxed serenity as he remembered another old willow tree, one far removed from the present dangers of war. It was a tree that had given him similar protection and concealment, but with a much different feeling of security. As he hugged the ground beneath the jungle willow's shielding boughs, Jimmy's mind began to conjure up images of that earlier willow tree, one that had long since given its final bow of boughs and returned to the earth from whence it came.

The old willow tree stood alone, only a short distance behind the big house and next to a grassy lane that separated the big field from a little stream that still trickles northward to Cribbs Branch. Like a shimmering tent of greenery, its beckoning lure seemed to invite anyone who might wander by to stop, if only for a while, and rest under its caressing boughs and cooling shade. Submerged in its shadow and between many Saturday and Sunday afternoon naps, it was there where Jimmy managed to summon up enough patience and determination to read all about Homer's *Odyssey* of Odysseus and Jonathan Swift's *Gulliver's Travels*.

Evening sunsets are especially beautiful when framed behind a lacy green screen of a willow's dangling boughs. Although Jimmy was generally under constant and strict instructions from his aunt to be stacking firewood or doing his school homework, he whiled away many evenings sitting under the limbs of that tree. But a young boy's time is never wasted while lounging under the lazily swaying branches of a willow tree and watching the final moments of daylight drift beyond the horizon. The memories of many evening hours spent sitting with his back to the trunk of that old tree, listening to the call of the whippoorwills, and counting the first sounds of waking night critters would one day be as valuable to Jimmy as all the hours that he would ever spend in any classroom.

Those were the days before television was to fully invade our lives and eventually destroy the ability of young people to create their own mental images from the works of nature rather than parroting the electronic images of man. People who fail to develop the potential of their minds soon become only receptacles for the thoughts of others, whether those thoughts are good or bad.

Each evening he spent under that old tree was as beautiful to Jimmy as all the evenings before, although each of the separate memories of the moments have since merged into a mental haze of tranquil indistinctions. However, there were a few instances when the beauty and serenity of that old willow was transgressed by its susceptibility to other and more peculiar forces of Mother Nature. This was especially apparent in autumn and spring. In autumn, the willow tree was subjected to the onslaught of just about every flying creature, local and migratory, that happened upon its welcoming branches. Beginning in early spring, it became a virtual Mt. Everest for any crawling thing that was capable of climbing anything higher than wiregrass or stronger than the stems of broom sage.

Opossums and raccoons have never pretended to like each other. That is understandable since opossums (in the South, the first 'o' is dropped) act and look very similar to members of the rodent family. Raccoons act and look much like cats (their tails are the big giveaway). Actually, opossums are marsupials (pouched animals) and raccoons are distant relatives of bears, hogs, and even dogs. But raccoons and opossums do have their social differences from their cousins. Raccoons don't go around searching for opossums to prey upon like cats do to rats. And opossums never seem to concern themselves about the presence of raccoons like rats do when they sense the presence of a cat. Under normal and undisturbed circumstances, raccoons and opossums go about the forest minding their own business and sticking pretty much to themselves. Nevertheless, when these two veteran cartoon professionals meet in what can only be described as a South Georgia version of a western box canyon, no playwright could possibly write nor any director ever stage a greater farce.

One spring afternoon, while Jimmy was involved in one of his many attempts at avoiding the drudgery of domestic duties, he managed to slip away from the supervisory claws of his Aunt Augusta and escape to his favorite refuge. After an afternoon of doing what boys do when left to their individual mental faculties and a homemade slingshot, he crawled under the old willow tree and fell asleep. As the setting sun began to release its slipping grasp on the horizon, a loud and argumentative chatter from somewhere above suddenly awakened him.

A treetop debate was in progress between a family of raccoons and an old mamma opossum with her offspring of spitting and grinning teenagers. Jimmy often wondered, but would never know, how they managed to get past him and climb the willow tree without waking him, but he would have enjoyed having witnessed the event. It is probably enough to say that pleasant days and willow trees are conducive to very deep sleep. But the raging racket of opossums and raccoons debating the finer points of high-rise real estate law is just as awakening to the body as willow trees are soothing to the mind.

Opossums are very adept at hanging from tree limbs that have some degree of substance and stability, but they have much difficulty maintaining a sense of balance on the dipping and yawing boughs of willow trees. But raccoons are the trapeze artists of the forest. And it seems that opossums and raccoons have both discovered the delectable taste of fresh cicadas. Cicadas are strange little critters whose song, when they begin to sing their mating call, can pierce the unprotected eardrums of nearby humans. They spend most of their lives buried in the ground before crawling out in early spring to inch their way up the nearest tree, side of a barn, fence post, or even a sleeping horse. After reaching an altitude that is suitable for their purpose, they attach themselves to the surface of their selected launch pads and begin the process of abandoning their drying and crusting shells. When their new wings are dry, they flit off into the night in search of a mate and to irritate the quietness of the night. It is during this time of metamorphosis and mating that cicadas become vulnerable and tender morsels, and objects of great search-and-destroy missions conducted by raccoons, opossums, and other foragers of the night. And for one special performance, Jimmy had a ringside seat.

The old mamma opossum mustered her young forces and established a defensive position on the largest and highest limb that she could find in the willow tree, one that barely supported their combined weights. Mamma raccoon took up a position on the same limb, but tactically positioned herself between the trunk of the tree and the opossums. Her young squad of raccoon infantry selected separate limbs of choice and continued feasting on cicadas.

Upon observing the German army's Siegfried Line crumble under his advancing armor during World War II, General George Patton remarked, "Defensive fortifications are eternal monuments to man's stupidity." Opossums are not very bright, but the expression on that old opossum's face seemed to hint of her realization that the General might have been correct in his assessment of the tactical superiority of the attack over the defense.

The raccoons wasted little time in seizing the opportunity to capitalize on their tactical advantage and quickly began making their move to consolidate their impending victory. The big raccoon that had positioned herself on the limb with the opossums began slowly inching her way out the limb towards the huddled and hissing mass of opossums. This kept the opossums occupied while her raccoon infantry closed in from two flanks. It was a classical pincher movement. One by one, and like little paratroopers jumping from an airplane, the young raccoons landed on the limb and joined their leader. The extra weight of all those opossums and raccoons on one willow limb forced it to bend all the way to the ground. The opossums stepped to the ground in unison, as if on cue from the director of a play. The limb full of raccoons, now void of opossums, rose back up into the mass of green willow leaves, and the raccoons resumed their evening dinner of cicadas. The family of opossums formed a single file behind their leader, each giving one last glance back at their masked victors before trailing off into the looming darkness of the forest.

In the fall of the year, the willow tree became a rallying point for all types of migratory birds. First came the doves that would use it as a resting place between foraging sorties to the big field in search of shelled corn that the harvester left behind, or peck at the dry seeds of beggar lice weed that grow along the fence around the big field.

When the sunsets turn rosier and the air crisper, crows come to disturb the autumn serenity. Crows are birds that have no respect for any other creature on earth, and they are completely void of manners. Yet, in their base and arrogant way, they are at least entertaining. Similarly, it is apparent that many humans have begun to excuse much of their own vulgarity and insolence in exchange for cheap entertainment that such antics provide. We would all be much better off had we left such disrespectful exploits of uncouth crudeness to the domain of crows and their cartoon reproductions like Heckle and Jeckle.

As autumn begins to scurry through the air, carrying with it gently falling leaves of the sycamore tree, crows fly in like poorly disciplined squadrons of World War I Spads and Sopwith Camels trying to land at a French aerodrome. Cackling, crowing, diving, and swaying through the air, they each selected a landing site in the tall oak, poplar, and sycamore trees that stretched high above the willow tree. About fifty crows made sloppy attempts to land in the top of the willow tree where there was room for not more than one crow. One of the crows did finally succeed in making a landing, but it looked like a drunken tap dancer trying to maintain some semblance of balance. A wispy willow tree has an amazing ability to repel attacks from the air.

Just as the most acrobatic of the crows managed to secure a grip on top of the willow, and begin to brag about his accomplishment, the entire flock of unruly aviators began screaming out their discovery of something that was invading the very place that they had just violated. The crows had spotted Jimmy's dog, Patchis, and she had now become the object of the crow's disdain. The squadron of crows formed into attack formations of twos and fours and began a continuous diving assault upon Patchis, nipping at her back at every pass they made.

Patchis was getting to be a middle-aged dog and experience had taught her that she must now accomplish with wisdom and cunning many of the things that she was once capable of doing with speed and youthful vigor. She trotted out in the field and, in full view of her dark haranguers, lay down on her side as if she were dead. The crows became braver and soon began landing on the ground and sauntering up to her apparent lifeless body, nipping at her white hair. The most foolish of the mob finally did what Patchis was waiting for one of her antagonists to do. It jumped on top of her and began pacing back and forth as if it was declaring victory over a deceased foe.

In a flash of white lightening, black feathers began flying through the air, grounded crows scurried for take-off positions, and a deathly silence fell over the gallery of crows that were observing the scene from their treetop bleachers. For a few moments, they watched in stark terror as Patchis gave them a demonstration in the finer points of field dressing a crow. Then, and as suddenly as they came, the sky darkened as the mass of blackness took to the air. The migration of crows continued on to wherever it is that crows go in November.

It seems that those creatures with the loudest mouths usually become the biggest cowards when the chips are down. It's a shame that there are still humans among us who are just as willing to follow that same dirty road to dishonor.

The mental picture of crows bobbing up and down on a darkening horizon snapped Jimmy's mind back to the reality of his present situation. The human figures in black pajamas and hats of woven straw were silently moving away in a single file of cautious motion. One by one, they disappeared into the impending darkness of a troubled land. Like the opossums, raccoons, and crows, they too were gone as suddenly as they had appeared. And again, it was time for Jimmy to leave another place of refuge under another willow tree, one that, one day too, will return to the earth from whence it came.

# Chapter XVII

## The Wings of Diana

Swiftly gallops the goddess of hunt
Riding the wind with eyes a front
Lunging forward to meet the moist air
Morning mist cooling our hair
Hoofs below pound rhythms so sure
If only this moment could ever endure
Upon the wings of Diana I flew
Bonded as one to a horse I once knew

Although Mr. Fet was transferred to the Army Air Corps at the beginning of World War II, it was his earlier and much longer career in the horse cavalry that was the life he loved most, and the one that he never really gave up. He held the rank of *Captain of Cavalry*, which meant more to him than any position that he or anyone else could ever hold, soldier or civilian. He was a real horse cavalryman, not a bit like those fancy-dressed Hollywood movie actors who have to use a double to stand in for them so that movie audiences will get the impression that the star of the movie is riding the horse. He was a member of the last authentic horse cavalry unit that was still on active duty during the years between the end of World War I and the beginning of World War II. He had even served as First Sergeant of the famous F Troop of the 6th Cavalry Regiment.

It was only natural that the first mile Jimmy would ride in his new life would be on the back of a horse. The day after he was born, his father picked him up at the Army Hospital at Fort Oglethorpe and paraded him on horseback through the regimental grounds and down to his troop area where he presented his new son to his old horse riding buddies. Today, every time Jimmy sees a horse and rider, it is no wonder that something deep inside his soul yearns to be the person sitting astride the saddle.

The United States Army, although diminished in size during the years between World War I and World War II, was going through a period of transition. It was slowly abandoning its horse and mule-powered army and inching its way closer to becoming the fully mechanized force that it is today. New tactics, strategies, and doctrines were being developed while old procedures and methods were re-evaluated and updated or discarded. By the late 1930s, horses were well on their way to obsolescence as a military necessity. However, a few horses would remain in active service to fill tactical voids that remained due to the fact that light-armored vehicles were not fully developed, heavy tanks were not yet dependable, and armed helicopters had not made it past the drawing board. The few mounted horse cavalry units that were still in service were relegated to reconnaissance missions and situations where army planners believed that any enemy the cavalry might face would be deployed without automatic weapons.

All debate about the role of the horse cavalry ended with the attack on Pearl Harbor and subsequent onset of World War II. Most of the horses that the army still owned were either sold at auction or sent to the post stables to be used by officers and their ladies for playing polo or other forms of pleasure riding. But, throughout the war, mules remained in honorable service to their country as beasts of burden. The ability of mules to negotiate the types of terrain that motor vehicles were unable to even penetrate gave them a temporary reprieve from the plow fields and glue factories.

The few horse cavalry units that remained in active service during the years prior to World War II were required to maintain their old proficiencies in the use of the saber and pistol in the mounted charge. That was Mr. Fet's specialty, and one of his responsibilities was to instruct other troopers in deployment and tactical operations of mounted cavalry units. He could ride a horse into a charge and mold his body to the saddle in a way that made it appear that no one was riding the horse. While at a full gallop, he could draw his M1911 Colt .45 service pistol, score seven hits with alternating shots from his strong and weak sides, reload with a fresh magazine, and score seven more hits. He would then wheel his horse around, holster his pistol, draw his saber, execute a reverse charge, and score all thrusts and slashes with his saber.

Shortly after old Charlie died, Jimmy and his father found a beautiful five-year-old bay colored quarter horse mare. She had a black mane and tail, was fast of gait, quick in the turns, obedient, and calm under the gun. The very first moment that Jimmy laid his eyes on her was an experience in love at first sight. He named her Diana after the Roman Goddess of the hunt. And after only a few weeks of training, she was responding to his slightest movements as if they were both embraced in the naked heat of tender love.

Western style rodeos were not a common event in South Georgia, but one did come to Claxton one summer, and it was held on the high-school football field. Not many people in the farming region of Evans County owned horses during the 1950s. Farm horses had already gone the way of cavalry horses and pleasure riding for city folks was still an expensive pastime that few people had time for, or could afford. Subsequently, most of the horses that were going to be competing in the rodeo arrived in trailers that were towed by the people who were working with the rodeo. Jimmy knew something seemed a little strange when he noticed that all the horse trailers were displaying out-of-state license tags.

Jimmy saddled Diana and rode her to town to see the rodeo and maybe even go for a swim in the waters at Bull Creek Bridge while on their ride back home. The people who were tending the entrance to the football field were members of a local civic club. Apparently, they believed that Jimmy was just another member of the rodeo when he came riding Diana up to the gate at the end of the ball field. No one said anything or seemed to notice as he rode through the gate, acting just like he was part of the show. He was even able to get all the way to the main arena and hitch Diana to one of the hitching rails where he could watch the rodeo from inside the fifty-yard line.

The rodeo had all of the events that western rodeos usually have; calf roping, bull riding, horseback acrobatics, lasso demonstrations, clown antics, and barrel racing. Jimmy didn't know much about barrel racing, but the procedure seemed simple enough to him. Mr. Fet had constructed a pistol and saber course in the little field behind the big house where he would often practice his old cavalry skills. Jimmy made the course more interesting by adding a few extra fence posts and several old wooden turpentine barrels. He and Diana spent many hours practicing together as they twisted and turned through all those barrels that were placed much closer together than the ones at the rodeo.

Jimmy's moment of opportunity came while he was watching the starter give the go sign to the riders and then timing their runs through the barrels. He noticed that the contestants were not wearing any identification numbers. That gave him the idea to wait until the last rider had cleared the gate before riding Diana up to the starting chute. When he and Diana approached the starting gate, the starter gave them a funny look but must have figured that there had been some change in the lineup. After what should have been the last rider to complete his run and have his time recorded, the starter gave Jimmy the go sign, and Diana blasted through the gate. All Jimmy had to do was to give her a few hints with slight shifts of his body and an occasional gentle cue with the reins. When they crossed the finish line, they had cut five seconds off the real winner's time.

The winning rider was a bit disturbed that both his thunder and applause from the crowd had been stolen, but the manager of the rodeo was much more forgiving. He tried to convince Jimmy to sell Diana to him and even said that he would be willing to meet any reasonable price. But the rodeo left town without Diana, and Jimmy was still reliving and enjoying the applause from the crowd as he and Diana began their eight-mile ride back to the *Pines*. He could even detect a bit more than the usual degree of sass in Diana's gait.

No matter how polite, well bred, or how well trained a horse may be, there will always be times when a horse abandons all pretenses at being either a gentleman or a lady. Sometimes a situation will arise that is not anticipated, which causes all sorts of events to occur in very rapid sequence. As well mannered as Diana was, there was still one thing she did that irritated Jimmy and let him know that she was not just any little filly with which a man could have his way. She would sometimes hold her breath while being saddled. That is a bad habit that some horses have, and it makes it impossible to draw the cinch tight enough around a horse's girth so the saddle won't slip off and slide down between the horse's legs, along with an unwary rider. But horses are not known to have long memories, and that makes it possible for a loose cinch problem to be remedied by leading a horse around in a circle before attempting to mount the saddle. The horse will forget about the saddle and relax its girth long enough for the cinch to be retightened.

One Saturday morning, Jimmy was in a hurry to saddle Diana and complete his fence checking and cattle counting chores out in the flatwoods. He wanted to get back early enough to be able go to town and see a special movie that was showing at the *Tos Theater*. Diana probably sensed that Jimmy was in a hurry and was about to abandon her and go have fun somewhere without her. She tightened her stomach against the cinch and, rather than taking time to walk her around, Jimmy decided to go ahead and ride her down the lane and through the gate at the edge of the flatwoods where he would stop and retighten the cinch before continuing his chores.

Everything was going as planned until they reached the flatwoods where Jimmy dismounted in the knee-high wiregrass and began tightening the cinch. It was there and then that the assault began. Diana was standing on top of an entrance to an underground hornet's nest. When she moved her hoof, the entrance to the hornet's den opened and all those hornets came buzzing out, every one of them as mad as a hornet and ready for a fight.

The worst thing that could possibly happen to a horse cavalryman, other than being thrown from his mount, happened. Jimmy was caught in the middle of an ambush while dismounted. He made a hasty attempt to remount, but his right boot hadn't quite found the far stirrup when the hornets found their targets. Diana lowered her haunches, sprang forward, accelerated to a high-speed gallop, and headed straight for the barn and the safety of her stable. Every ounce of Jimmy's weight was on one side of the saddle as he attempted to reach the other stirrup with his right leg draped over the saddle. The loose and flopping saddle rolled to the left and his body caught the first pine sapling as Diana brushed against its bark at full gallop. The next pine tree captured the saddle and Diana was free except for her bridle, bit, and reins, which were streaming backward in the wind and flapping against her withers.

Nursing a dozen hornet stings, a fractured arm, several abrasions, and dragging a broken saddle, Jimmy limped back to the barn. He took a nice cool dip in the horse trough before his

Aunt Augusta drove his mutilated carcass over to Claxton where Doctor Hames began the task of repairing the damage. After completing their mission at the doctor's office, they drove back to the *Pines*. Jimmy had a new cast on his left arm and no memories of that special movie he wanted to see.

As soon as they arrived back at the big house, Jimmy limped out to the barn to check on Diana and see how she had managed to cope with the events of the day. She seemed fine except for a few welts on her inner thighs and evidence that one kamikaze hornet had met its doom on the inside of her lower lip. Diana glared at Jimmy as if she thoroughly understood the predicament they both had somehow managed to survive that day. And ever since that day, Jimmy never again experienced another time when Diana would hold back her cinch when it was being tightened. Maybe horses do have good memories after all.

About a month after Jimmy graduated from high school, he saddled Diana for the last time and rode her over to Hagan. He had made earlier arrangements to sell Diana and all his saddle gear to the school bus driver, the one who had been so tolerant of his antics over the years. Babe Todd paid for his new horse and leather gear and Jimmy apologized for making his life so miserable during all those years when he was riding school bus number one. Jimmy then walked the railroad tracks to the little gas station in Claxton where the Trailways bus always stopped twice a day. He bought a one-way ticket to Savannah, joined the United States Army, and was immediately shipped off to Fort Jackson, South Carolina where he began basic army training and a new career. He has never again been in a situation where or when it was convenient or practical to own and properly care for a horse. He still waits that day.

Jimmy's father used to say that caring for a horse is a responsibility that every man and woman should be required to experience before being permitted to have children of their own. He believed that people who are unable to meet the high standards of care that horses demand would never be able to live up to the responsibilities that are inherent in caring for children. He once said, "Horses are a lot like children; they both require dedicated attention from those who are responsible for their welfare. Although it is a shame to ruin a good horse, it is a greater shame to ruin a child. Show me a person who respects horses and I will show you a person that can be trusted and respected."

Over the years, Jimmy came to realize that his father knew what he was talking about. Children who spend their formative years in public daycare centers and horses that are kept in public stables will both soon begin displaying undesirable personality traits. If every prospective parent were to give those words a little thought, they might think more soundly about having children, and even more soundly about the practice of allowing strangers to raise their children for them.

# Chapter XVIII

## A Dog Named Patchis

After his long career in the horse cavalry and another four years in the Army Air Corps during World War II, Mr. Fet finally came back home to the *Pines* where he became the local expert on horses, fox hunting, bulldogs, and game chickens. When Aunt Augusta received word that he was on his way home, she drove Jimmy and his brother over to Claxton to meet their father when he arrived at the Seaboard train station. As they were driving up to the station, Mr. Fet was already standing on the platform holding a well-worn olive drab colored B-4 bag in one hand and cradling a white English Bull Terrier puppy under his other arm. He informed his welcoming committee that he had named the puppy Patch Eye because it had a black patch over one eye, just like the dog that is in all those *Little Rascals* movies.

They loaded Patch Eye and Mr. Fet's gear in Aunt Augusta's 1940 Ford and then backed the car up to the freight dock. Mr. Fet went in the freight office and soon came out carrying two little red fox kittens in his arms and saying something about how they were going to revolutionize fox hunting in South Georgia. Aunt Augusta informed him that those little creatures could do anything they wanted, but if they did it in her car their revolution was going to be over before it ever got started. Jimmy's father knew that he was already walking on thin ice for staying up north for a couple of weeks looking for horses and dogs rather than coming directly home after the war. Stopping by Anderson's grocery store to get a Union Bag and Paper Company grocery sack to put the little kits in so they wouldn't make a mess in Aunt Augusta's car was an act of compliant self-defense on Mr. Fet's part.

Patch Eye sired many litters of puppies during his long life at the *Pines*. Mr. Fet's favorite was the result of a cross between Patch Eye and a Staffordshire terrier. He gave Jimmy one of the female puppies that was a snow-white mirror image of Patch Eye, except she didn't have a patch over one of her eyes. Jimmy named her Patchis in honor of her sire and, from then until he left the *Pines*, that dog was Jimmy's constant companion, personal guard, and keeper of thousands of secrets.

People of crude upbringing, whether they live in Georgia, Maine, California, or anywhere else in this world, seem to have several characteristics in common. They all act like they know everything there is to know about trucks, dogs, and women, and they usually rank them in about that same order. Jimmy's grandfather taught him to never brag about himself, never flaunt anything he owned, and always treat people with respect, at least until they demonstrate that they don't deserve respect or don't want it. He believed that high character and fine personal qualities would reveal themselves soon enough without the need of formal announcements. He qualified that a bit by explaining that crude people often attempt to take advantage of others and, accordingly, respect does not mean we should tolerate such abuse. Take action when action is warranted, but take it with sufficient force, speed, and self-assurance as to be effective the first time. Mr. Fet added a little to that sage advice by saying, "Never tax your reserves by allowing your enemy an opportunity to mount a counterattack."

Jimmy began to understand what they were trying to tell him after hearing about an incident that happened on the road between Bellville and Mendes. A man stopped his truck on the side of the road, grabbed his wife by her arm, and yanked her out of the truck. He began slapping her about the head in a most brutal manner before forcing her to get in the back of the truck and ride in the cargo bed with their children. After a short, but profane demonstration in vocal obscenity, he drove off with his dog riding up front in the seat beside him. He stopped the truck again, got out, walked to the rear of the truck, and slapped one of their children. When his wife said something in apparent disapproval of his actions, he pulled her from the back of the truck and began beating her again. He stopped the truck again and got out to relieve himself in a drainage ditch alongside the road. His wife used the opportunity to reach in the cab of the truck and pull out a shotgun that was stored behind the front seat. She drove away with all her troubles behind her; face down in that watery ditch.

The county sheriff said he knew all about that fellow. "That sort of thing was bound to happen to him one day. And there's no good reason to put anybody in jail for doing something that had to be done." The sheriff took the woman and her children to the bus station where he bought them a one-way ticket to another town in another county where some of her relatives lived. That was an example of a few of the types of people that Jimmy had to ride with on the school bus for the next twelve years.

There was one particular boy of ill-breeding and coarse conduct who had been a real sore spot in the posterior region of Jimmy's pants ever since the two of them first met at school. He was larger than Jimmy, somewhat older, and had failed his second try at the third grade. His father worked as a sawmill hand at a lumberyard near their home, just outside of the town of Bellville. While most farmers prudently saved for the future, took care of their families, and prayed for the right combinations of sunshine and rain, this family had a regular, yet modest, weekly income. Nevertheless, by sunrise every Sunday, every cent of their money would be spent on the usual kinds of redneck entertainment and liquid refreshments at one of the beer and wine joints on Highway 280 just across the Cannochee River Bridge on the Bryan County side of the county line.

Instantaneous gratification was a concept that Jimmy was to learn about much later in life when it would gain popularity in the form of a government welfare system that forces sober people to pay for the cost of drunkards who no longer have to worry about how to pay for their own drunkenness. Any system that guarantees an income for everyone without requiring any effort on the part of able recipients has to be one of the worst sins that humans have ever committed against their collective dignity.

When Jimmy was in the fourth grade, his teacher often asked her students to bring to school some item that might be of interest to the other students. Each student had to be prepared to explain to the other students what their chosen object was and why it was they had decided to bring their particular item to school. Jimmy had a James Audubon book entitled, *Birds of America*, which was filled with colorful pictures of birds and detailed descriptions of each bird. He decided to bring the book to school and explain the differences between red-headed sapsuckers and red-headed woodpeckers. He was aware that the crude kid had developed a shine for his book by the way he kept looking at it when they were on the school bus that morning. He was sure the kid didn't have any academic interest in birds, but had probably seen how colorful the book was and just wanted to have it. A larcenous mind is one of the unfortunate results that can occur when ignorance, greed, and laziness are combined. Jimmy shouldn't have been surprised when his book turned up missing from his desk later that day.

That same afternoon, as the school children were getting on the school bus for their ride home, Jimmy saw the dust cover of his book dangling from the inside of the crude kid's jacket where he had made an obviously unsuccessful attempt to hide it. When he confronted the thief with the fact that he knew he had his book, the big kid pushed him away and ran towards the school bus. Jimmy caught up with him just as he was getting on the bus, grabbed the big kid by the collar of his shirt, and yanked him away from the bus so hard that the thief landed face first in a big mud puddle. The thief jumped up spitting water and cursing like a sailor on a short leash. Since Jimmy was standing between the thief and the bus, it was difficult to determine if the kid was coming after him or just trying to get back on the bus. But since the kid was bigger, Jimmy decided that was reason enough for not taking any chances. As soon as the big kid came into range, he gave the brute three of his best punches straight to his solar plexus. The big thug crumpled to his knees like a ton of bricks and then fell face down in that mud puddle again. Jimmy secured his book, threw the thief's jacket in the middle of the mud puddle, got on the bus, and took his seat just like nothing had ever happened.

The school principal, hordes of teachers, and the bus driver arrived on the scene and began trying to sort things out. As often happens, circumstantial evidence will outweigh the truth of a matter. That larcenous jerk got off by telling a lie about how he had just found Jimmy's book and was about to do the righteous thing and give it to the bus driver. He inaccurately reported, "Jimmy just came up to me and hit me for no reason at all!" The principal marched Jimmy to his office and gave him a paddling for beating up on that lying little redneck. Yet, Jimmy still felt good about it all. He had learned the truth about that little future prison inmate, and he also knew that the kid now knew about him, and they both knew that Jimmy would always be able take him in a scuffle.

After that incident, every time that loudmouth crude kid got on the school bus, he would sit on the front seat behind the bus driver where he thought he would have a safe place from which to taunt Jimmy. But rednecks never learn. Their short memories, desires for quick gratification, and desperate need to appear important will soon divert their simple minds. They just can't resist the temptation to try to do things that far exceed their level of mental competence. That bigmouth kid kept on talking about his big bad *German Police Dog* that his uncle had given him after coming home from the war in Europe. His uncle was always bragging about how he had served with the U.S. Army's Occupation Forces in Germany after World War II. Later, Jimmy learned the real story. A military court had tried the kid's uncle, convicted him, and sent him to prison. After serving his sentence, the army gave him a dishonorable discharge for his crime of raping a young German girl.

That kid's incessant carrying on about the ferocity of his mutt finally got to the point that he was even beginning to insult Patchis. They were on the bus riding home from school one afternoon when the kid started bragging about how his big bad dog could make Jimmy's dog whine and howl like a little girl that was being violated by a big man. Only those were not his precise words; they were much cruder.

That did it! There was no way Jimmy was going to take any more assaults upon him, his good dog, and now upon the sanctity of womanhood. He decided that it was time for that redneck to be taught a lesson in a way that would make him understand that all he would ever be in life was a piece of warm cow patty that decent people wipe off their feet before entering a clean house. "I tell you what. If that so-called German police dog of yours can beat my dog in a fair fight, I'll let you have that .22 rifle of mine, the one you say you want so much. If my dog beats your dog, you must tell the bus driver about you being the one who stole my bird book."

"Okay, that'ud be fine wit'n me."

That stupid kid failed to realize that the bus driver had been listening to everything the two of them had been saying. The driver now knew which one of them had actually been telling the lie about that bird book. Several years later, when Jimmy was in college studying criminal law, he learned that such exclamations are examples of what the law refers to as a *'spontaneous declaration.'* Such freely given confessions are admissible in courts of law as an exception to the hearsay rule. Jimmy imagined that Sir Arthur Conan Doyle would have been proud of him for the way he had extracted that unintentional admission of guilt from that little criminal.

The deal had been struck and only the time and place needed to be fixed. During recess the following day, the two of them agreed that the battleground would be in front of Bay Branch Church at six o'clock on Friday evening, right after they would be getting home from school. The church was roughly half way between the *Pines* and where the redneck kid lived, and since it would be on a Friday, neither of them would have to worry about homework, not that the redneck kid ever worried about such things anyway. And since the bus stopped at the kid's house first, Jimmy would have to hurry to get to the church on time.

When the school bus stopped at the head of the lane in front of the big house on the afternoon of the big event, Jimmy had already formulated his plan for how he was going to escape from his Aunt Augusta's custody. He had secreted a change of clothes in the loft of the well shelter the evening before and made sure that Charlie would be in the corral next to the barn and not out grazing in the big field. As soon as Jimmy jumped off the school bus, he executed his plan with flawless precision. He cut left past the mailbox, jumped the fence between the big field and the mulberry lane, and then made a dash for the well shelter where he quickly changed into his riding clothes. Charlie must have known something was up. He was standing next to the tack room when Jimmy went in to get his saddle. There was no problem with Patchis being ready. As usual, she had met Jimmy at the head of the mulberry lane just as the school bus was pulling to a stop.

Patchis was three years old and in her prime. Charlie was getting old, but was still in great condition. Off they went to Bay Branch Church, Charlie at a trot, Jimmy astride Charlie, and Patchis resting on a pillow between the saddle horn and Jimmy's stomach. They arrived at the church a few minutes early, which gave Jimmy a little time to water Charlie and Patchis from a water spigot behind the church. He even had time to trim some of the grass that was growing over the edges of his grandmother's grave. And, for a few moments, he remembered how she and Eloise had made it their personal challenge to make sure that he learned how to read, not just read, but read well and often.

After a few minutes, the loudmouth crude kid came riding up on his bicycle and leaned it against a tree in the churchyard. Behind him straggled a hot and thirsty-looking German shepherd dog that was struggling against a long rope that had one end tied to its neck and the other end attached to the seat on the boy's bicycle. Jimmy asked the kid if he wanted to let his dog have a little water and rest for a while, but the kid retorted with, "Naw, I drug him heah so's he'ud be good n' mad. Let's fit 'em rat now."

The redneck kid drew a large circle in the sand and then held his dog at one edge of the circle. Jimmy went behind the church to get Patchis from where he had purposely tied her to the water spigot so she wouldn't see the other dog before the fight. Jimmy knew that keeping a dog from seeing its opponent before a fight is a technique that makes a dog react with a higher degree of ferocity than a dog that doesn't perceive its master to be in imminent danger.

Patchis sensed her duty the moment both dogs caught the first glimpse of each other. Her bristles went up and she bared her teeth. Jimmy told the kid to let him know when he was ready to release his dog, but as the words were leaving Jimmy's lips, the kid yelled, "Git 'im" and released his dog. Patchis flew across the sandy circle and met the other dog in its own corner. In less than thirty seconds, that big bad *'German Police'* dog lay motionless in the very spot where the kid had just released it.

That loudmouth crude kid claimed that he didn't have to live up to their bet because Jimmy had cheated. He even tried to convince Jimmy that he didn't have to tell the bus driver about him being the one who stole the bird book. His justification was that Jimmy never mentioned anything about his dog being one of those "real fittin' dawgs." He even demanded that Jimmy give him his rifle as payment for his dog. Jimmy never really expected the kid to rat on himself. Besides, delayed gratification is much sweeter than any immediate, yet brief, taste of some small victory. Ever since the time when Tommy stole Mr. Fet's watch, Jimmy knew that, when in a tough spot, feeling the quick pain of truth is much better than telling a lie that will give only temporary reprieve before the certain onset of some greater misery.

The morning after the dogfight, Jimmy saw the loudmouth kid's father sitting in his truck in the pine grove and talking to Mr. Fet. Their discussion seemed to be very agitated. Jimmy watched the truck leave as it rattled through the pine grove, turned right, and headed back up the road in the direction of the crude kid's home. Jimmy was already feeling the pangs of guilt about what he had allowed to happen the day before, and he knew by the look on his father's face as he was walking back to the front porch that he was soon going to be answering some tough questions.

"Jimmy, that man tells me you killed his dog. Tell me about it."

"That boy of his told me the dog was his. Patchis actually killed his dog and this is how it happened. Remember when I got a paddling for fighting at school? Well…"

After Jimmy finished telling his story, his father looked at him, shook his head from side to side, and said, "Son, you failed to realize that it's not that dog's fault for having been forced to live with humans that are below his intelligence, breeding, and social standing. Furthermore, if you had some unresolved problem with that boy you should have taken care of it yourself. You should never demand that anyone do anything that you should do for yourself, not even a dog like Patchis. Pride is an honorable emotion when it comes from doing honorable deeds, but you should never confuse pride with the base satisfaction of revenge. However, you and Patchis probably saved that German shepherd from a miserable life that is undeserving of a member of such a fine breed."

Although Mr. Fet's speeches were usually punishment enough for Jimmy's frequent mistakes, misdemeanors, and general acts of thoughtlessness, they were always highly educational. Nevertheless, a few months later, Jimmy sold his rifle to that kid at a price that no redneck has ever been known to resist, at least five dollars more than anything is worth.

The following Monday morning after the dogfight, the school bus was passing Bay Branch Church on its usual route to Bellville School. The bus driver winked at Jimmy and suggested to him that he might be having a much better day at school. It seems that, sometime over the weekend, the bus driver had spoken to the school principal. When the school bus arrived at the schoolhouse, the principal called Jimmy to his office and apologized for giving him a paddling. He still insisted, however, that the theft of the book should have been reported to him rather than Jimmy taking matters in his own hands. Jimmy's teacher appointed him class monitor and assigned him the duty of ensuring good order and discipline be maintained in the classroom when she was not in the room. *Ahhh*, he thought, *My first command!*

The last time Jimmy saw Patchis was when he came home on furlough after having served two years in Europe with the 8th

Airborne Infantry Division. Although Patchis was getting quite old by then, she still enjoyed their walks through the flatwoods and along the back lane among the scrub oaks and persimmon trees.

A few weeks after leaving home to report to his new duty station in Kansas, Jimmy received a letter from his aunt informing him that Patchis had disappeared only a few days after he left home. She wrote that she saw Patchis get up from her cool spot under the magnolia trees where she always waited for the school bus and then raced Jimmy back to the house. She said the last time that she had seen Patchis was when she saw her walking though the pine grove out towards the flatwoods, and she suggested that perhaps a snake had bitten Patchis.

When Jimmy came home for the Thanksgiving holidays, he walked south through the flatwoods and then back along the lane among the scrub oaks and persimmon trees. Not far from the decaying remains of an old willow tree stump, he found her bones, a bit of dried skin, and a few tufts of her white hair that were scattered among the wiregrass and scrub oak trees. He gathered up her remains and buried them under the scrub oaks and persimmon trees, which still grow along the grassy lane where she spent many of her days searching forward, guarding Jimmy's flanks, and bringing up the rear.

Jimmy sat down under an imaginary shade where an old willow tree once stood and permitted his mind to take him back to earlier days. For a few more moments and a few more times, he rode a horse named Charlie and a horse named Diana through a few old adventures. And always with them was a dog named Patchis.

# Chapter XIX

## A Place and a Friend

There was once a time when the crossroads at U.S. Highway 301 and Bay Branch Road, just five miles south of Claxton, was a busy little place. But those were the days before Interstate 95 cut a wide swath through parts of Georgia where virgin land had never before been witness to things that travel on wheels. After the last few miles of the new interstate highway were completed, most of the traffic between New York and Florida moved east where new life was breathed into the coastal cities of Savannah and Brunswick. It was not long before the little towns along U.S. 301 began to look like old deserted towns in western movie scenes. The few towns that managed to survive were fortunate to have been located where the new interstate highway intersected the few roads that connect the coastal marketplaces with the inland agricultural centers. But most of the general stores, gas stations, and roadside watering holes that once invited tourists to stop for a tank of gasoline, a *Coke*, and maybe a three-pound bag of pecans were left to fend for themselves until finally dying from terminal economic malnutrition.

A man named Grady Blocker once owned one of those little stores. It sat in the southeast corner of Bay Branch Road and U.S. 301, and it had two large murals painted on the sides of its cinder block walls and two signs hanging over the front entrance above a manually operated gasoline pump, one advertising *RC Cola* and the other promoting the freshness of *Claussen's Bread*. The store was conveniently stocked with the kinds of things that people usually run short of before making their usual weekly or monthly Saturday afternoon shopping trips to Claxton. The shell of the old store is still there, but it now wears only the signs of its neglected past.

Blocker's Crossing was only three miles from the *Pines* down a deep-rutted white sandy road that once served as the main connector between Reidsville and Savannah. That was before the Seaboard Railroad Line came through Claxton and made U.S. 280 the main route to Savannah. The railroad elevated Claxton to the ranks of one of the main towns along the few major routes between Savannah and Georgia's agricultural interior. The old Reidsville/Savannah Road was renamed Bay Branch Road, and a wooden sign tacked to a post at Blocker's crossing still points the way to Bay Branch Church.

Mr. Blocker sold many different items of household necessity and personal convenience. He even sold things that every boy and girl just must have, even if it costs them their last dime. With much anticipation of some final reward, Jimmy transported many a dime down that road and deposited it in Mr. Blocker's old manually operated cash register, an old *Dutch Masters* cigar box. Favorite items on a country kid's menu were boiled peanuts, *Butter Logs*, *Moon Pies*, *Baby Ruth* candy bars, *Nehi* orange or grape flavored sodas, and a bottled chocolate drink that had to be shaken with enough violence so as to loosen the chocolate syrup that was caked to the bottom of the bottle. Mr. Blocker even sold such things as fireworks and black powder, the kind of powder that is stored in little wooden kegs and intended for use in muzzle-loading firearms.

Jimmy stepped off the school bus as it stopped at the head of the mulberry lane, which was the main entrance to the farm for trucks, tractors, and other farm vehicles. The lane began at the edge of the flatwoods, crossed the main road, went past the tool shed, well shelter, barn, and ended at the little field behind the oak grove, just north of the big house. Mulberry trees lined the entire length of the lane. In spring and summer they were always alive with all kinds of birds that constantly fought over the abundant supply of sweet purple mulberries.

Jimmy waited for the trail of dust that had been following the bus all the way from school to finish settling before he crossed the main road. The wet gray dust caked to his sweat-drenched flannel shirt as he used his sleeve to brush the fine sand from his eyes. When he looked up, the first thing to catch his attention was the sight of Uncle Jeff reaching up and pulling something down from beneath the eaves of the well shelter. *Rats! Jeff found my stash of firecrackers.*

By the time Jimmy arrived at the well shelter, Jeff had already pulled several fuses from the largest of the firecrackers. But Jeff simply smiled at Jimmy and said; "Don't worry, I won't tell your aunt about the firecrackers. I just figured that there's no sense in having a bunch of these little bangers sitting around here when we can use them to make one really big boomer." Jeff didn't usually get excited about much of anything, but the idea that he might be able to create a giant mushroom cloud over the big field seemed to be tweaking a renewed interest in his old days in the army. Heck, Jimmy was ecstatic!

Uncle Jeff knew what he was doing when he was working around explosives. When one of the neighbors needed to have an old tree stump removed that was causing too much interference when plowing their fields, Jeff would set and blow dynamite in a way that made those stumps pop up like corks from champagne bottles. Jeff had a few blasting caps and several feet of fuse left over from his last blasting project and had decided to use the blasting caps, the powder from the firecrackers, and a keg of black powder that he got from Mr. Blocker's store to construct something that, today, would land him in the Atlanta Federal Penitentiary for at least twenty years. But then was then and now is now. Back then, most people rarely worried about what other people did on their own property as long as they didn't hurt anyone other than themselves.

Jeff and Jimmy worked on that bomb for most of the evening, and Jeff worked on it all the next day while Jimmy was at school. They decided to name their creation after the two bombs that had been dropped on Japan only a few years earlier and had ended World War II. *Little Fat Boy* was completed on Friday afternoon, and Jeff said the job had been finished just in time. The big show was going to make its opening debut and final act on the following Saturday afternoon.

One of Grady Daniel's daughters was married to an Air Force pilot who was one of the first pilots to fly the F-84 Thunder Jet. That was back when jet-powered airplanes were fairly new and few people in Evans County had ever seen one. The pilot would notify his wife when he was going to be flying over the county and then she would call home to tell her family. The word would soon be passed around to all the local folks so they could have an opportunity to come out and see the big air show.

The pilot always entered Evans County air space by flying in low from the west and screaming along Bay Branch Road past all the Daniel's houses. He would then pull up in a steep and fast rolling climb over the big field. Although the famous pilot, Chuck Jaeger, had broken the sound barrier in an experimental rocket only about a year earlier, jet airplanes were still not capable of achieving such speed. Nevertheless, the loud roar of that jet sure sounded like it was breaking the sound barrier, and its loud thunderous roar seemed to always be centered in the middle of the big field. Apparently, that was what had given Jeff his big idea.

When the jet was over Bay Branch Road, about where Josh and Martha Murphy lived and where Herbert Daniel would build his house a few years later, Jeff gave his electric spark generator a firm twist. His timing was perfect. The rumbling boom of that homemade bomb that Jeff had buried in the middle of the cornfield magnified the thunderous boom of the jet. It even made the tall pine trees in front of the big house shake like a field full of broom sage in a stiff wind. A giant plume of dirt, smoke, dead corn stalks, and who knows what else reached upward. It looked like the whole mess was going to overtake the jet as it spun upwards toward the high cirrus clouds of autumn.

Just as things were getting pretty loud, Preacher Stewart and his mule drawn wagon turned off the main road and ambled through the gate at the end of the mulberry lane. He hitched his mule to a fence post next to a pecan tree and walked over to where Jeff and Jimmy were standing at the entrance to the big field. They were looking up at the cloud of black smoke and debris as it drifted over the barn, releasing its fallout and peppering the barn like a hailstorm. Preacher Stewart eased over to where Jeff was standing with his mouth wide open and still clutching the spark generator tightly in both hands. He stared straight at Jeff, like he always did when he was talking to someone or something, and said, "Dat flyin' thing neva' dropped no bums befo' did it, Mista Jeff?"

Blocker's Crossing was the place where Jimmy first met someone who would become his friend. Although fate would direct them towards separate destinies, Jimmy was to later know the pains of guilt for failing to keep in touch with him for over thirty years. They met right after the two of them had been riding their horses among the pine trees, gall berry bushes, and palmetto fronds in the flatwoods south of Claxton and Daisy. Jimmy was on his way back from an overnight camping trip in a place that everyone around those parts called the *Area*. The Area was what local people called the great expanse of land that is better known today as Fort Stewart, which is the largest single landmass military reservation east of the Mississippi River.

Along one of the dirt roads leading to the Area is an old gristmill and pond called *Groover's Millpond*. The pond was home for some really huge largemouth bass, and it had a really great swimming hole below the millrace. It was a serene scene that was reminiscent of a Norman Rockwell painting, but one that could actually be experienced in real life.

The two boys rode up to Mr. Blocker's store about the same time. They dismounted, led their horses over to an old bathtub, opened the water spigot, and offered their horses a drink of fresh water. After exchanging casual greetings, they walked around each other's horse displaying the usual youthful airs and very obvious common interest in anything equestrian. Jimmy's new acquaintance commented on how he thought Diana appeared to be a horse of excellent breeding. Jimmy mentioned the fact that both horses were wearing bridles with straight jointed snaffle bits; an indication that their owners were riding well-mannered mounts. They introduced themselves like real adults and went in Blocker's store where they shared a sack of boiled peanuts and a *Coca-Cola*. After that day, the two of them often met at Blocker's Crossing and rode their horses through the flatwoods. They would talk about their families, horses, and their plans for the future.

Those were the days when all schools in the county were being consolidated and the doors of the old rural community schools at Antioch, Canoochee, Daisy, and Bellville were being closed one grade at a time, and the students were being bussed to the big school in Claxton. After Jimmy completed the seventh grade at Bellville, he was transferred to the consolidated school where the students were assigned to different classrooms by alphabetical order. The students from the old school at Bellville had to make new friends in a new environment. That wasn't so bad for Jimmy since he and his horse-riding friend would now be attending the same school.

Jimmy was impressed with how much energy his friend always displayed and how he pushed himself beyond normal limits to accomplish every task, whether assigned or self-assumed. Every eighth grade class in the world is full of fourteen-year-old boys whose intellects are in constant battle with their emotions, but that didn't seem to apply to Jimmy's friend. He seemed to know where he was going and how he was going to get there. It was as if he was able to see into his own future and somehow knew that he had to make the most of his life before something might happen that would be beyond his ability to influence.

One afternoon, the two boys were sitting on the steps of the school lunchroom and talking about the things they usually talked about when they were out riding in the flatwoods. As if he had been commanded to speak in obedience to some god of destiny, Jimmy's friend suddenly blurted out, "I'm going to be captain of the football team, and when I graduate, I'm going to go to a military school and become an officer in the United States Army."

Jimmy commented that he would also like to be an army officer, but didn't know if he would be able to make the football team. The only football that he had ever touched before was one that he used for sharpening his shotgun shooting skills, and that football actually belonged to his brother. Uncle Jeff would throw the football over the well shelter and Jimmy would practice shooting at it with his shotgun. His shotgun was loaded with shells that had the lead shot removed from and the shell casings and then reloaded with cracked corn. He got to be a pretty good wing shot, but never had much practice at catching the football. Nevertheless, Jimmy figured that catching a football and running on flat land might be easier than catching watermelons and loading them on a truck, and he sure had plenty of practice doing that. After their discussion, Jimmy and his friend decided they would show up for the summer football tryouts when the coach would be picking prospective players and assigning preliminary positions for the next football season. Jimmy was picked for defensive end and his friend showed definite talents as a quarterback. While his friend's high school football career was just beginning, Jimmy's was about to take a turn for the worse, even before he had a chance play in his first game.

Aunt Augusta went into one of her tizzies as soon as she discovered that Jimmy was planning on joining the football team. Her mind had long since been made up about those over-stimulated football players and those cheerleaders that wore short skirts and therefore surely had loose morals. She was not about to let him get mixed up with that bunch of depraved deviates. She even tried to talk him into getting involved in other extracurricular activities, like the glee club, theater, or maybe tennis. This was coming from a kindly little old lady who was destined to become the most avid wrestling fan that people in Evans County had ever known.

Jimmy's plans to be a football star may have been in the process of derailment, but not before he was lucky enough to play in at least one game. His moment of glory lasted only part of a half-time period, but what a period it was. It was even worth the weeks of restriction and confinement to the house and barnyard after his aunt discovered that he had failed to spend the night with a friend in town, like he had promised her, but had gone out of town with a busload of football players and cheerleaders.

The Claxton Tigers were behind at the end of the first half. The first string quarterback had sprained his ankle early in the second quarter and the star halfback had a dislocated shoulder. Jimmy's horse-riding friend suddenly found himself in the game as the quarterback and the first string defensive end had suddenly become one of the offensive end receivers. Just before the referee blew the whistle to signal the beginning of the halftime period, the Tiger's coach was looking like he really needed someone to replace his defensive end. He looked at

Jimmy and asked, "Can you suit up?" Jimmy ran to the locker room, quickly suited up, and ran on the field with the team just as the second half was beginning.

The new quarterback threw two touchdown passes and ran in another touchdown on a quarterback sneak. Jimmy intercepted two pass attempts by the other team, one for a touchdown and the other for a fifty-yard gain that set up a short drive to the end zone by the substitute fullback. The Tigers went home with a victory and Jimmy's friend went on to be captain of the team and one of the most dedicated, polite, and honorable men that anyone could ever know. However, by order of the Supreme Commander of the *Pines*, Jimmy's football career had just come to an abrupt end.

Out of pure teenage spite and a demonstration in displaced aggression, Jimmy challenged the reigning captain of the tennis team to a match. He was a smart-alecky kid who had been cursed with a rumor about him taking some kind of ritual pleasure in spending his nights ironing his underwear. Jimmy beat him in two sets on Sunday afternoon and then joined the school band the following Monday morning.

Aunt Augusta was happy about the fact that Jimmy was no longer on the football team where he would be exposed to all those sinful shenanigans she had conjured up in her mind. But, what the heck, there were just as many good-looking girls in the band as there was on the cheerleading squad. He had even heard that one of the girls in the band had a crush on him. It was time to make the best of a bad situation. Besides, as his grandfather often said, "One must look at defeat only as another opportunity in which to excel."

Things really did begin to work out after that. Jimmy got to go to all the football games, albeit on the band bus. He even discovered that girls in the band like to do the same things that his aunt had been accusing the girls in the cheerleading squad of doing. She used to tell him, "People who have music in their hearts never have time to think thoughts of the Devil." She never realized that the back of the band bus was a great place to do things that teenagers are bound to do, and it doesn't matter whether or not they are cheerleaders, football players, musicians, or just little devils.

That experience taught Jimmy two valuable lessons. Prejudice and self-righteousness can often blind people to the more important issues and facts of life, and girl trombone players have great lips. And what about his horse-riding friend? He continued his high school football career as captain of the team and even joined the tennis team and beat that smart-alecky kid too. He lettered in football, tennis, basketball, and track.

A few years later, the two friends were home on leave from the military. Jimmy's friend was a recent graduate of the Citadel and had just received a commission as a Second Lieutenant in the United States Army. Jimmy was a Sergeant with the First Infantry Division at Fort Riley, Kansas and was still thinking about his plans for the future. Neither of them owned a horse anymore, so they borrowed a car from a friend and took a drive through some of the old familiar roads in Evans County. They talked about their families, horses, and their plans for the future. It quickly dawned on Jimmy that his friend was already an officer in the United States Army while he was still an enlisted soldier. He felt better after his friend told him that he wished he had enlisted in the army before going to college. He said that it would have given him more time to gain experience and have an opportunity to serve with the kind of people he was now required to lead. The following day, Jimmy returned to his military post and doubled his college subject schedule at Kansas State University. He wasted no more time in beginning the process that would lead to him earning a commission in the United States Army.

That summer was the last time Jimmy would ever see his old horse-riding friend again. After graduating from Officers Candidate School, he served in various military units in different parts of the world while his friend did the same in other parts of the world. Jimmy first heard the news about his friend soon after completing the School of Americas in Central America, the Special Forces School at Fort Bragg, North Carolina, and was on his way to Vietnam. It was the kind of news that blows an instant void in a person's life. His old horse-riding friend, Captain William D. (Bidd) Sands, who during one summer night's drive caused him to reevaluate his life and refocus upon old goals, had been killed in Vietnam while engaged in combat against a regiment of the North Vietnamese Army.

Jimmy didn't receive the news until days after his friend's funeral, and it would be another thirty years before he could bring himself to visit his friend's grave. He had driven by it many times when he was home on leave and many more times during the years after retiring from the army. Unexplained feeling of undeserved guilt, combined with uneasy fears of one's own mortality, is an escape mechanism that helps some people avoid having to deal with their own frailties. But finally, on the 4th of July 1998, Jimmy stepped through the gate of a little cemetery that sits on the side of the old Sunbury Road, just south of Daisy, Georgia. He stood quietly by his friend's grave. Beside him was his son, the only person on earth with whom he knew he could bear the moment, and he wept.

Jimmy was like most men that he had known during his career in the military. They always found it difficult to grieve. If and when they did, they never let anyone know about it, and they never discussed it. It seems that there is some quality ingrained in men who understand that it is their duty to display strength and courage around people with whom they know they might someday have to lead in harm's way. And grief is one of those emotions that can often be misinterpreted by those who rely upon their leaders to insulate them from the disillusionment of panic and the terrible fear that they might fail as men.

No one can say for certain whether or not grieving is a good thing or bad thing, but many manly things that are important to young men often become less important to older men. Some are even futile. Jimmy finally understood that it was his own fear of revealing his personal weaknesses that had made him hide his grief from others. But now that most of the reasons for displaying such strength had passed with the years, there was little need to restrain old repressed grief, which is often dug up by ghosts of memories past. It might have been the discovery of that knowledge of his on self that gave Jimmy the strength, perhaps the wisdom, to succumb to a higher strength and finally approach the place where his old friend had been waiting so long for him to come and visit.

Bidd Sands now rests next to a field surrounded by woods where two young boys once rode their horses through the flatwoods and talked about their families, horses, and their plans for their future. It is a place that is now marked in remembrance of the dedication and determination of a young man from Daisy, Georgia who tried so hard to be a winner, yet never realizing something that his friends always knew about him; he was always a winner. It is a place where they can again meet and remember riding their horses through the flatwoods among the pine trees, gall berry bushes, and palmetto fronds. It is a place where they can still talk about their families, old horses, and their old plans for a future that so quickly and harshly became the present. Death may have taken the life of a friend, but it has mercifully spared the memories of those fortunate lives he once touched.

# Chapter XX

## *Pete's Moonshine Still*

It was in the fall of 1957 when Pete decided to liquidate the production side of his moonshine business and concentrate his efforts on expanding his interests in distillery design consultation, product distribution, network marketing, and his highly popular special events catering service. His decision to direct his interests more to the less risky functions of his business proved to be a much more profitable business arrangement than was his old production and direct sales techniques. It was also a decidedly safer move in view of the fact that the Georgia Alcohol Beverage Commission and the Federal Bureau of Alcohol Tobacco and Firearms were finally getting around to cooperating with one another rather than competing in their efforts to control the boot-leg production and sales of alcohol spirits of the drinking kind.

The sports of hunting and fishing have always been an important part of the lives of country boys who were lucky enough to have grown up among the pine woods, sandy oak ridges, and along the slow-moving creeks and rivers of Southeast Georgia. However, there are some people who have lived more sheltered lives and believe that hunting and fishing are unnecessary sporting pastimes that the world could easily do without. There are even others who say that such activities should be banned all together. Actually, hunting and fishing are activities that can be of valuable assistance in educating young people, building their character, and instilling in them an appreciation for the laws of nature and ethical human conduct. The special and unique knowledge of how to dress quail, doves, rabbits, and squirrels has given many a country boy a leg up on city boys during anatomy experiments in science classes. Gathering Mother Nature's bounty with respect for her gifts to mankind also builds a kind of reverence that is good for the soul.

Hunting and fishing, when learned, practiced, and supervised under wise and proper adult tutorship, are helpful tools in teaching young people how to appreciate and develop the kind of responsible relationship that humans should have with the natural world that surrounds them. No one can honestly say that they have never met a well-bred hunter who was not also a conservationist and whose appreciation for a good hunt and fine catch were not equal to his appreciation for classical music, good wine, and great literature. However, we have all met a few of the other types of people who, regardless of their financial successes or self-assumed social status, are creatures of crude breeding. They exist as parasites in every segment of society, and they remind us of the despicable Yahoos in Jonathan Swift's *Gulliver's Travels*. When we discover such creatures in our midst, the best we can do is to single them out and deny them access to what they have chosen to deny others by way of their unethical and destructive conduct.

Aunt Eva and her husband, who everyone in the family called Unkie, lived in Avondale Estates, a little village just northeast of Atlanta. It is a beautiful little town that was built in the English Tudor style of architecture. Unkie and Aunt Eva loved to drive down to the *Pines* every year and spend a few days relaxing from the hustle and bustle of the Atlanta area.

Unkie enjoyed hunting quail and Aunt Eva enjoyed designing and directing landscape projects. As much as Jimmy tried to avoid the drudgery of planting, transplanting, re-transplanting, and re-re-transplanting various species of vegetation during her visits, she at least managed to force upon him much of her tremendous knowledge of horticulture and other botanical subjects.

Unkie was an expert wing shot, and no one ever recalled seeing him miss a bird on the rise. He was such a good shot that he could bag his limit well before the other hunters in a hunting party. But Unkie was a gentleman. He would space his shots in a way that gracefully allowed other hunters a fair opportunity to bag a few birds. Good hunters are never greedy and, although the dogs would point and flush several coveys of quail during a morning's hunt, only a few birds from each covey would be harvested. Years later and after Unkie died, the shotgun that he used on his hunting trips was passed on to Jimmy. It has since been passed on to his son who now owns that old 20 gauge, straight cylinder bored, 2½-inch chamber, model 12 slide action shotgun that was manufactured in 1913 by Winchester Arms Company.

During the 1940s and 50s, South Georgia had a very large and healthy quail population. The farming techniques that were employed back then permitted the beggar lice weed and other favorite foods of the quail to grow along fencerows and in the untilled corners of fields. Although quail are very prolific breeders, they nest on the ground where their natural enemies can feed upon their eggs and young chicks that have not yet developed the ability to fly. At best, about ten percent of a covey of quail ever manages to survive the first year and carry on the annual reproductive cycle.

A covey is a single brood of birds that are hatched from a pair of adult quail, and one covey usually consists of from twelve to fifteen birds. Occasionally, when environmental conditions are favorable for producing higher populations of quail, two and sometimes three young coveys will join together and create one giant covey of perhaps thirty to fifty birds. Anyone who has not been startled by the sudden and explosive rise and fluttering flight of a covey of bobwhite quail has been missing out on one of the most thrilling experiences that nature can provide.

Southern bobwhite quail are very territorial and, unless under unusual pressure, they rarely extend their range beyond more than five hundred yards in any direction from their point of home reference. Their home reference may be the corner of a field, a small grove of pine saplings, or some brushy area that provides good cover, food, and adequate concealment. That point will always be within not more than three hundred yards straight flight to a thick growth of protective cover where the birds can take refuge in the event a predator or some farmer's machinery invades their home turf.

Jimmy once found a covey of thirty quail that had been caught in a poacher's trap. The trap was constructed with tobacco sticks tied together in a way that made the trap form a pyramid. A trench had been dug in the ground and a board of about eight inches wide placed over the trench. The trap was positioned over the board in a way that allowed the board to serve as a bridge over the trench, just inside the trap. Cracked corn was sprinkled outside the trap, down through the trench, and up inside the trap. The entire covey of quail had followed the trail of grain leading into the trap. Once the birds were in the trap and had eaten all the grain, they walked in a circle around the inside edges of the trap with their heads up and searching for a way out. With just one of those traps, a poacher could wipe out an entire population of quail in just one breeding year.

Before Jimmy was sixteen years old and it was legal for him to drive an automobile, he knew of several college students that hauled moonshine in order to make enough money to pay for their tuition at Georgia Southern College. They would pick up bulk loads of moonshine at predetermined locations in Evans County and haul it over to Bulloch County where they would deliver it to the local distributor that controlled that area. The distributor would pay the hauler, bottle the moonshine, and control the local market. There never was much trouble with the local law enforcement officials or federal or state revenue agents. Those agencies usually concentrated their anti-bootlegging efforts on locating and destroying the larger illegal stills. Their usual tactic was to locate an active still upon receiving a tip from a fire tower attendant or after bribing some local moonshine operator into squealing on one of his competitors. With their expertly gained intelligence, the revenue agents would hide in the bushes most of the night and try to arrest the still operators when they came back to their stills to begin the process of distilling their illicit joy juice. Usually, the moonshiners were about two weeks and two counties ahead of the revenuers, and all the revenuers ever got in return for their efforts was a bad case of woods chiggers and hundreds of mosquito bites.

A successful bust of a moonshine operation always led to a lot of newspaper coverage and film clips showing agents breaking barrels with axes, chasing violators through the woods, and giving inflated estimates as to the worth of the illegal booze that they had managed to keep off the streets as a result of their professional efforts. Much like local, state, and federal narcotics agents do today, revenuers of yesterday went for the easy targets and those that would get them the most publicity. More pictures of their ill-gotten gains created more publicity. More publicity resulted in more effort. More effort justified more money for their budgets. And more money meant more and higher paid agents that could be hired to fight what was an obvious increase in the illegal trade of moonshine, drugs, or whatever.

Like most country boys of those times, thoughts of crime, evil and corruption on either side of the law was far from Jimmy's mind. He preferred to hunt and fish during the day, read at night, and spend his Saturday evenings in town trying to impress the girls who were always congregated at the 301 Soda Shop. He also enjoyed spending time with Pete and listening to him tell about his narrow escapes from the clutches of the law and about his Saturday night forays in town. Pete liked to go to a place called *The Wagon Wheel* where he would spend his moonshine profits on the local ladies of the evening.

It was a cool Friday morning in September and Jimmy was hunkered down in a clump of palmettos on top of a little hill overlooking Cribbs Branch. The dove season had just opened and he was in the best location for taking pass-shots at morning doves as they flew back and forth between Dick Waters' cornfield and a line of trees along Cribbs Branch. He was watching a pair of doves flit slowly across a stand of scrub oaks when he noticed a familiar green truck, one that belonged to the new state game warden that had been recently assigned to the county. It was then that he remembered he had failed to replace the wooden shot-shell plug back in his shotgun after cleaning the shotgun the night before.

Federal game laws classify doves as migratory birds. That one fact places them under the dubious jurisdiction of the U.S. Department of Wildlife. Hunters are prohibited from taking more than twelve birds in a single day and further prohibited from taking more than three shots in succession at any controlled species without having to reload their shotgun. Apparently, some expert in the federal government didn't know that it is darned near impossible to hit a bobbing and weaving dove with less than three shots. Even if a hunter was that good, he would still have to stop hunting after bagging his daily limit of twelve birds. Federal bureaucrats; go figure. At any rate, the plug for Jimmy's shotgun was back at the house and he was sitting in the middle of a palmetto clump under a persimmon tree. He was dead certain that, with no plug in his shotgun, the game warden would be coming around the edge of the field in less than five minutes. Jimmy really did respect game laws and never had any intentions of breaking them, but at that moment, he was confidant that he was about to be arrested and sent to the big federal penitentiary in Atlanta. He was going to be a federal felon and not yet a high-school graduate.

No self-respecting country boy would ever allow himself to be caught without having a good knife in his pocket. Jimmy was always mindful of his grandfather who often quoted his favorite poem about knives. "Buck horn handle, Barlow blade, sorriest knife ever made." A good knife was important, and Jimmy had a genuine U.S. Army issued TL-29 wireman's tool set that he had bartered from one of the soldiers that were stationed at Fort Stewart. During the Korean War, the flatwoods was often full of soldiers that used the flatwoods around the farm as a training and bivouac area. The tool set came with a leather sheath, wire cutters, and a good quality knife that Jimmy kept sharp as a razor, just for such emergencies.

He reached over his head, sliced a limb from the persimmon tree, cut a five inch long piece of straight wood from the limb, and then whittled his new plug down so that it would fit in the magazine of his five-shot slide-action shotgun. No sooner had he installed his field expedient plug in the shotgun than the game warden came driving up in a cloud of dust. The warden slammed down hard on his brakes, slid sideways, and immediately sank his right front wheel in a very deep and large stump hole that had been burned out by a recent forest fire. The warden stepped out of his truck, sauntered over to Jimmy, and looking like he had just done something normal, said, "Boy, I seed you shootin' at them birds way over yonder. You got a plug in that thar' shoot-gun of yorn?"

Jimmy stood up and brushed the persimmon shavings off his lap while resisting the temptation to respond to the impossible scenario that the game warden's grammar had just posed. "Yes sir, I sure do. Would you like to see it?"

The game warden looked down at the pile of wood shavings at Jimmy's feet and mumbled, "Naw, I can see what's left of yore new plug scattered all around you. Cuttin' it a bit close ain't you, boy?"

"Yes sir, about as close as you came to stopping that truck somewhere between here and China."

Considering his precarious situation, Jimmy immediately knew that had not been such a wise thing to say. He quickly turned cooperative and told the game warden how to get to the nearest house where there would be a tractor that might be big enough to pull his truck out of the hole. The warden began walking across the field towards Dick Waters' house and Jimmy decided to move his dove shooting spot closer to Cribbs Branch.

Jimmy stalked his way down the hill and quietly approached the head of a little stream that fed into Cribbs Branch. Out of the corner of one eye, he caught a momentary glimpse of something red as it quickly flashed behind a fallen tree. Supposing that it might have been the head of a wild turkey, he quickly ducked behind a clump of fox grape vines and waited for whatever it was to make another move. Thinking that the turkey must have slipped away, he eased up and continued down the hill towards the branch. The object suddenly popped up again over an old pine log. It was then that Jimmy recognized that it was Pete wearing a red cap. Pete's familiar voice whispered excitedly, "Mista Jimma, dat you?"

"Yeah, is that you, Pete?"

"Yeah, I seed you wid de law and thunk maybe yuse dun told him 'bout my still?"

"Shucks, Pete, I always knew you had a 'shine still, but I never knew where it was. Even if I did know, you ought to know I wouldn't tell anyone, not even my Uncle Jeff."

"Yo' Onkle Jeff done be knowin' all 'bout it, and he ain't tellin' nobody neither."

Pete and Jimmy spent the rest of the afternoon sitting in the bushes next to Pete's still while taking occasional sips of some of Pete's finest *second run* and watching Dick Waters and that new game warden trying to pull the warden's truck out of that stump hole with Dick's tractor.

It was about a month later when Jimmy heard that Pete was home in bed after somehow and very mysteriously being involved in a serious accident. He saddled up Diana and rode over to Pete's little house where he found him sitting on his front porch. He had bandages wrapped around one leg, a big white cast on the other leg, and a pint of his best and most recent vintage sitting on a little table next to his beat up old lounge chair. Jimmy asked him what had happened to his legs. Pete explained that he had fallen asleep one night while he was supposed to be tending his still. Things got a little too hot and the still blew up, scattering parts of his still all over Cribbs Branch. One of the heavier pieces of the still landed on top of Pete, breaking one of his legs and cutting a big gash in the other.

Jimmy suggested to Pete that he should consider getting someone to help him operate his still. Pete said it didn't really matter anymore because he had already decided to quit making the stuff and start being a middleman. He said he thought that was where the real money was anyway.

As Jimmy mounted Diana's saddle and was about to turn around and head back to the *Pines*, Pete called to him, "I knowed I shutna' used so many o' dem lite'ner knots. Dey shore duz burn hot, don't dey, Mista Jimma?"

# Chapter XXI

## Wild Thing

There is an old story about a wildcat. It is a story that is still often heard being told in hunting cabins, sports bars, and other places of questionable benefit where men like to gather and enjoy drinking adult beverages, swapping tales, and trying to impress their buddies. It is also the kind of story that is fun to tell and even provides the teller a feeling that his listeners might believe that he actually lived the tale. The story is about a prank that is often credited to people who live in parts of the world where country boys and wildcats have never been concurrently indigenous. It is even close to becoming a part of American folklore in the way that it evokes a bit of envy in those who wish that they had actually done the deed, like the stories about Daniel Boone or Davy Crockett. But, only in these pages can be found the original and true story that tells about how it all came to pass.

It all began in Evans County, Georgia in the spring of 1958 and was finally consummated on a Saturday night in July, about a month after the class of '58 graduated from Claxton High School. Anyone who might wish to verify this story is invited to contact one of the few participants who actually witnessed the events as they unfolded, and who might still be alive and willing to confess to the dastardly deed.

Young people of the 1940s and 1950s never regarded school as only a place to learn reading, writing, arithmetic, history, and civics. It was also considered a tactical headquarters from where they could go forth on reconnaissance missions to discover and experience all the flavors of life. The only difference between the youth of then and youth of today is that the earlier generation had a much deeper sense of responsibility, duty, and obligation that extended well beyond their mindless acts of the moment.

Regardless of all the shenanigans that children might have pulled in those days, they at least made an honest effort to not go beyond an established point of demeanor, a level of decorum that had been instilled in their souls bit-by-bit and day-by-day by their caretakers of the post-war culture in which they grew up. They may not have been able to define character in its purest terms and academic meaning, but words like respect, honor, trust, and integrity were part of their active vocabularies. However, their youthful vigor did occasionally cause them to transgress beyond that which was considered appropriate. Yet, it was their instilled sense of morality and character that caused them to own up to their mistakes and be willing to take personal responsibility for their actions. Sometimes, the owning up would occur only after a few of the more vigorous offenders were finally confronted with the certainty of disclosure. Sadly, however, good intentions sometimes failed to shield them from the deadly results of some of their most innocent indiscretions and youthful inexperience.

The automobile was the culprit. It gave young people of the 1950s a new dimension to their lives, one that their parents had yet to fully understand and devise an effective method for protecting their children from themselves. A new and deadly phenomenon had begun to reveal itself with the development of automobile engines that could out perform the crude roads of the times, and even the minds of young drivers. Young people were dying on the roads at an alarming rate while public safety officials were presenting gruesome images of blood, flesh, and exposed bones via poorly staged driving safety films. It was a well-meaning effort to scare young drivers into being 'safety conscious.'

Many adults, then and even now, have never learned that such scare tactics don't work on teenagers whose social survival depends so much on their ability to demonstrate to their peers that they are not afraid of anything. More than classroom lectures on whatever topic might be in vogue, teenagers need to be forced into situations where they are required to demonstrate personal responsibility and problem-solving skills in a framework that provides for gradually decreasing controlled environments and which is based upon their ability to demonstrate acceptable levels of performance. This kind of supervision and attention can only be provided in the home, reinforced in schools, supported by communities, affirmed by the states, and acclaimed by a nation.

There once was a red-headed kid named Bobby who rode school bus number one to and from school. He was about seventeen years old when Jimmy was ten or twelve, but Jimmy thought how adult he seemed to be when he was talking about things having to do with cars and girls. One Friday afternoon, he and a few older boys were sitting in the rear of the bus talking about what a great time they were going to have during the coming weekend. But when Monday morning came, Bobby didn't get on the bus, and he never got on it again. He was killed in an automobile crash on U.S. Highway 301 sometime after getting off the bus that Friday afternoon. At his funeral, many adults lamented about how such a terrible thing could have possibly happened to such a fine boy. They said he was a good boy, very smart, and what a shame it was that such a thing could happen to someone who could handle a car the way Bobby knew how to handle one.

Jimmy knew that Bobby didn't die because he was a bad person or because he was stupid, or because he was a bad driver. He died because he was an inexperienced young human being who had not been trained on how to pay attention to details in a way that would permit him to recognize the really important things that might occur around him. He had never been required to demonstrate to anyone that he had developed the skills necessary to survive on his own in a new and powerfully mobile culture. Jimmy was sure Bobby's parents had told him to be careful before driving away from his house that fateful evening. But no teenager that Jimmy ever knew, other than the ones he would have later in his life, had ever been required to explain to another adult just what *being careful* really means to them.

Although he was not witness to the deadly event, Jimmy knew why it happened. It happened for the same reason it happens today. Most adults allow their teenage children to drive around with a carload of their friends without ever having required them to demonstrate to some responsible adult that they are *proficient* drivers and not just *skillful* drivers. No parent likes to admit his or her guilt, but their failure to train their children when there is both opportunity and responsibility to do so is an example of what the law refers to as contributory negligence.

The summer after high school graduation is a time when feelings of confusion and fear of confronting imminent reality begin to trouble every new graduate. It is an emotional period when young people are forced to realize that it is time to leave their friends and familiar places. It is the time when they must go out in the world and become the adults that they always claimed to be. This is the first real jolt of adulthood, and it brings with it a sudden awareness of an impending emptiness that causes young people to do strange things. The urge to have one last wonderful fling, to taste a kind of togetherness that was previously taken for granted, and to mark the moment forever in their memories can be irresistible. Avery Coley and Jimmy did just that. It was their last hurrah before riding into the sunset of their youth to meet the sunrise of adulthood.

While Jimmy was on one of his many excursions in the flatwoods, he discovered a wild bobcat that had somehow managed to get caught in a poacher's trap. Since the person who owned the trap had obviously been trespassing on the *Pines'* property, he brought the whole irate, hissing, screaming, and clawing mess back to the well shelter and put the cat in an empty chicken coop. After dining on a few meals of wild rabbits, squirrels, and tame yard chickens, the bobcat eventually regained its strength and was soon in need of a larger cage.

Jimmy told Avery that he was going to set the cat free in the flatwoods, but Avery wanted to keep it for a while so some of their friends who lived in town could have a chance to see a real wild bobcat. Since one of Avery's brothers used to raise raccoons in their back yard, he suggested that the cat could be kept in one of the old raccoon cages. So, in the spring of 1958, the bobcat moved into his newly remodeled condominium on East James Street.

By the middle of the summer, the cat had grown much too large for the raccoon cage and it became evident that it should be released back to its natural habitat. Jimmy and Avery couldn't allow such a noble gesture to be as simple as just turning the cat loose in the flatwoods. That great deed of emancipation had to be accomplished with a bit of flair.

After Sara and Thomas had died a few years earlier, Tommy, Temp, and Cleo moved to town to live with one of their aunts. Avery and Jimmy decided to bring Tommy into their confidence since he was the one who had adopted the cat and assumed the job of feeding it after it moved to Avery's back yard. Although racial segregation was still common in most schools during the 1950s, Tommy, Temp, Avery, and Jimmy never allowed the finer points of custom and tradition to get in the way of their activities. They had always been a good team when it came to doing things they had always been doing in the way they had always been doing them.

Tommy came up with what he thought was a better plan. He believed that Avery's plan to turn the bobcat loose in the swimming pool behind the 301 Soda Shop was not such a bright idea. There would be too many people there and no way of determining which one of them might decide to be a hostile witness in case things went wrong. The crime might be traced back to them. He was also correct when he said that any black fellow who got caught with a bobcat anywhere near a swimming pool with a sign on the gate that says '*White People Only*' would probably cause more problems than the good people of Evans County could handle. Furthermore, Avery and Jimmy had no wish to have any more trouble with the law after that little incident at the city water tower a couple of years earlier. Considering the fact that Tommy was much more experienced in practical matters having to do with the law, they decided to go along with his plan.

There was once a popular watering hole that sat on the west side of the highway between Claxton and Metter. Although it has long since been demolished, it was one of those roadside joints where people of different backgrounds, cultures, and races could mingle together without having to be bothered with such impediments as local traditions, blue laws, and old prejudices.

The place specialized in barbecue, beer, and wine. However, if a customer gave the right sign to the right person they could get a take-out bag with a bottle or two of first-rate moonshine poked down in the bottom of the sack and covered with a box of barbecue. White folks were always stopping by to get some of that 'real fine barbecue' and drink a few shots of branch water at the bar, which was constructed of two old wooden doors and six empty fifty-five gallon oil drums. They would purchase an extra pint or two to take home with them so they could brag to their more bashful friends about their 'close connections' with the local underworld. That was the place that Tommy decided would be their target.

Tommy used to work as a cook for the man who owned the barbecue place, and it was well known around the county that Tommy's pork barbecue was the best anyone around those parts of South Georgia had ever tasted. He used combinations of vinegar, pepper, and special spices in a way that made every morsel of his barbecue taste like it was the first bite of heaven. But Tommy made the mistake of teaching one of the owner's relatives how to cook his barbecue. Fairly soon, Tommy was out of a job and it was only a few days later when the new cook's barbecue became an Old Family Tradition', at least according to the new sign that was painted on a four-by-eight sheet of plywood and nailed to the wall over the front entrance facing the Metter Road. It was understandable that Tommy would be upset, and Avery and Jimmy were not about to let an old friend down. The plot began to thicken.

Temp was an expert junkyard picker and landfill scavenger. That earned him the mission of locating a container that would be capable of transporting a highly agitated bobcat without the entire town learning about it. Avery worked at Brown's Drug Store and could afford to keep a 1949 two-door Ford Custom in reasonable running condition. He was placed in charge of providing a reliable means of transportation. Tommy assumed the responsibility of gathering essential elements of information that related to such things as terrain, enemy force structure, and avenues of approach and egress.

Since it was Jimmy's idea to have that cat in the first place, he would be the one to make the final delivery of the package and, if necessary, jump in the Canoochee River. He was a good swimmer and seemed to have a talent for being able to move fairy effortlessly through swamps during the night. If their plan started to fall apart, he was to jump in the river, swim downstream, and decoy any pursuers while Avery, Tommy, and Temp made their getaway in Avery's car. After things cooled down a bit, they were to pick Jimmy up a ways down stream at the bridge just north of Claxton where U.S. Highway 301 crosses the Canoochee River.

The usual nightly routine at the barbecue joint was that the owner would close about midnight and make deliveries of barbecue and spirited liquids to the back doors of certain select cash-paying white customers who lived in town. His entire work force of kinfolk would pile in his old beat-up, coal-black, four-door, 1951 slip-o-matic Buick. Each of them would be holding in their lap several boxes of steaming hot barbecue or a case of fresh-run Canoochee River joy juice. Tommy sure had done an excellent job of gathering the essential elements of intelligence for the operation.

Temp secured an old brown and tan checkered cardboard suitcase that someone had tossed in the Evans County landfill. Tommy was the only person who could get anywhere near that bobcat. He carefully stuffed the cat in his new, albeit cramped and temporary, living quarters.

They were in position close to the river and behind a clump of ty-tys for not more than twenty minutes before they saw the lights at the barbecue place being turned out. That was the signal for Jimmy to make his move. That old Buick would be coming down the road in less than two minutes. He grabbed the suitcase that was weighted down with forty pounds of internal anger, ran across the bridge, and placed it broadside and right on top of the centerline of the highway where no one could possibly miss seeing it, not even a blind person. No way was Jimmy going to risk taking a swim in the Canoochee River when he was wearing his new penny loafers. He ran back across the bridge and jumped in Avery's car only seconds before the shimmering headlights of the Buick began lighting up their ambush site.

The Buick rounded the curve, straightened out, and its high beam lights soon began ricocheting off the suitcase. There was a sudden and piercing sound of squealing brakes and tires as the car came to a sliding halt next to the suitcase. The left rear door swung open and a long dark arm reached out and grabbed the suitcase by its broken handle. That old traditional barbecue family's newfound prize was yanked inside the Buick. The door slammed shut as the overloaded Buick slowly straightened out and accelerated down the road, straining against its worn out shock absorbers and groaning and moaning noises coming from its out of time straight-six engine and slipping transmission.

That old Buick made it about two hundred yards down the road and on the bridge before it fishtailed, slid sideways, and then came to a tire-warping sideways halt, right in the middle of the bridge. All four doors popped open in unison, and boxes of barbecue, bottles of moonshine, and six members of that old traditional barbecue family came flying out of the Buick. Every one of them dove over the bridge rail. Their screams seemed to trail behind their moonlit images as each of them splashed into the dark waters of the Canoochee River. It was a strange sight with sounds more eerie than anyone could imagine coming from a thousand banshees in a Boris Karloff movie. The bobcat, apparently disgusted over his most recent experiences with the human species, trotted over the bridge, slipped down the embankment, and disappeared into the darkness of the ty-tys and briar bushes.

There are times when justice is sweet, but as with some romances, the real story must remain secret, at least until the heat is off and the memories of the damaged parties have had a chance to dim. There is an old saying, "With time comes forgiveness." With a little luck, maybe it will come with a bit of forgetfulness.

# Chapter XXII

## The Bridge

Under bridge slowly creep
Dark waters running deep
Shielded from light of day
Fish down under never stray
Long it held vehicles in flight
Planks roaring and trusses tight
Gone with time plank and pier
But bridge holds memories dear

When traveling along the back roads of rural South Georgia, it would difficult for a traveler to fail to notice the many churches that are sprinkled throughout the pine tree covered countryside. When flying above and looking down, they seem to be sprinkled everywhere, nestled in little cleared areas among the pines like little whitecaps on a shimmering green ocean. Most of these old country churches were built at intersections of old land trade routes or near ferry crossing along major rivers. Over the years, the roads in front and along the sides of the churches were made wider and wider in order to accommodate the increasing traffic and changes in modes of transportation.

Today, many of the little country churches are so close to the road that the views of drivers of vehicles are blocked when approaching the intersections. During the colonial period, churches and trading posts were intentionally located near transportation centers, and it was common for families to ride their horses, wagon teams, or boats to the nearest church where they would spend the day socializing. In those days, the Unitarian Church was a prominent church because it embraced many faiths and it wasn't practical to have a church for every denomination.

After church services, the men would conduct their business and the women would spend the afternoon socializing before their families had to leave early enough to get back home before dark. Since it took such a long time to travel to and from church, few churches conducted Sunday school classes for children. Most of the churches had only one room, which made it even more impractical for scheduling religious sessions for children, especially at the same time as for adults.

The periodic trips to the nearest trading center and church were all-day affairs, a tradition that many southern denominations continue today, even in this age of the automobile. The southern practice of having an annual 'dinner on the ground' after morning church services originated in the days when it was necessary for people to bring their own meals to church. They would bring their favorite dishes and spread them out on long make-shift tables for everyone to share under the oak trees and tall pines that shaded the grounds around the church. Going to church in those days was not just a religious experience, but also a social affair that continues today as weekly events for most rural church congregations.

Like the country churches of old, Bay Branch Primitive Baptist Church had only one room and no Sunday school classes for children. That presented Aunt Augusta with a dilemma after deciding that Jimmy and his brother needed to catch up on some of the religious training they had missed as a result of not being under her influence before coming to live with her. She accepted the idea that they wouldn't be going to Sunday school at Bay Branch Church during the regular school months. After all, she could always use homework as an excuse to ruin their weekends during the regular school year. But she was not someone to allow the convenience and happiness of children to get in her way, much less those of her heathen male siblings. She was going to make sure that her adopted boy's first summer living with her would establish a standard by which all future summers would be measured. She was going to see to it that they went to Sunday school every Sunday. So, she kicked off every summer by sending them to a two-week religious educational experience that was known as Vacation Bible School.

Aunt Augusta was aware of Mr. Fet's habit of driving to town every Sunday morning when decent people were supposed to be in church. She didn't like the idea of him hanging out with certain characters of lesser moral inclinations and general conduct than would ever meet her approval. Armed with her knowledge of Mr. Fet's weaknesses in matters of the heart and body, she moved to capitalize upon his stronger senses of duty and obligation. Besides, he had already admitted that he was in dept to her for taking care of his two boys while he was in the war. She figured it would be a plus for him to feel even more guilt for not providing his boys with the kind of mother that met her approval.

She devised a scheme that was about to permit her to take every bird in the covey with only one shot. She arranged things in a way that allowed her the convenience of going to both the adult Sunday school class and regular church services at Bay Branch Church. Her plan called for Jimmy and his brother to be in a structured Sunday school program and, at the same time, their father would be chained down with domestic duties. All that and she would still get her Sunday paper without having to drive eight miles to town after attending services at Bay Branch Church. Besides, she needed to get back home early enough to have enough time for cooking her famous Sunday dinners that she always cooked after church services.

Mr. Fet was assigned the mission of driving his two boys over to the *First Methodist Church* in Claxton where they were required to attend Sunday school every Sunday of every year and where Vacation Bible School was held every day for two weeks in the month of June. After dropping his boys off at the church, he had to go to *Brown's Drug Store* and pick up the Sunday edition of the *Savannah Morning News and Evening Press* before all the papers were sold out. That would leave him with only a few minutes for visiting his friends of ill repute before having to drive back to the church and retrieve his boys. She even placed an additional nail in all their coffins by demanding that they be back home in time to eat dinner with the preacher or whomever it might be that she had decided to invite to Sunday dinner at the *Pines* after church services.

Mr. Fet was not about to stand idly by and allow his sister to beat him out of his weekly Sunday morning brunch and cocktail hour with his gang of fox hunting buddies. He devised a plan of his own that would not only meet her time restraints, but even place him in good stead with her. He took on a project that came to be one of the most notable improvements in the local scenery around the Bull Creek and Bay Branch communities. His finished product served the public well until Governor Talmadge's road building program caused the destruction of one of the most wonderfully scenic and useful recreational parks to have ever graced the many country roads in South Georgia.

There once was a wooden bridge on the dirt road that connects Bay Branch Road to U.S. Highway 280 at the town of Hagan. The bridge stood just below a giant earthen dam that held back the waters of Bull Creek and created what is still known today as Smith's Pond. The old bridge was made of heavy wooden pilings and thick planks of timber that rattled like thunder every time a vehicle passed over it. There was a large pool of water with a clean sandy bottom on the downstream side of the bridge. The pool of water was kept purified by the water that rushed from the spillway every time the dam gates were opened to let off excess water from Smith's Pond. This naturally aerated pool of running water had a large shallow area at one end that made it easy for non-swimmers and a deep area for the more experienced swimmers, much like a modern swimming pool. This old swimming hole that had been witness to the naked dampness of many a young swimmer was five miles from the *Pines* by automobile but not more than three miles by horseback. Both horse and boy spent many summer hours lounging and frolicking together in the cooling water that was kept purified by hundreds of cypress trees growing in the pond above the bridge and dam.

It took only about two trips over that bridge and past the swimming hole to and from Vacation Bible School before Mr. Fet had everything all figured out. He quickly developed his plan of action, mustered his troops, and began the execution phase of his plan. The only problems that had to be solved were issues involving time management and how to convince his fox hunting buddies to change the location of their Sunday morning social meetings. Anything, he assured them, would be an improvement over the loading ramp and leaky shed behind Chick Sike's feed store. Jimmy knew something organized was about to happen when his father managed to get both of his brothers involved in the physical aspects of the project. In just one day, they cleaned an area around a giant oak tree that shaded the swimming hole, built four picnic tables, constructed a shed with a shingled roof, and mounted a rainproof bulletin board on the side of the shed.

The *Bull Creek Swimming Pool, Roadside Park, and Fox Hunting Social Club* opened to the public right after graduation ceremonies at the First Methodist Vacation Bible School, class of the summer of 1947. The time management problem was solved when Mr. Fet recruited Will Kicklighter. Will lived in an apartment above *Mincey's Dry Goods Store*, which overlooked *Brown's Drug Store* where the Sunday newspapers were sold. Will's job was to pick up the Sunday paper, drive by the vestibule at the First Methodist Church and pick up the weekly Sunday school lesson pamphlet, and then drive out to the swimming hole to meet the *Claussen's Bread* and *Coca-Cola* truck drivers before they arrived with the refreshments. Mr. Fet knew what he was doing when he invited those truck drivers to be charter members of the club. All Mr. Fet had to do was to drop Jimmy and his brother off at the swimming hole while he was on his way to town to pick up a few essential items before heading back to the festivities that would soon be commencing at Bull Creek Bridge.

It didn't take long for the membership of the club, both active and casual drop-in, to grow to the point that the food and beverages improved over the usual cold cuts and soda pop. They were soon eating hot grits, biscuits, gravy, scrambled eggs, and even barbecue. Although there was an assortment of soft drinks available, Pete would drop by with a few containers of his adult-grade beverage. The Sunday school lessons at the bridge consisted of Mr. Fet making sure that his two boys were familiar with the Sunday school lesson of the week. It would have been indicative of very poor planning had they been unable to provide appropriate responses to questions that their aunt was surely going to be asking them just as soon as they got home. "What did you learn in Sunday school today?" The nice thing about the Methodist Church is that it can be counted on to be consistent in publishing advance copies of the weekly sermon topics and detailed outlines of every Sunday school lesson.

Aunt Augusta was impressed with the newfound civic-mindfulness of her three brothers. Every time she drove over the old bridge on her way to town she would comment on how glad she was to see some proof that her brothers had actually done something nice for the community. "We sure could use more little parks like that around this county. I only wish they hadn't stopped after building just that one." Jimmy was sure that she was also thinking about what a positive influence she was beginning to have on his father as a result of her decision to get him more involved in the raising of his two boys. At any rate, Mr. Fet certainly seemed to be developing more interest in the weekly Sunday school lessons, especially in the summer during those two weeks of June.

It was several years later and many trips to the old Bull Creek swimming hole were behind Jimmy when he saddled up Diana and rode across the Sara Ace Branch towards the old bridge. Governor Talmadge's road building program was in full swing and the road in front of the *Pines* had been paved all the way from the Bellville Road to Blocker's Crossing at U.S. Highway 301. The road-paving crews had just begun work on the Hagan road, and it wouldn't be long before every dirt road in the State of Georgia would be graded flat and topped off with a layer of black tar and granite gravel.

Jimmy could hear the grinding roar and rhythmic pounding of the earth moving machinery as Diana trotted around the edge of Smith's Pond and up the incline to the top of the dam overlooking the bridge. He looked out past the spillway to where an old wooden bridge once stood high above a pool of inviting waters. Horse and boy stood there for a few moments and listened to the thundering rumble of the ghosts of past horse and wagon teams, tin Lizzies, and modern automobiles as they rolled over the bridge's old warped and splintered timbers. Even today, if you listen carefully, you can still hear the ghostly echo of their reverberating thunder. A fourteen-year-old boy has very few good thoughts about progress when he has just witnessed one of his childhood memories being turned into a muddy ditch fed by a concrete culvert.

Jimmy gave Diana a gentle tug on her reins and they turned around and headed up Bull Creek to take a swim in the Island Hole. Maybe the road crews would never be able to find the Island Hole, and maybe it would always stay hidden there among the ty-tys and briar bushes, waiting for a boy and his horse to come along and dawdle away the summer days on its grassy banks.

# Chapter XXIII

## Music

Jimmy's grandfather used to tell stories about the days when he was a young man and enjoyed playing the fiddle. But old age and arthritis can be evil conspirators as they begin to attack a once active body. Day by day and like a musical crescendo slowly reaching its final climax, pains that were barely noticeable at first keep creeping up on their victim until the body suddenly cries out, "STOP! I can't do this anymore!" Even as the years passed and his motions came to be noticeably slower and more deliberate, Mr. Jim would still have moments that recalled his lost years of youthful agility and gaiety. Every now and then, when he would hear the mournful cries of a fiddle coming from the radio, he would hold his arms out from his sides and break into a little dancing jig. In his best square dance hog-calling twang, he would sing, "Chicken in the bread pan picking up dough. Missus, will your dog bite? No child no."

Jimmy once asked his grandfather whatever happened to his fiddle. In the way in which old people seem to accept the finality of things past, he explained, "When it is over it is over, and when it is over you shouldn't try to hang on to it. Just remember and savor the good times you had. Someone gave that fiddle to me a long time ago, but when it began to spend more time in its case than in my hands, I passed it on to someone whom I trusted would do it justice. Maybe that old fiddle is still being played somewhere by someone who will pass it along to someone else."

Jimmy often wondered where that old fiddle might be. Did it find a permanent home, or did it come to rest in some old attic, waiting for a new chance to play? Perhaps it is deep down in some dark landfill where it waits to be discovered in some future archeological dig. It would be nice to know that it is still alive somewhere, maybe squealing out notes in a country band or singing softly from a more formal concert stage in some great hall of acoustical perfection. Wherever it is, and even as musical styles change to suit the changing tastes of changing generations, there will always be hope that it still sings a few of the old songs it once sang.

That was the first music appreciation class that Jimmy can remember ever having. Although the experience should have prompted him to want to have a fiddle of his own, he chose the guitar as the instrument with which he would try to unleash his hidden musical talents. Playing the fiddle would have been enjoyable, even if it did seem a bit impractical for a person to play a fiddle and sing at the same time. The guitar was a different story. Gene Autry, Jimmy's hero, sure seemed to be having a lot of fun playing his guitar and singing songs to all those pretty girls who were always in his movies.

There is one thing that every six-year-old kid understands about grown-ups. When they want something for themselves, they manage to get it with something they call money. Therefore, it seemed the practical thing for Jimmy to do when he went up to his Aunt Augusta and demanded that she use some of her money to buy him a guitar for his upcoming birthday. After a few minutes of vocal clarification on the subjects of good manners, purchasing priorities, and the availability of local financial assets, she conceded that it was about time for him to be introduced to the world of music. Jimmy was satisfied knowing that he had at least been successful in arranging for his seventh birthday to be a profitable one. Although he knew the guitar would be hidden in Aunt Augusta's closet until his birthday, he could hardly wait for the postman to arrive with a big package that he knew was going to be just for him.

Jimmy never was able to determine just how things got so mixed up. He clearly pointed out in the Sears and Roebuck catalog exactly which guitar it was that he wanted for his birthday. He probably should have been tipped off when the mailman never delivered a package of the right dimensions during those long weeks leading up to his birthday. Nevertheless, he would never forget the words of soliciting encouragement that came from the adults that were surrounding him as he opened a little box that was not more than two feet long, four inches deep, and eight inches wide.

Encouragingly, Aunt Augusta said, "Look, it's a little guitar; just like the one you wanted."

Jimmy retorted with, "Rats, this is no guitar. This stupid looking thing is a ukulele. How could you have made such a mistake?"

The ukulele had a big palm tree painted on it and a picture of some goofy looking red-headed man that was sporting a big smile. It even had the man's signature scrawled under his picture. The reality of Jimmy's situation was not apparent to him at the time, but he had just been caught in that great chasm that lies between the kind of music adults like and the kind of music that young people like. To him, Arthur Godfrey could never come close to being as good a musician as Gene Autry was, not even on one of Gene's bad days and on one of Arthur's best days.

Most people love to listen to music, but few of them possess that special ability to actually hear the subtle tones, pitches, and slight variations in harmony. Even fewer possess the kind of talent that is necessary for creating good music or to accurately reproduce the music of others. Nevertheless, that should never keep anyone from trying to reach their musical potential, howsoever deep it might reside somewhere deep down in the pits of their souls.

At least Aunt Augusta spent a lot of time reaching for her talent. She would spend an hour or so every day sitting in front of her old upright Baldwin piano pounding out church hymns and old Nelson Eddy and Jeanette McDonnell songs. Aunt Edith was more into classical music. She even took weekly voice lessons when she was not on duty at the Central of Georgia Railway Hospital in Savannah. Every time she came home for a visit to the *Pines*, the two of them would sit together on the piano bench and begin their duet. Aunt Augusta would thrash out the notes and chords of their chosen musical selection and Aunt Edith would turn the pages as they both sang. They created combinations of piano sounds and vocalizations that resonated through the house like what must surely have been the same wailings that drove Odysseus' sailors mad enough to crash their ship upon all those rocks.

Jimmy enjoyed music and often wondered what is it that resides in only a few people and gives them the ability to perform in ways that are not possible for other people to even contemplate. People have always referred to the fruits that come from the labors of such people as *talent*. But what is talent, and from where in the body or mind is it stored or generated? How does talent function in such a way as to give only a few human beings the ability to become true artists, those unique individuals who are capable of giving the product of their souls such special personal and original interpretations and which makes all worthy art so very rare and such marvels to hear or behold?

It seems there are many talents that human beings are capable of possessing, but most people fail to develop the one talent that is most peculiar to them. The talents that most people usually talk about are those that can be displayed through the mediums of music, sculpture, or painting. But there are other human attributes that are exhibited in ways that are not usually thought of as being expressions of talent. The ability to reason, to think conceptually, and to predict the actions of other humans each appears to be rooted in some innate talent. Such talents are often confused with ordinary skills that can be acquired through training.

People who are limited to using only their basic senses of sight, smell, hearing, taste, and touch don't seem able to fully understand talent, and those who possess any of the various talents seem to be the only ones that are capable of fully appreciating them and relating effectively with other people who are likewise talented. Perhaps this might explain why one talented musician and another talented musician, having never before met the other, are capable of coming together and creating music without ever having to speak a single word to the other. Such talents are true gifts, but they are usually possessed at the expense of some other ability. The true artists of music, granite, and canvas are special people who are often otherwise incapable of functioning in an appropriate manner when in normal social circumstances. Other expressions, such as those demonstrated from the stage or podiums of political oratory, are only well-honed skills that can be reproduced by most people of acceptable intellect and determination.

The fact that a person may possess a reasonable level of intelligence or a graduate of some fine arts school doesn't automatically make that person a talented artist. As much as that educated but untalented person might try, he or she will never reach the high level of accomplishment that only the truly talented are capable of reaching. Untalented students of music might eventually master the fundamentals of musical theory and may even develop their learned mechanical skills to a level that will allow them to be capable of reproducing, with acceptable similarity, the musical works of others. They may even become teachers of technique and theory. But as financially successful or famous as such people may become, they will never be true artists. From such truth came the old saying, "Those who can, do, and those who can't, teach."

After his disappointing episode with the ukulele, Jimmy was offered a consolation prize. He would be permitted to take piano lessons the coming school year when he would be entering the second grade at Bellville School, provided that he behaved himself. They just didn't get it. He didn't want to play a ukulele or the piano. All he ever wanted to do was play a guitar, ride horses, and be a regular hero like Gene Autry. No, there would be no piano lessons for him. He could still remember when he was in the first grade only a few months earlier. The only students that were taking piano lessons were girls. He was not about to put himself in a position that would cause him to have to defend his manhood even before he knew what manhood meant. His musical career would just have to be put on hold for a while. And it would be another seven years before he would play another note on anything other than a homemade kazoo, one of his father's hunting horns, or Uncle Jeff's old army bugle.

Just as it was an act of defiance when Jimmy refused to take piano lessons, it was in defiance of his aunt's efforts to keep him off the football team that forced him to pursue a mediocre musical career. There was just no other way out of his predicament. Aunt Augusta would never permit him to play football or any other sport that might place him in close association with low class ruffians, and certainly not one that allowed him to be anywhere near those cheerleaders and their loose morals. Furthermore, there was no way he going to go along with her suggestion that he play tennis or join the glee club. And he certainly would never submit to taking one of those stupid courses that everyone knows is for students who don't have the coordination and skills necessary for participating in organized extracurricular activities. No one suspected it then, but it would be a few more decades before people would discover that it was those types of people who would be ruling the world with their computers. Anyway, there seemed to be a compromise in the making, and joining the school band seemed to be the only way for Jimmy to pretend to accept Aunt Augusta's authority and still be able to achieve some semblance of victory.

'Cymbals! I was supposed to be playing the trombone and sitting next to that good looking girl with those great lips!' But there Jimmy was, standing between some kid that was beating on a big drum that was strapped to his stomach and two other kids who were rattling two sticks together on top of a couple of smaller drums. The only instructions the bandmaster had given him was to slam those two cymbals together every time the fat kid hit the big drum and make dog-gone sure that he kept his eyes glued to the bandmaster and his baton. Every time the bandmaster pointed his baton at Jimmy he was to slam those cymbals together real hard, hold them over his head, and wave them around in the air. The bandmaster believed that it didn't matter how well anyone could play melody. They would never be able to be an accomplished musician until they learned how to follow rhythm. Therefore, his policy was to make everyone who wished to be in the band to start out in the rhythm section.

Mr. Weit knew what he was talking about. Jimmy finally got out of the rhythm section and moved up from third, second, and finally to first chair trombone. He became a student teacher, composed original compositions, arranged musical scores, and even won a prize at the state music festival for conducting a full concert arrangement of Richard Wagner's *Zueignug* (*Dedication*). The crowning glory of his high school musical career was to receive the John Philip Sousa Award, which is presented each year to the graduating student that made the greatest achievement and had contributed most to the high school music program.

During his tour of duty in the military service as a United States Army Bandsman, Jimmy grew more and more aware of the fact that his true talents lay hidden somewhere else, in some endeavor not of the musical kind. He soon realized that, although determination and hard work can usually deceive most people of lesser ability, the truly talented are always able to determine when another person's music comes from force and sweat or just naturally bubbles up from some innate pool of talent. That one seemingly simple little leap from accomplished technician to actualized talent never came to Jimmy. It was time for him to leave music as a profession and embrace it only as an enjoyable pastime.

Jimmy gave his trombone away a few days before leaving the 437th Army Band and reporting to Officer's Candidate School where he would begin a new direction in his life. He gave his trombone to someone he thought might enjoy it at the time. He hoped that person would treat it well and maybe even pass it on to someone else who would enjoy it. And just maybe, like that old fiddle that once belonged to his grandfather, his old trombone might still be somewhere playing a few of the old tunes it once played.

# Chapter XXIV

## Christmas

Wondrous days of Christmas past
Children wish them to ever last
Simple things they wanted then
When dreams were real for children
Tucked in bed the night before
Little minds see gifts galore
Perhaps a doll or spinning top
Things made in Santa's shop
Shade of night please quickly rise
And reveal my wondrous prize
Santa Claus must surely be real
But mom and dad will never reveal

The mind of a three-year-old child is an empty space that gathers information like a dusty road gathers dust kicked up by everything that passes over it. When a child is about five years old, its little brain suddenly turns into a black hole, sucking in every piece of information yet harboring little respect for the significance of anything that it absorbs.

"Jimmy! Watch out for that *crystal* lamp!"
"Don't let Jimmy near that *crystal* bowl, he'll break it!"
"Careful Jimmy, you almost broke that *crystal* goblet!"
"Oh my Gawd, Jimmy broke the *crystal* vase!"

It seemed as if crystal was in every room of the big house that Jimmy and his brother were allowed to visit only on special occasions before their aunt adopted them. Jimmy wasn't even sure what crystal was, but a lot of it was always on tables that he couldn't see over, especially the ones that were covered with pretty lace cloths that had ruffled edges hanging down from them. Those dangling linens, cottons, and silks were convenient handles for steadying himself as he navigated from room to room and exploring every crevice of the big house. It was no wonder that terror was the first emotion that rushed through his little neophyte brain every time he heard the word crystal being mentioned.

The first time that Jimmy heard the word *Christmas*, it sure sounded a lot like crystal.

"Jimmy, what would you like for Christmas?"

Mental images of clear looking and easy to break objects, and the reason that chaos would break loose if he so much as looked at them, prompted a zombie-like catatonic spell to come over his little body every time he heard that word. No Sireee! He didn't want anything to do with *Crystalmess*!

He lived in mortal fear as each day before Christmas was counted, announced with happiness, and received with glee by everyone in the house, even by his younger brother who was yet to discover the horror that crystal would soon bring to his life. As the days were marked off the calendar, Jimmy feared the day of his impending demise, that terrible day when crystal would be all around him. There was no doubt in his little mind that they were planning to kill him and bury him in a big pile of crystal, the same pile of crystal that was so indelibly printed upon the movie screen of his little brain after an earlier and very traumatic experience with crystal. He was still suffering from visions of razor-sharp pieces of crystal scattered all over the floor right after he gave cause for a vase to fly off a tea cart, the one that he thought he could push around the living room like the one that his Aunt Augusta pushed around in her flower garden.

Christmas Day finally arrived. It came early in the morning when it was still dark and cold outside the covers of Jimmy's bed. He imagined that Hiawatha would have been proud of him as he blew hot breaths of vapor that condensed in the cold air and floated off into the darkness of his room like little puffs of white smoke. His morning fantasies were suddenly interrupted when his bedroom door opened and he was snatched from the warmth of his covers and dragged clawing and screaming down the hall to the great living room. That was where the Christmas tree was waiting, along with almost every piece of crystal in the house. Each piece was perched so delicately yet threatening on every table, shelf, and windowsill in the great room. "Come on Jimmy, you're just going to love what we have for you. Sanka coffee has been here."

Yeah, that's what I said, *Sanka coffee*! Having never before heard about Santa Claus, and being totally unfamiliar with the material benefits of Christmas, Jimmy's infantile brain clamored for the most recognizable sound that came even close to resembling anything like the words, Santa Claus. You see, Aunt Augusta drank Sanka coffee, and she drank a lot of it. Those dark brown and rusty-orange colored coffee cans were everywhere, inside and outside the house. They were on the porch rails, in a circle around the sycamore tree in the back yard, stored in rickety stacks in the pantry, and even hidden under Jimmy's bed, his brother's bed, and Mr. Jim's bed. Each can was destined to serve its final and corroding days as some useful, but not very attractive purpose. They were turned into flower pots, nail buckets, grease containers, or as emergency receptacles for the men in the house to use instead of having to take night-time trips down a cold hallway, across the freezing screened-in back porch, and to the icy bathroom next to the pantry. The women got to use the front bathroom, the one where they didn't have to break a layer of ice in the commode before the darned thing could be flushed.

And that was the way it was on Jimmy's first Christmas at the *Pines*. The little red wagon with the wooden side rails took a lot of the sting out of his fear of dying under an avalanche of crystal. He even became addicted to Santa Claus about as much as Aunt Augusta was addicted to her no-caffeine Sanka coffee.

The Christmas seasons after that first horrific holiday experience were much more enjoyable. When Jimmy was old enough to carry a small hand saw and tall enough to navigate through the barrier of wiregrass and gallberry bushes that guarded the flatwoods from the intrusiveness of immature human beings, he was permitted to accompany Mr. Jim on his annual Christmas tree hunts. They would search for a well-rounded and evenly shaped cedar tree, one that was tall enough to reach almost to the ceiling of the living room. Every time Mr. Jim spotted a young tree that was not yet tall enough to cut, he would clear all the other vegetation away from it so it would have more space to grow. That practice guaranteed there would always be a supply of well-shaped cedar trees for future Christmas seasons.

The hunt for a proper Christmas tree always took place on the first Saturday in December. The tree trimming and decorating would take place that same evening, except for the placement a white angel on top of the tree. That ceremony customarily took place the following day after church services and Sunday dinner. Jimmy didn't know whether or not other people in the world performed such rituals in preparation for Christmas, but he had read a story about some children who lived up in Vermont and who went riding a horse-drawn sleigh through the snow looking for a Christmas tree. The pictures in the story made them all seem so happy. After they found their perfect tree, they tied it to the back of the sleigh and dragged it home through a deep layer of fluffy white snow. That made Jimmy wish it would snow in South Georgia so he would be able experience the same kind of enjoyment.

A few years after his father brought old Charlie back to the *Pines*, Charlie became a forced, although not unwilling, participant in Jimmy's plans to build a sleigh that would enable him to duplicate the experience of those Vermont Christmas tree hunts. Actually, the finished project was not such a bad looking device. It even seemed to work quite well during a test run in the sandy field next to the tool shed. A large metal rim from an old wagon wheel was cut in two pieces so that the two bowed halves could be used as runners for the sleigh. The seat for the sleigh was borrowed from an old metal riding plow and bolted to the top of two wooden cross beams that connected the two runners. A pulling bar was attached to the center of the sleigh just behind the two runners in a way that made it serve as an attachment point for a one-horse single tree that had been scavenged from an old side-busting plow.

All Jimmy had to do to place the contraption in operation was to harness old Charlie to the front of the sleigh, take the reigns in hand, and give Charlie the usual go signal. The go signal is a clucking sound that is produced by quickly snapping the inside of the cheek away from the tongue and teeth. The resulting sound, which is traditionally used to make all beasts of burden go, is created in a chamber that is formed between the teeth and one cheek when they are separated at sufficient speed as to create a frequency equal to the resonance point of the pulpy flesh surrounding that part of the mouth. Most people are capable of doing it, it's just that they don't understand or care about learning the physics of it all.

Most boys of around nine or ten years old have plenty of initiative. They even believe that they have sufficient skills for building almost anything. They are lucky that most materials that are required to complete their projects are rarely available.

When they do happen to acquire them, they are usually even luckier to have some adult show up at the right time to prevent a second invention of the airplane, sailboat, moon rocket, or the occurrence of some great human disaster. Jimmy assumed that the adults around him at the time had decided that his sleigh project could do no harm.

The cedar tree that was to decorate the living room at the *Pines* on Christmas of 1950 had already been identified. By then, Jimmy had been given his grandfather's job of going forth to the flatwoods and delivering a tree to the living room where it would serve its proper role in the season's festivities. His older cousin, Jean, who had been attending the Henry Grady School of Nursing in Atlanta, had just arrived home for the holidays and immediately assumed her old job as the family's chief tree decorator.

Jimmy hitched Charlie to his new '*sleigon*' (a cross between a sleigh and a wagon), strapped a hand saw on one of the breast collar knobs on Charlie's harness, and then gave his best sounding *cluck-cluck*. Although it was very cold that December, there was no snow on the ground like there was in that story about the children in Vermont. Nevertheless, the sleigon was sliding smoothly over the dry wiregrass, broom sage, and gallberry bushes as he and Charlie headed out to the flatwoods.

Jimmy cut the beautifully shaped cedar tree low to the ground, tied the cut end to the back of the sleigon, and then headed for home with a comfortable feeling of satisfaction flowing through his young body. When he arrived at the gate that was between the two magnolia trees in front of the big house, he pulled back on Charlie's reigns and quickly jumped off the sleigon. Every member of the family was gathered on the front porch and waiting to inspect the new Christmas tree and its strange looking conveyance. Jimmy hitched Charlie to one of the magnolia trees and turned to accept the accolades that he was sure he would be receiving for bringing home the new Christmas tree. No one uttered a word. Jean finally broke the silence by asking a question that seemed to be directed towards no one present at the moment. "Now just how am I supposed to decorate a piece of ugly scrub brush like that?"

Jimmy turned to take a protective, albeit more unbiased, look at the tree, only to discover what briar bushes, gallberry bushes, pine saplings, and two miles of flatwoods palmetto fronds can do to a cedar tree after it has been dragged unmercifully through them. Vermont snow and Georgia flatwoods have very different effects on the tender green limbs of Christmas trees. Jimmy's family did a nice job of consoling him, and they even went ahead with the ritual of decorating what was left of the tree. After the tree had been adorned with all the colorful decorations of Christmas, it seemed to display a big smile in one of the many bare spaces where its greenery had been scraped away. As usual, the ritual of placing an angel on top of the tree was saved for the following Sunday evening. But when the angel was placed on top of the tree, the tree's best effort to support the little angel was insufficient for the task. The little angel's head kept drooping over with her face looking down towards the floor, as if in thoughtful payer.

It was many years later and Jimmy was a grown man with a family of his own. Many Christmas seasons had passed since that memorable Christmas at the *Pines*, and many Christmas trees had since graced their living room. It was a dark and stormy night (I always wanted to write that too) and the first Saturday night in December of 1977. Jimmy arrived home from his office late in the evening and was met at the door by his concerned family. They were quick to remind him that they did not yet have a Christmas tree, but were unanimous in agreeing with Jimmy's suggestion that they not go out with him in such bad weather to search for a tree in the country that gave us the custom of the Christmas tree.

Among the last of the picked-over trees that were remaining at a tree dealer's roped off space along a narrow German cobble stone street, he spotted one small limb-shredded cedar tree that seemed to be begging for a home. When he arrived back home with the tree, his family was understandably disappointed and a bit unsure about keeping the pitiful looking thing. One member of his family was even more vocal in stating his personal opinion regarding the effect that tree was going to have on his Christmas. "This tree is ugly. It's going to ruin our Christmas!" Nevertheless, and considering the fact that there were few other choices, they decided they would just have to make the tree do. They spent a stormy evening adding twigs, taping up branches, and adorning the tree with an array of Christmas colors and little hand-carved German ornaments. One of the ornaments was a little wooden hand-carved horse-drawn sleigh that had two little children sitting in it. As always, they waited until Sunday afternoon before placing a little white angel on top of the tree.

The little tree that had been given new life was placed next to a window that framed it against an outside world of white snow. The weight of the little angel made the top of the tree bend down in a way that caused the angel to face the floor, as if in thoughtful prayer. Jimmy could make out the shape of a little smile that was formed in the tree between the spaces of its sparse limbs and slender trunk. And he recalled a Christmas past and another little shredded cedar tree that was barley able to support the weight of a little white angel. And he remembered the story about that family in Vermont, and how a horse and sleigh had delivered their Christmas tree. That Vermont family could never have had a happier Christmas than the one his family was having on that snowy Christmas day, so far from the *Pines*.

# Chapter XXV

## Requiem for a People

When Jimmy was a young boy growing up at the *Pines*, he lived with a constant understanding that he was experiencing many things that most young people would never have a chance to learn, much less have an opportunity to actually experience for themselves. Soon after he learned to walk, he was riding horses, tending cattle, mending fences, loading melons, culling tomatoes, grading tobacco, and communicating in a cryptic version of English that was being spoken by the local black population. This dialect of the southern rural Negro, later modified by the urban black experience, was the original form of a dialect that would be discovered by cultural grave diggers some fifty years later and given the suspiciously sounding label of 'Ebonics.' Actually, this language of the plow fields and turpentine trails is only an example of the mundane and innocuous differences that exist among all races, cultures, and customs. Although they are often only reflections of an exaggerated attempt by some people to adapt to their present surroundings, such differences are sometimes a problem for other people who criticize others and like to point out their differences in an effort to divert attention from their own inadequacies. In the course of human events, such differences are often brought crashing together in times of social upheaval. Tragically, there has always been and always will be a few people who are willing to exploit and manipulate such differences in the human condition for purposes that are usually evil.

The Canoochee River springs from the geological fault line above Emanuel County and flows southeasterly through Candler, Evans, Bulloch, Liberty, and Bryan Counties. It empties into the Ogeechee River about a mile west of Kings Ferry, which is an old and well-known swimming hole south of Savannah on U.S. Highway 17. The Ogeechee River originates a few miles south of the city of Athens in what is known as the Piedmont region of Georgia. It flows southeasterly and parallel to the Savannah River where it creates a large delta of black muddy marshland as it slowly meanders its way to the Atlantic Ocean near Ossabaw Island. Like other marshy deltas along the coastal South, these marsh islands and tidal creeks became home for many people who had been forcibly exiled from their native lands, and then again from the land that they were forced to adopt.

Jimmy was also quite fluent in *Geechee*, a mixed dialect that can still be heard spoken by many of the people that inhabit the few dry spots along the banks of the lower waters of the Savannah, Canoochee, and Ogeechee rivers, and even along the tidal waters as far south as St. Simons Island. Many of the white settlers that first came to the coastal region of Georgia were from Scotland and Ireland. Upon hearing their present day descendants speaking Geechee, an English teacher might understandably suspect them of being an uneducated people. Many were and many still are, but that should not give cause to condemn a people for uttering the few vocal remnants that still remain of the tongues of their forefathers.

If you listen very carefully to Geechee and other sub-dialects of Southeast Georgia, you should be able to distinguish the faintly familiar sounds of their Gaelic origins. The contractions of *ain't, tain't,* and *hain't,* when used in expressions like ain't (am not), ain't dunnit (did not do it), tain't dun yet, (not quite finished), we'uns ain't got (we do not have), and hain't ner (I have never) were brewed from the stout language of the pubs of Ayrshire where Robert Burns spent his nights writing, drinking, and staggering home over the Brig o'Doon. However, not one person has yet to suggest that Geechee might possibly be some lost language from Scotland or Ireland, or that it should be taught in schools as a cure-all for low self-esteem.

Geechee is very different from *Gullah,* a dialect that sometimes can still be heard spoken by some of the black people who live along the lowlands of South Carolina north of the Savannah River and extending up the coast to the mouth of the Edisto River. This is an area of the coastal South where many black people once lived in almost complete seclusion from the influences of a changing world that was only a few miles from their hidden world. Gullah is a low country dialect that is representative of progressively corrupted attempts by slaves and their descendants to speak the English language. Over the years, their speech became infused with sounds that were vaguely reminiscent and only faintly suggestive of their old African tribal dialects. Their quickly changing language was further modified and diluted by exposure to countless other combinations of words and verbal fragments of other languages and dialects. Without benefit of having been recorded and preserved in writing, the old African words soon lost their original forms and intended meanings.

A few researchers have been studying this mutated dialect for many years while never realizing that the few Gullah speaking people who still live along the coastal tidelands sometimes jerk the white man's mental chains by telling them that Gullah is descended directly from their old African tribal languages. Such a thing is easy to believe when one desires to be known for restoring lost cultures. Some supposedly present day customs and traditions are often only creations from borrowed dreams about past cultures.

A few culture creationists, in apparent pursuit of personal notoriety, have been busy trying to convince the world that the utterances from the lips of Gullah people is some lost African language that was somehow kept in sterile preservation through succeeding generations of the descendants of slaves. It has also been proposed that Gullah might be a menagerie of Creole dialects or even a blend of African and Atlantic Coast Indian languages. It is a shameful indictment of the human intellect that so many people have turned the study of some languages into a sociological hunt designed to give some contrived meaning to a people's ethnic identity, especially when their authentic cultures are special enough.

Gullah is an example of what happens to the human remnants of a 'caretaker society' when that society, through whatever means, is altered to the extent that it no longer provides the kind of support and attention that had been traditional, expected, and even necessary under the circumstances. Because of similarities in sounds, it is much like taking the Vietnamese word *toi* and claiming that it is the English equivalent of *toy*. *Toi* is actually the Vietnamese equivalent of the English noun, *I*. The Vietnamese word *toi* is pronounced exactly like the English word *toy*, the English word for a child's plaything. Therefore, if we accept such strange skewering of logic, The Vietnamese language must be some lost English dialect, or visa versa. We'uns ain't so ignert da'we cain't 'ave a liddle fun wid fur'ners.

It was recently reported that some people from the United States government have set up camp on St. Simons Island and are attempting to dig up evidence proving that Geechee, like their ideas about Gullah, is another preserved language of African slaves. They probably will never lend any consideration to the possibility that the Geechee spoken by the black people of earlier times just might have been the result of their attempts to speak the heavy brogue that they heard being spoken by the Scots who settled that part of the Georgia coast.

It is too bad that, when visiting parts of the world that are different from the places that are familiar to them, some people often bring with them pre-conceived notions and assumptions about things of which they understand very little. They frequently voice ill-concocted opinions without bothering to study the area that they are visiting or to even ask questions of the more informed local inhabitants. On the other hand, local populations often demonstrate their own xenophobic tendencies by resisting what is only the innocent presence of strangers.

Although the First Amendment to the Constitution of the United States guarantees all Americans the right to express any opinions they may wish to express, one fact remains; no one can justly claim a *moral* right to speak authoritatively on any subject about which they know little or nothing. Biased opinions that are purposely designed to support social agendas have always been a curse upon the accurate recording of the history of mankind. Playing with the minds of tourists and local city slickers has been a recreational pastime of rural southern white folks and black folks ever since the days of northern carpetbaggers and those scoundrel southern scalawags.

Most of the people who still live in those heretofore forgotten and practically impenetrable coastal swamplands of Georgia and South Carolina are descendants of slaves. After the War Between the States was fought and won, allegedly to free the slaves, the northern liberators quickly abandoned any previously trumped up concerns over the plight of the poor southern Negro. They hastily went off in hot pursuit of other and more profitable spoils of their victory. The forsaken dependents of other people's bad ideas were abandoned with nothing more than their innate instinct of how to live off nothing but their surroundings. Fearing for their safety, many of the newly freed slaves fled into the swampy wilderness and isolation of the coastal lowlands where, for several generations, they were insulated from the influences of the white man's civilization.

For nearly a hundred years, these inhabitants of the southern coastal tidal banks lived on rice, fish, shrimp, and oysters. Their seafood diet was supplemented with half-tame yard chickens, feral pigs, and a never-ending supply of backyard-grown collard greens. Food never was a serious problem, and the occasional meat of a raccoon, opossum, or snapping turtle provided a little variety in table fare. For the most part, these people were relatively untouched by the outside world until they again became a desirable source of cheap labor that was needed by the white man to fuel a changing southern economy.

Rickety old surplus school buses could be seen making regular early morning stops as they picked up groups of transient workers waiting at designated collection points along U.S. Highway 17. The men worked as deck hands on fishing boats, headers on shrimp trawlers, field hands, turpentine dippers, sawmill workers, and log swampers. The women toiled as house servants for the new genteel classes that were beginning to emerge in the expanding coastal cities of Charleston, Savannah, and Brunswick. Many served as maids and servants in grand hotels and opulent homes that had been built on the barrier islands by such notables as the Baruchs, Nobles, Vanderbilts, and other barons of the American Industrial Age.

The busses would return late in the evening and deposit their human loads along the dirt roads that led into the wilderness from the main road. The little sandy trails seemed to disappear into an infinity of misty darkness that quickly and gently engulfed the live oak trees and saltwater marshes. The women always wore their traditional white cotton muslin head wraps and shawls. The men wore wide brimmed straw hats that had been bleached to a dingy yellow from long days of toil under the hot southern sun. As they trudged their way home through the darkening sea of swaying head-high marsh grass, they looked like little whitecaps and clumps of floating marsh grass bobbing up and down on a moonlit ocean.

Land developers eventually moved in after new technology provided them with an effective means for penetrating the swampy domain of Francis Marion, the famous hero of the Revolutionary War and who was also known as the *Swamp Fox*. These new invaders of the South were the first since General William T. Sherman. And instead of merciful muskets and cannons, they came armed with eviction notices and bulldozers. Local fat-cat politicians scrambled over themselves as they crawled in bed with the land developers and traded their souls to the pimps of progress. Tax levies were increased far beyond the ability of the poor black residents to pay on lands that the white man once considered worthless. After seizing their land for failure to pay taxes on land that had never before been taxed or tilled, they sold it to the highest 'bidder' at rigged public auctions.

This once pristine home to ancient moss-laden live oak trees, salt marshes, and generations of mosquitoes soon fell victim to the machines of progress as it was cleared acre-by-acre of all insect, animal, plant, and human life. Marsh grass and tidal creeks disappeared as developers hauled in truckloads of rip-rap and fill-dirt to build new roads, golf courses, housing developments, shopping centers, and all the trappings of a civilization gone amuck. Giant paper mills and electric power plants moved in with their insatiable thirst for fresh water that was needed to feed their giant pulp boilers, chlorine vats, and cooling towers. They drilled forty-eight-inch diameter wells deep in the underground fresh water aquifer that for ages had held back the salty Atlantic Ocean. The natural and ancient artesian wells that once spouted unbroken streams of water into the air along the Georgia coast were soon sucked dry, leaving much of the black population without a convenient source of fresh water and everyone else with a new problem of saltwater intrusion in the crumbling and dying aquifers. Even General Sherman would have never considered committing or even condoning such dastardly deeds upon the land that he once conquered.

After the beaches and barrier islands had been made more accessible for people and their automobiles, and air-conditioning was installed in the motels, the construction crews were soon replaced by the camp followers of cultural destruction, social workers and junior league anthropologists. Hoards of these neophytes from academia filled in the blank spaces of their plagiarized graduate theses and pre-written doctoral dissertations as they recorded their 'discovery' of a unique people who had been forced to live on the fringes of a new civilization. Inflicted with a lust for academic notoriety and to get published at any cost, they easily convinced themselves that the local black people were communicating in what was obviously some lost African dialect or perhaps even a new African based language.

The people who were living along the few high spots of the coastal wetlands, separated by patches of white sand and black muddy tidal creeks, were just a bunch of poor, uneducated, yet hardy and resourceful black folks. Much like the aboriginal American Indians, they had been pushed to the edge of the world by the ever-expanding civilization of the white boy. These castaways from a defunct feudal system were communicating in a menagerie of sounds that they had collected over the years without benefit of written scriptures. Vague and distantly familiar sounding vocal reproductions were passed down to succeeding generations. And each generation further modified and attenuated what was already an intellectually limited mixture of very bad English, Scott-Irish brogue, remnants of multiple African dialects, local improvisation, and a uniquely sounding oral adaptation that is caused by the obvious physical difference between the lips of white folks and the lips of black folks.

The African tribal dialects of the plantation slaves have long since been forgotten. Even today, it is almost impossible to distinguish the accent of second generation Hungarians whose parents came to America after the Hungarian revolution of 1956. It took only a few years for their children to be completely assimilated by the dominant American culture. Their grandchildren have now been left with only a few pages of textbook knowledge about their language and heritage. It would therefore be only gratuitously charitable to credit the descendants of slaves, much less their slave grandparents, with the ability to keep their varied African dialects alive during a period of history when their survival depended solely upon a mandated and enforced requirement that they respond to instructions and communicate in the English language.

Those poor, dominated, and displaced people who had been exiled for so long to the southern coastal wilderness just did not possess the acquired education and skills that were necessary for them to develop and sustain such linguistic ideals. While the old dialects of the Scottish and Irish settlers gradually became less pronounced through voluntarily assimilation, the African tribal dialects of the slaves were quickly forced into oblivion; beginning with the yokes of their own tribal brothers and followed by the whips of English and Dutch slave-ship masters. It all ended with the final slam of the slave auctioneer's gavel.

Charles Darwin's laws of natural selection and survival of the fittest apply to languages and cultures as well as to plants and animals.

Printed in the United States
48332LVS00004B/206

9 781413 787375